Reckoning and Ruin

Reckoning and Ruin

A Tai Randolph Mystery

Tina Whittle

Poisoned Pen Press

To my brother dearest Tim, the best "big" brother a "little" sister could have, and to Lisa, Patty, and Rich, my ever-awesome sibs-in-law (and sibs-in-heart).

And to my other mom and dad, Yvonne and Gene, who welcomed me into their lives over three decades ago, and who continue to support me in everything I do. I am so grateful for your presence in my life, and for the love you have shared with me and mine.

Acknowledgments

It takes a village to write a book, and I have an excellent one. And even though I put a lot of stock in words, I know that words can never truly demonstrate how blessed I am to have such smart, talented, generous people in my circle:

The Mojito Literary Society, made up of Annie Hogsett, Susan Newman, Katrina Murphy and Laura Valeri; my fellow Sisters in Crime, including the members of my home chapter, the Low Country Sisters in Crime (especially Donna Kortes, our dynamic president and can-do maven); my always supportive friends—Toni Deal, Sharon Hudson, Theresa Moore, Danielle Walden, and Robin White. Kira Parker, a woman of mystery in her own right; my UU Womenspirit sisters; and—of course—my excellent and forbearing family: my parents, Dinah and Archie; my parents-in-law, Yvonne and Gene; my sibling and siblings-in-law, Tim and Lisa, and Patty and Rich, plus my wonderful niece and nephews—Connor, Sydney, Drew and Hayden.

Special thanks goes to Kathy Bradley, who guided me through the legal issues in this book, and Jonathan M. Bryant, who lent his historical expertise and listening ear to this endeavor. They are fine writers both, and I am grateful for their encouragement and wisdom. I also absolve them completely of any responsibility for the mistakes I surely made.

Much gratitude to the fine folks at Poisoned Pen Press—especially Barbara Peters, Annette Rogers, Rob Rosenwald, Suzan

Baroni, Diane DiBiase, Tiffany White, Pete Zrioka, and Beth Deveny—a writer's dream team that serves writers and writing in exemplary fashion. I am also grateful to my fellow PPPers—the Posse—for their smarts and generosity and unwavering support, and to my agent, Paige Wheeler, for the quickness of her brain and the goodness of her heart.

And—as always and forever—much love to my husband, James, and daughter, Kaley. I couldn't do this thing without you.

Chapter One

Trey's head snapped back. "Ow!"

Gabriella ignored him and pressed her hand harder against the nape of his neck, her eyebrows knit in concentration. She had him sitting backwards in a kitchen chair, shirtless and annoyed, while she poked and prodded the muscles across the top of his shoulders.

I stayed on the sofa with my *Garden and Gun* magazine, not saying a word. Through the terrace doors, a spring sunset flickered behind Atlanta's Midtown skyline, gilding the black and white apartment with golden light. This was not how I'd envisioned my Saturday night—up on the thirty-fifth floor instead of down in the vibrant scrum of Buckhead. But I guessed from Gabriella's cocktail dress and sky-scraping Louboutins, she'd had other plans too.

She was barefoot now, her lips pursed prettily. She was Trey's bodywork therapist, alternative medical adviser, and former lover. The first two were fine by me. The last one sucker-punched me every time I saw her place a deceptively delicate-looking hand on his bare skin.

I licked my finger and turned another page. "Is it bad?"

Gabriella blew one red ringlet from her forehead. "I am still evaluating."

She moved her hand across the plane of his upper back to his left arm, then pushed her fingers into the muscle of his shoulder.

Trey closed his eyes and curled his hands into fists. If he'd been a cursing man, obscenities would have been spilling from his lips.

He grimaced up at her. "Well?"

She slipped back into her shoes. "Not dislocated, and not torn. But you have severely strained the acromioclavicular."

"Does it require a doctor?"

"No. But you will need to treat it with care for a while." She left him in the chair and opened the leather carry case on the counter with a snap. "How did this happen?"

Trey shot a look my way. I buried my face in my magazine.

Gabriella caught the look. "I see. You will need to take more care, especially with your more…energetic activities. You're predisposed to subluxations, and every injury—"

"Increases the risk of further injury, I know."

"Then behave as if you do." She smacked two bottles on the counter. "Turmeric and boswellia capsules. Liniment and tape. Ice tonight, then moist heat."

"I know how to deal with this."

"I was explaining for Tai, since she is to be stuck with you this evening, not I, *par la grâce de Dieu.*" She turned to face me. "He can't drive for twenty-four hours and must leave the holster at home for a week. Is he fully stocked on painkillers?"

"Everything from aspirin to oxycodone."

"Good. That shoulder will hurt *comme de le merde* in an hour." A rueful smile twitched at the corner of her mouth. "Of course, fifteen milligrams of oxy, and he will be utterly useless to you for the rest of the evening."

"Yeah. I figured as much."

She closed her case and slipped the strap over her shoulder. "But congratulations on the occasion, nonetheless. A year together is a year together, yes?"

Across the room, Trey reached for his tee-shirt, black hair mussed, blue eyes prickly with pain and simmering anger, although I couldn't tell if his wrath was directed at me in particular or the world in general. He and I were supposed to be celebrating that year together. Had started celebrating, in fact, before our unfortunate tangle and tumble. Now he was a tornado of irritation.

Gabriella nodded toward the hallway, my cue to follow her. I did, shutting the door behind me as I walked her to the elevator. She carried herself like the ballet dancer she'd once been.

"I understand your enthusiasm, *ma chère*, but you must be more gentle with him. The hypermobility—"

"The what?"

"Hypermobility. Double-jointedness, yes? Surely you have noticed?"

My brain sifted through several very specific memories. "That explains some things."

"*Probablement.* But it also predisposes him to injuries like this, especially if he is overtraining, which from the state of his deltoids, I am guessing he is. Has the PTSD returned?"

When she said it, the acronym sounded exotic, flowing with French trills and gliding vowels. *Peety-Essdie.*

I shrugged. "It's hard to tell."

"Have you consulted your brother? He has a specialty in this, yes?"

I felt the knot tie up again. Yes, my brother Eric was a cognitive behavior psychologist, and he did indeed specialize in post-traumatic stress rehabilitation. And yes, he knew the situation exceedingly well, having once served as Trey's occupational therapist. But I was reluctant to approach him. Asking my brother's advice about Trey invited him to offer advice about me, and that never went well.

"Eric recommended some books on clinical exercise physiology, which is why Trey has upped his training regimen into the Iron Man zone."

"Is this regimen working?"

"Yes. No. Maybe." I shook my head. "I can't put my finger on it. He seems…I don't know. Like he's trying too hard."

"Have the nightmares returned?"

"No."

"Is he sleeping properly?"

"Yes."

"And sexually—"

"Working just fine, thank you."

She examined me almost as keenly as Trey did. They'd been together for over five years when I came along, three of those years before Trey's car accident, two of them after. And yet she seemed to hold not one hint of resentment against me. Quite the opposite, in fact, something I found terribly suspicious. But according to Trey, she'd saved his life. Since he wasn't a man to exaggerate, I tolerated the phone calls, the herbal remedies, and the vegan soup she brought over regularly. I remained skeptical, though. And watchful.

She tilted her head. "You are upset he is not spending as much time with you, yes?"

"I didn't say that."

"No, you did not, true enough." She crossed her arms and tapped one crimson-tipped fingernail against her shoulder. "Let me guess. His schedule is becoming tighter and more regimented. More work, more training, less time to be your significant other."

I started to argue, but realized she was right. Our now-defunct dinner was to have been our first date-date in over a month.

Her expression was one of commiseration. "You must be patient. Recovery from a traumatic brain injury is a complicated process."

"I know that, but—"

"You and your *folie du jour* have made his life interesting, yes. And that is good. But interesting can be problematic at times."

I wasn't sure I'd heard her correctly. "My what?"

"Your hazards and exploits. Trey cannot help wanting to protect you, and this sometimes involves him beyond his capabilities. You must not let your life choices interfere with his well-being."

"What exactly are you trying to tell me?"

She smiled with infuriating patience. "When I was a little girl, I visited my grandmother in Provence every spring. One day I found a butterfly struggling to free itself from its cocoon.

I wanted to help it, but *mémère* told me, "Non. It is the struggle that makes it strong enough to fly.'"

I stared at her. "That's your contribution to the situation, a butterfly story?"

Her lips compressed in a straight line. "Then here is the story without the pretty butterfly. This isn't about you. Your wants, your needs, the way you wish things were or were not. What matters is Trey. And right now, he is stable and functioning. I am determined to make sure that does not change."

She got in the elevator and punched the first floor button. I grabbed the door before it could close.

"Are you threatening me? Because that sounded like a threat."

Her eyes flashed. "We do not need to threaten each other because we both want the same thing."

"That thing being Trey?"

"That is not what I mean!"

"I think it's exactly what you mean."

"I meant…ugh! Now is not the time for this discussion. I am late for dinner with Jean Luc." She straightened her back, smoothed the anger from her perfect face. "If you would kindly step back, please."

I hesitated only one second, then pulled back my hand and let the doors close.

Chapter Two

Back in the apartment, I locked the door behind me, engaging the drill-proof deadbolts with more force than purely necessary. Trey eased himself to standing, wincing as he straightened.

"Your ex is asking for it," I said. "And she'd better be glad I… why are you giving me that look?"

He narrowed his eyes. "Because this is your fault."

I put my hands on my hips. "You're the one who fell out of bed."

"I did not fall, I was pushed."

"You were not pushed, you fell and landed where there was no bed."

"Because you pushed me where there was no bed."

"Because you…" I closed my eyes, counted to three, then opened them. "Never mind. This isn't a real argument. You're hurt and sexually frustrated, both of which make you belligerent. I feel your pain, boyfriend, believe me. So let's not take it out on each other."

He grimaced and rubbed his shoulder. I knew he'd landed badly the second he'd hit the floor with me on top of him. I'd felt the unnatural give in the shoulder, the full force of my weight coming down on that one precarious joint. I'd banged my elbow up, bruised my knee, but he'd been hurt worse. And things had been going so well up to that point.

He stamped his way to the bathroom, tee-shirt balled in his hand. I followed, propping myself next to the sink while he rummaged in the medicine cabinet. His body was taut with muscle, but the accident and the SWAT ops and a decade of Krav Maga had taken their toll. He was no longer a cocky twenty-something, and had the scars and pinned knees and titanium-screwed spine of a hard-lived thirty-five years.

I took the PT tape from the shelf along with the scissors. "Let me do this."

"I can—"

"Just let me."

He hesitated, then nodded. I stood behind him and traced a line from his shoulder blade down the curve of his upper arm. The deltoid lay on top of the joint, a finely honed slice of muscle connecting the bicep in the front and the trapezius in the back, and I followed its contours.

"There?"

He nodded again. The grumpy was burning out, replaced with an exhausted composure. I cut off about eight inches of tape, scissored it into a Y shape, then stretched it along the top of his shoulder. I crisscrossed that with another length of tape along the scapula. The result resembled an exotic tribal tattoo, slick ebony against his pale Irish skin.

I cut off a final strip of tape. "You sure you're okay?"

"I will be in the morning."

"No, I mean the other kind of okay."

Trey sucked in a breath as the last piece of tape pulled the injured muscle into place. "You need to keep the tension—"

"At sixty percent, I know. If there's one thing I've learned from a year of being with you, it's how to use kinesiology tape." I smoothed the final result with my thumb. "And you didn't answer my question."

"Oh." He dipped his head forward, exposing the back of his neck for me. "I'm okay. Work has been challenging, that's all."

"Work with Phoenix or work with Garrity?"

"Both."

"Anything serious?"

"The usual at Phoenix. Marisa wants me more involved in the client intake process."

I couldn't actually blame Marisa; if I'd been his boss, I'd have wanted him out from behind his desk too. He was Phoenix Corporate Security's top premises liability agent, a math-heavy endeavor involving actuarial tables and crime foreseeability studies—the part Trey loved—and showing up at client meetings to explain things—the part Trey hated. But clients were quick to sign contracts if Trey was present. Everybody wanted an Armani-clad bad ass on their team.

I returned the tape to the cabinet. "How about things with Garrity?"

"Good. My LINX clearance came through."

"Meaning?"

"Meaning I'm authorized to generate my own AMMO reports now. I still have to be supervised, of course. But I can start moving into quantitative analysis, predictive policing."

I recognized the acronyms. AMMO was the Atlanta Metro Major Offenders task force, a combined effort between the Atlanta Police Department and the FBI, currently headed up by his friend and former partner, Dan Garrity, which is how Trey got hooked up with it. LINX was some kind of official law enforcement database, one he'd been unable to access until he passed the second tier of training. Which apparently, he had.

"Congratulations," I said.

"Thank you."

I smiled at his reflection. "I'm glad you have cop work to do again. I want everything to be good, you know?"

"I know. So do I."

"Us things, too."

His eyes crinkled. "Us things are good for me. Are they good for you?"

"Yes. Of course. It's just that…I don't know."

Trey frowned, then turned around so that we were face to face. He put his hands on my hips, which took me by surprise. Trey rarely initiated physical contact, but the doctors always said the same thing—that even though his frontal lobes would never fully recover from his injury, his brain would develop new coping strategies. I knew this, and it still caught me off guard sometimes, the tiny infinitesimal steps he took into a recovery that looked different every single day, but which tonight looked like his thumbs resting lightly on my waist.

"What's wrong?" he said.

"Nothing. It's just that you've been working fifty hours a week, plus volunteering with Garrity, plus training." I gave him my serious face. "And I know that staying super-busy is your favorite coping device when you're not okay."

He bristled only the slightest. "A structured schedule is a significant part of my recovery complex."

I reached behind him and pulled the eucalyptus rub off the shelf. The stuff smelled to high heaven, but worked wonders on stressed and strained muscles.

"I simply want to make sure that you're not decompensating. Because Gabriella thinks I'm a destabilizing influence."

"She said that?"

"Sort of." I massaged some of the liniment into the corded tendon on the left side of his neck. "Am I? You have to tell me if I am."

He considered. "I wouldn't say destabilizing."

"What would you say?"

"What's another word for 'chaotic'? One that doesn't sound as…"

"Chaotic?"

"Right. Because that's not the right word." He dropped his eyes. "I know this wasn't your fault. I said that because I was frustrated, and tired, and…you know."

"I know."

I wrapped my arms around him gently, trying not to aggravate his injury. My reflection gazed back at me alongside his scarred and taped shoulder. Spring was the reenactment season, and hundreds of hours on the mock battlefield had tanned my skin, lightened my dark blond hair with honey-gold streaks. Even my eyes seemed lighter—a gray-flecked green now instead of the deeper hazel—and I saw new wrinkles at the corners. I was no longer a twenty-something either, thanks to my last birthday.

"You need to lie down," I said.

"Okay."

"I'll get the ice pack."

"Okay." He raised his eyes. "I really am sorry. About tonight."

I kissed him on the chin. "It's all right. I would have preferred champagne and dinner to liniment and oxy. But I'll take you however you come."

Chapter Three

Trey was asleep fifteen minutes after the meds hit his system. I looked up *comme de le merde* in the online French-to-English dictionary and decided that was for the best. I picked my red dress up off the floor and re-hung it in the closet—it had spent approximately ten minutes on my body—but I opened the champagne. Poured myself a glass and hoisted it in a toast to the bedroom door.

"Cheers, boyfriend. I'd like to say this is an unusual way to end a date, but we both know it's not. Here's to us anyway."

I slid open the door to the terrace and stepped into the night. Down below, Peachtree and Piedmont streets glittered like rivers of dirty diamonds. I suddenly panged for a cigarette. There was no tobacco in Trey's apartment, of course, and I'd been smoke-free for almost five months, but down below, there was anything I could have wanted, from the gritty and grungy to the luxuriously illicit.

I stared up at the slate gray sky, a city sky, familiar now. This spring marked not only a year with Trey, but a year in Atlanta, a year with my gun shop and its Confederate clientele. From spring to spring, like the Civil War itself, bookended between two Aprils. And in the morning I'd be on the reenactment field again. But until then, I savored the rising night breeze, closed my eyes...

And heard the doorbell.

I grumbled to myself as I padded back inside and peered through the peephole. Garrity stood there, running his hand through his already messy red hair.

I unlocked the door and opened it a crack. "Go away. You can't have him. Tell your task force they can—"

"I'm not here on AMMO business."

"Then why…Wait a second, you're supposed to be in Alabama. With your kid. Doing dad-and-kid things."

"Yes. And I want to be in Alabama. But I have to get this last minute thing straightened out, which I can't do in the hallway. So let me in, okay?"

I stepped back and opened the door wide. In his navy suit, Garrity looked like an FBI recruitment poster, but he still wore the gold Atlanta PD detective shield pinned to his belt.

He fixed me with an accusatory glower. "Neither of you are answering your phones. I've been calling for over an hour."

I heard the beeping then, both our cell phones, like dueling banjos. "Sorry. I was on the terrace and Trey's asleep."

He glanced toward the bedroom. "You wore him out already?"

"You could say that."

Garrity plunked down on the leather sofa and put his feet on the coffee table, examining the apartment with his typical bemusement. I plopped on the sofa next to him.

"So what are you doing here if you don't want Trey?"

"I need to talk to you."

"Crap. What have I done now?"

"Nothing for once." He pulled an envelope from his pocket. "But I figure you might be able to explain why I'm getting a letter from Ainsworth Lovett's office wanting to set up an interview with his investigator."

"Who is Ainsworth Lovett?"

He stared at me. "Seriously? You've never heard of Atlanta's most notorious criminal defense attorney?"

"I'm not a criminal, so no, I haven't. Why is he notorious?"

"Because he takes on the worst of the worst. He hates the death penalty. Hates mandatory sentencing. Hates anything that makes my job easier. And he's taken your cousin Jasper as a client."

"What the…? Give me that!"

Garrity handed me the letter. I read it quickly, and saw that he had spoken true—Jasper now had a genuine, spit-shined, top-notch lawyer. This was the same Jasper who'd led a white supremacist militia group in rebellion against the Ku Klux Klan, and who was now a guest of the Chatham County Detention Center awaiting trial on charges from criminal trespass to felony assault to conspiracy to commit murder. The same Jasper who'd tried to kill Trey and me, and who'd come damn close to doing it. Which was why he was in state-sponsored rehab for a shattered wrist and ankle, courtesy of the three bullets Trey had pumped into him. It was a clear case of self-defense, backed up with two eyewitnesses and a security camera, so no charges had been filed against Trey. But I knew that could change.

I threw the letter on the coffee table. "This is bullshit!"

"My reaction exactly. Have you heard anything from anyone down Savannah way?"

"Not a word. Trey and I have already given our interviews. Last time I talked to the prosecutor's office, they said we were out of it until the trial."

"So has this investigator, this…" Garrity peered at the letter. "This Finn Hudson person. Has he contacted you? Or Trey? Or anybody else connected with the case?"

"Not that I know of. I left the shop early, though, and didn't get the mail. I'll check tomorrow."

"What about Trey?"

"He hasn't said anything. Neither has Marisa, and you know if Boss Lady got a letter like that, she'd be screaming bloody murder about it. That woman does not like surprises, especially not legal ones that involve Phoenix Corporate Security, and she'd have Trey in her office ASAP if she—"

Trey's phone rang. I picked it up, peered at the screen, and felt my stomach drop.

Marisa.

Chapter Four

Marisa got right to the point, as usual. "Where's Trey?"

"Asleep. He's—"

"Wake him up and put him on."

I tried to keep the annoyance out of my voice. "Let me rephrase. He pulled his shoulder, and now he's in a drugged stupor. Can I take a message?"

Marisa exhaled in frustration. She didn't much like me, a feeling I returned, plus she seemed to think I was a trouble magnet. It made our relationship antagonistic, touchy, and difficult to navigate.

"Is he okay?" she said.

"He's fine. Gabriella doctored him up and now he's sleeping off some heavy-duty narcotics."

"Oh." She paused, and I could almost hear her foot tapping. "So perhaps you could help me."

"You got a letter from Ainsworth Lovett's investigator, didn't you?"

"Worse. Trey got a letter and has scheduled a meeting with this investigator without telling me."

I was momentarily flabbergasted. "But Trey would never—"

"I'm looking at his desk calendar right now, and I see an appointment on Monday morning at eight-thirty for—surprise, surprise—Finn Hudson."

That *was* surprising. Trey was scrupulous in all ways procedural. "Perhaps he just—"

"Did you get one of these letters too?"

"I don't know yet."

Marisa's tone grew stern. "I don't want either of you talking to this person, do you understand? Defense council cannot compel you to cooperate."

"This has all been explained by the prosecutor, trust me."

"Good. Because this is not the kind of situation Trey needs to be involved in. Tell him to stay out of whatever Lovett and his minion are stirring up. And tell him to call me first thing in the morning."

"Perfectly happy to do so. But I could also let you talk to Detective Garrity, who also got contacted by this investigator person, and who is sitting right beside me."

I shoved the phone at Garrity. While he dealt with Marisa, I rummaged in my tote bag for more nicotine gum. Then I got my phone and looked up Finn Hudson, PI. His website popped up instantly, heavy with respectable blues and professional reds. His photograph dominated the space—a sturdy white guy with a high forehead and a salt-and-pepper comb-over. I imagined he'd once been a federal agent, or a police sergeant. Something bossy and rule-bound. There was no résumé, no other photographs beyond that nondescript headshot. Finn Hudson obviously liked to keep a curtain between himself and the world, which I supposed is what made him the kind of investigator a criminal defense attorney would hire.

Garrity threw Trey's phone on the coffee table and rubbed the bridge of his nose. "Marisa wants to know the same thing I do—how can Jasper afford the services of a big-gun lawyer like Lovett?"

"I don't know. As far as his family is concerned, Jasper might as well be dead. Not that the Boone family is rolling in the big bucks anymore. The Feds snatched the marina, which not only put the kibosh on the smuggling, but the legitimate business too."

Garrity rubbed his chin. "You think that militia group he created is funding this?"

"I doubt it. Most of them are in jail too, waiting for their own trials."

Garrity grimaced in distaste. Jasper's co-defendants were all dirty cops. There was nothing Garrity hated worse.

"What about the KKK?" he said.

"They booted Jasper from their ranks, so there's no money coming from that direction. Of course there are hundreds of KKK groups in the US. Any one of them could have decided that Jasper's brand of race hate is exactly what their mission needs."

"Enough to throw a couple hundred thousand his way? 'Cause that's what a lawyer like this costs."

I shook my head. "I don't know. What did Marisa think?"

"She was as polite as a glacier just then, but she told me she'd have *somebody's* balls for breakfast if anyone from Ainsworth Lovett's office sets one foot into Phoenix on Monday morning."

"Somebody meaning Trey."

"That was the gist of it. And I don't blame her. Savannah was complicated business, especially where Jasper and your uncle were concerned, and she and Phoenix got tangled up pretty bad." He lowered his voice, gentle. "Fess up, Tai. Is there something you're not telling me?"

"No. I thought we were almost done with all this. I *want* to be done with all this."

"You had any more cryptic messages?"

I felt an involuntary shiver down my spine. "No."

"No more photographs?"

I shook my head. The photo I'd received was innocent enough—a candid shot of me, my back to the camera, taken at the top of Kennesaw Mountain with Atlanta shimmering in the distance—except that I had no clue who'd taken it, nor who'd written the message on the back: *And all the kingdoms of the world and their glory.* From the Bible, where Satan tempted Jesus at the top of the mountain.

Garrity squinted at me with his cop eyes. "Are you sure? No weird e-mails, no strange customers?"

I visualized my clientele down at the gun shop. "No stranger than usual."

"Odd phone calls?"

"The past few months have been quiet. I work, Trey works or runs or lifts weights or hangs out with you down at the FBI."

Garrity caught my tone. "Is something going on with him I need to know about?"

"He's over-scheduled for sure, but he assures me all is well."

Garrity took his feet down from the coffee table. "I don't know what's brewing, but you want to be on top of it, I promise you, before it turns into a three-ring circus."

"I thought I was done with bloody circuses."

"There's always another bloody circus." He pushed himself up, gave my shoulder a reassuring squeeze. "Call me when you find out what's going on."

"I will."

I walked him to the door. I suddenly realized that I missed Garrity too, that he and Trey regularly retreated deep into their law enforcement world, which was the one place they could still understand each other. But when Trey talked about their official work, it was necessarily redacted, the juicy parts off-limits to a civilian like me. Like so much of his life, so much of his past. Suddenly I felt even more like an outsider.

I stopped at the threshold. "Garrity? Can I ask you something completely off topic?"

"Shoot."

"Why did Trey and Gabriella break up?"

He shook his head as he stepped into the hall. "You'll have to ask Trey."

"I did, a long time ago. He said they didn't have that kind of relationship, and I said what kind, and he said the kind that breaks up, and I said, what does that mean, and he stared at me for a while, then walked off."

"See? Clear as a bell."

"Garrity—"

"For real, Tai, I'm not the person to ask. I don't know shit about relationships. Ask my ex-wife." He put his hands on his hips. "I know this one thing, though. They were never really a couple-couple. Trey is a one-woman man to the middle of his marrow. But Gabriella? The woman's as fine as china, but she doesn't have a monogamous bone in her pretty little body."

"Are you telling me I need to be watching out?"

"I'm telling you what I know. You decide what to do with it." He gave me a weary smile. "One whole year together. Doesn't seem that long and yet it seems like forever."

I returned the smile. "I suspect Trey would describe it exactly the same way."

Chapter Five

Trey always slept deeply, even without a dose of oxy in his system. His mouth softened and his forehead unwrinkled, smoothing the furrow that deepened between his eyebrows when he was annoyed or frustrated or confused.

I lay on the bed face to face with him, ran my fingers through his hair. "Trey?"

No response. I stroked his forehead, heard the deeper inhale, the interrupted rhythm of respiration. After a few seconds, his eyes fluttered open.

"Hey," I said.

He licked his lips. "Hey."

"You coherent?"

"What?"

"Guess not." I propped up on my elbow. "How's the shoulder?"

"Better."

He smelled like menthol and shea butter, and the skin on his neck was still cool from the ice pack. His eyes were half-lidded, his voice slurred with painkillers and sleep.

"Trey?"

"Hmmm?"

"I need to ask you a question."

"A what?"

"A question. About the investigator from Ainsworth Lovett's office. Marisa said you'd made an appointment with him on Monday."

"With who?"

"Finn Hudson. The PI who works for Jasper's new attorney. You're meeting with him on Monday."

He shook his head. "No, no. That was blue." Then he closed his eyes again.

I sighed. Gabriella was right. He was totally useless. I pushed myself up, but he reached over and tangled his hand in my hair, running his fingers deep into the curls. There was something about my hair that enraptured him. Sometimes I woke up to find he'd wrapped one finger around a tendril at the nape of my neck, closing it into his fist like a keepsake.

"Come to bed," he said.

"In a minute. I need to do something first."

"So come to bed now, then come to bed in a minute."

I shook my head at him, amused despite my frustration. "You're not making any sense."

"Of course I am."

He ran his thumb along my bottom lip, his touch so light I felt shivers racing across my skin, like a breeze stirring up still water. This was his prime tactic for seduction, the almost innocent caress. Never overt, always an invitation. Always irresistible.

"You're supposed to be taking it easy," I said.

"This is easy," he whispered, rolling to his back. "Very very easy."

I straddled his hips, careful of the injured shoulder as he stretched out underneath me, warm and willing. Half submission, half seduction, total surrender—to me, to desire, to the languid, oxy-hazed pleasure of the moment. I bent to kiss him, my hair falling in a curtain around us.

As it turned out, Gabriella was wrong. He wasn't *totally* useless.

◇◇◇

I left him in the tangle of bedsheets, slipping his shirt over my head as I went to his desk. I flicked on the reading lamp, and it made a warm circle against the shadows of the living room. The black furniture and blank white walls always seemed so stark without Trey. He provided a flesh and blood beating heart in what was otherwise a hollow space, as empty as a vacuum.

I sat in his chair and got a mechanical pencil and yellow pad from the top drawer. There were no places in the apartment off limits to me, the whole of his present life open. And yet there was the whole of his past, a vast unknown territory. Trey had instructed my brother to turn over his entire psychological profile to me, to help me understand the intricacies of his brain, but the MRIs and cognitive reports hadn't revealed who he'd been before, the Trey that Garrity and Gabriella knew and loved and missed.

I shook off the unsettled feeling, switched on Trey's computer, and looked up Ainsworth Lovett's website. I printed off pages of it, mostly FAQs and explanations of terms, and then started collecting articles on his past cases. The more I read, the more I understood why Jasper appealed to him—the good lawyer had a taste for tabloid fodder.

His previous client list was a roster of sadism. The LaSalle brothers, accused of killing their parents and feeding their remains to the family koi collection. The Boxing Day Bomber, a quasi-terrorist who'd blown up a rec center the day after Christmas. The San Diego Succubus, accused of sleeping with and murdering five men, every single one slaughtered in the bed she'd lured them to.

And now he'd sicced his investigator on Garrity and Trey. Not me, not yet anyway. But my politely threatening letter was coming, that was certain, was perhaps already at the shop, waiting for me.

I slumped back in the chair. I'd thought I was almost done with Jasper Boone. My first cousin. My most frequent nightmare.

When we were little, I'd spent countless afternoons with him and his brother Jefferson, the three of us playing hide-and-seek in their marshland backyard. We were all three tow-headed, tanned as dark and supple as leather, running buckwild while our parents drank whiskey sours on the deck and watched the sun melt over the Wilmington River.

Their mother was my mother's younger sister, who abandoned Uncle Boone and the boys the summer I entered middle school. My family abruptly stopped visiting soon after. I never understood why, only that this fell into the category of "grown-up reasons" and that there was no bending them.

I eventually learned it had something to do with the underbelly of my uncle's successful marina, which not only made a good respectable living, but also channeled its fair share of marijuana and moonshine and illegal tobacco into the Lowcountry. My parents had been well-off in the gated community way, but Boone had been rich in the twenty-acre private waterfront estate way. And despite the cold war my parents had decreed, I secretly visited his place almost every weekend during my late teenage years, usually sneaking home some moonshine in a Mason jar.

Until Boone went to prison for manslaughter, the result of a bar fight gone bad wrong. Until his membership in the KKK came out. He underwent a prison redemption, as they say, seeing the errors of his racist ways and denouncing his former associates. He didn't repent of his other criminal activities, however, which was why he went to prison the second time, getting out early thanks to an incurable lung condition and compassionate parole. IPF, the diagnosis said. Idiopathic pulmonary fibrosis.

My parents were dead now, but Beauregard Forrest Boone, once upon a time the most dangerous man in Chatham County, was still alive, though we hadn't spoken since that night in the fall, barely five months ago. What was there to say? His own son had tried to kill him, and his other son too. How could we even begin to talk about that?

The memories of that rain-slashed night were vivid still, though. Trey and Jasper and me…and Hope. She was the fourth player in that final act, a vital witness currently serving time at the Chatham County Detention Center for her own crimes. We had complicated history, Hope and I, and I'd bid good riddance to her. But if Lovett was stirring up the pot, then I knew I'd have to talk to her again. Back to Savannah, back to all the hungry ghosts haunting its shadows and stones.

I threw down the letter and lowered my head to the desk.

Not again.

I didn't think I could do it again.

Chapter Six

The next morning Trey woke up groggy and still in pain, but not quite as edgy. This happy state lasted until he talked to Marisa. I shimmied into khaki pants while he paced in front of the terrace doors, cell phone to his ear.

"No, an appointment written in *blue* means I need to update you on something. An appointment in *red* is for face-to-face meetings…. But I wasn't meeting Hudson, I was meeting *you* to inform you…well, actually yes, that *did* seem like something that could wait until Monday, hence my putting it on the calendar for then."

I pulled on the white long-sleeved shirt that completed my official shop uniform, deciding to skip the sneakers and go for the heavy-duty work boots. I'd be in-field all day with both infantry and cavalry units, which meant the staging area would be a slop of churned mud and horse manure. I was not going to come out of the day smelling—or looking—like a rose.

Trey shook his head. "Of course I wouldn't schedule a meeting without approving it with you, which is…why would I need a color key on my own desk calendar?"

The conversation continued in this vein for several more minutes. I checked my phone. Another text from my helper Kenny, the third that morning, saying that he'd arrived at the shop and had his truck almost loaded. It was his first time prepping by himself, and he was consumed with the jitters. I wasn't worried. Kenny knew the shop's on-location routine, especially set-up and takedown, and he'd been active in the reenactment community since he was a toddler. Plus he was nineteen, with a nineteen-year-old's energy.

Trey exhaled loudly. "Of course. I understand. I'll have it for you by five."

He hung up. He was still wearing the workout pants and tee shirt he'd put on before he'd been forced to admit a morning run was beyond his capabilities. He could pace, however, and so he did, like a tin soldier wound far too tight. I was still worried about his shoulder, worried enough to want to stay home, but a teensy part of me couldn't wait to get out the door. He'd been nothing but complaints and thwarted energy since he'd gotten out of bed at six, as usual. When he got in such a mood, he was *not* a pleasant companion.

I pulled on a boot. "What does Marisa want by five?"

"A 302 on Ainsworth Lovett."

Phoenix code for an information report. I'd had to fill out one for every extracurricular event I'd involved Trey in that somehow also involved Phoenix. I'd created 302s on car chases and boat chases, skulls and reticulated pythons. They felt old hat to me now.

"I assume you're doing this from home since you can't drive," I said.

"I can access the Phoenix data bases remotely, but to get a full background, I need to access LINX, and to do that, I need to be at the field office, and I can't do that until Monday." He threw himself in his desk chair, drummed his fingers on a legal pad. "You said Garrity had heard nothing from the Savannah detective on the case, correct?"

"Yep."

"Or from the prosecutor?"

"Yep again. But I'm not surprised. Savannah Metro is fruit-basket turnover right now—new police chief, new recruits, new procedures, all of them pushing that whole "racist bad cops in an underground militia" stink as far away from themselves as possible. If they could mash a button and make Jasper and all his co-defendants go poof, they would."

Trey had a mechanical pencil in hand now, beating a steady tap-tap-tap against the wood, and he was spinning the chair in a tight arc, back and forth. I recognized the look in his eye. Perseveration was the clinical term, but it meant that once Trey caught the scent of something, he became incapable of dropping it. It wasn't all due to the accident—Garrity's stories of the pre-TBI Trey revealed an individual with a sharpened sense of focus, an extreme talent at concentrating. It had served him well as a sniper, and it served him well now, even if it stuck in high gear sometimes.

I stood up. "Regardless, nothing's happening today. So stop… oh heck, hang on."

I pulled my phone out of my pocket and sighed. Kenny. I put the phone to my ear, but he started jabbering before I could even say hello.

"Miss Tai! I can't find the tent!"

I pressed a hand against my forehead. "Crap. I forgot. Raymond Junior across the square borrowed it for some party he's having at the restaurant."

"What am I supposed to do?"

"Bring the back-up tent."

"But—"

"And bring the mail! Don't forget the mail! Even if you forget the tent, don't forget the mail!"

"But—"

"You'll be fine. I have faith in you, Kenny."

I hung up before he could work himself into a lather. I propped a hip on the edge of Trey's desk. He was staring out the window, tapping the pencil, two seconds from lather himself.

"Was there a letter?" he said.

"I don't know. I'll check when I get there and call you back."

"You should have asked him now. I need to put that information in the report. You should have—"

"No, no, no. We are not doing this." I put my hands on his shoulders and looked him square in the eye. "You are grumpy as hell, and there is not a thing I can do about it. And if I don't get out of here, I am going to grumpy up too. And then it will be the OK Corral of grumpiness, and neither of us will walk away unbloodied from that."

He narrowed his eyes. "A point."

"I will call when I get there. And then I'm going to watch the Blue and the Gray pummel each other. And you are going to take some more oxycodone, wash it down with that nasty anti-inflammatory tea Gabriella left, and lie down with the ice pack. And then maybe, just maybe, you and I can have a civilized conversation when I get back. Deal?"

He started to fold his arms, then winced. "No, it is not a deal. I have a 302 due by five today."

"Lucky for you, you've got a proactive girlfriend." I pointed to his desk. "Everything I could find on Lovett and his investigator, printed and stapled and tucked into folders. All it needs is a summary and some collating, and you've got a fine Phoenix-worthy information report." I took a deep breath. "So go back to sleep, okay? And then I'll come back and rub some liniment into that shoulder and we'll have a nice quiet dinner, just the two of us. How's that?"

His expression softened the tiniest bit, and he mumbled something that I was going to take for acquiescence. I pulled the pencil from his fingers and tossed it on the desktop, then pointed toward the bedroom. He heaved a sigh of protest.

But he went.

Chapter Seven

I was late, thanks to an overturned truck full of crab legs right before my exit. It was on fire when I got there, and had three lanes blocked and all of I-85 smelling like a Red Lobster. I was running when I got to my spot outside the reenactment field where the various sutlers set up shop. The kettle-corn guy was already selling his wares, his giant copper cauldron fired up like the noonday sun, the smell of sugar and oil heavy on the morning air.

Kenny waited behind the table, trying desperately to keep everything from blowing away. He was dressed in his butternut infantry uniform, his kepi covering his short brown hair, his glasses falling halfway down his nose. Today's skirmish wasn't a reenactment of any particular importance—on this April morning one hundred and fifty years ago, the Confederacy was slouching its bloodied and disgruntled way toward surrender at Appomattox Court House—but I didn't want him to miss muster.

"I'm here, I'm here, I'm here!" I threw myself behind the table. "Did everybody get their pick-ups?"

The wind riffled up a pile of shop pamphlets, and Kenny slammed a hand on top of them. "Yes, ma'am. Except for Mr. Reynolds. He insisted on waiting for you, as usual."

Reynolds Harrington liked any excuse to play Rhett Butler to my...well, not Scarlett O'Hara, for sure. But Reynolds liked a female foil, and I was the best he could get this morning.

I thunked a plastic bin of antique bullets on top of the pamphlets. "Did you remember to bring the mail?"

"Yes, ma'am. I left it in the back of the truck so's—"

I hurried to his truck and flung open the gate. And then I froze. Smack dab in the middle of the tee-shirts sat a bouquet of red roses. They were the color of heartblood, rich and velvety, and the cut crystal vase fractured the morning light into yellow-white shards.

I felt the first whirl of vertigo. "Kenny? Where did these come from?"

"They came to the shop after you left yesterday. But you gave me strict orders not to call you last night unless it was an emergency, and roses weren't, so I kept them safe until today."

I'd been waiting for this shoe to drop, for my mysterious stalker to make contact again. I'd been expecting another photograph, though, or a mysterious letter written in code. Not roses.

I peered among the petals. "Did you see who brought them? Was there a card? You didn't touch them, did you?"

"Miss Tai—"

"There might be fingerprints. They can get DNA from fingerprints now, and—"

"Miss Tai, I swear it's like you never got flowers before." Kenny plucked the card from the leaves and extended it my way. "They're from Mr. Trey."

I blinked at him and accepted the card. There was Trey's signature, in that proper Palmer method handwriting he'd learned in Catholic school. I felt a blush rising, and a squirmy ripple of pleasure.

Kenny noticed both. "Aw, that's sweet, right there."

"Yeah yeah yeah." I slipped the card in my back pocket. "So where's the mail?"

Kenny pointed. I snatched it up, yanked off the rubber band, and sifted through it. Sure enough, there was a letter from Ainsworth Lovett's office. I ripped it open and pulled out the triple-folded paper, skimming it quickly.

It was the same letter Garrity and Trey had gotten, and just like theirs, this Finn Hudson person wanted to interview me.

Right. Like I had anything to share with someone trying to defend that son of a bitch who'd tried to murder me and mine. I crumpled the letter into a ball and threw it back in the truck, then pulled out my cell phone to call Trey.

A booming voice came at me from behind. "Tai Randolph, you are tardy!"

I turned around and popped my hands on my hips. "Reynolds Harrington, I told you about sneaking up on me!"

The man behind the voice was short and round, with silver hair falling across his forehead. He had a neatly trimmed beard and eyes like a satyr and an unlit cigar champed between his teeth. He'd been a charmer in his day, back when "wealthy scion" counted as a respectable career option. Now, after his sister's death, he was the head of the Harrington Foundation, charged with preserving the finest private collection of Civil War relics in the Southeast.

He took my hand in his, pressed a kiss to my knuckles. "You are a vision, m'dear."

"And you are a liar." I gave him the up and down. "And a Yankee to boot. You got galvanized, I see."

"The Union side needed a few good men, so today my impression will be of Federal infantryman Lance Henry Harrington—no relation—who first fought with the Illinois 86th Infantry in Chickmauga, honing my martial skills in Buzzard Roost and Snake Gap Creek before taking a Minié ball to the chest."

"So you die today?"

"Alas, I am doomed to perish on the field of glory." He scrutinized me. "Why don't you ever wear a nice dress like the other young ladies? A pretty calico, maybe a gingham?"

I laughed. "I'm doing an impression of a woman impersonating a Confederate infantryman."

He dropped his eyes to my chest. "Female infiltrators usually bound their chests to disguise their…ah…assets."

"There's not enough gauze in the metro area to disguise these assets."

I reached into the back of the truck and unwrapped Reynold's latest purchase—a genuine Confederate cavalry saber, quite possibly a Froelich, which made it easily worth the five grand he'd paid for it. That he was neither cavalry nor Confederate today bothered him not one whit.

I slipped the belt around his ample waist, cinched the buckle. "Quick question before the bugle—what do you know about Ainsworth Lovett?"

"Idealistic liberal from an old-money conservative family. Takes on the scandalous cases no decent lawyer would touch, mostly to piss off said family. Why do you ask?"

"He's Jasper's new lawyer. And his investigator is trying to set up an interview with me and Trey."

"Well now, that *is* a game changer." He sheathed his weapon in its matching scabbard. "Are you ready to dig around in that again?"

"Ready or not, I'm about to start."

The bugle sounded, calling him to arms. "Lovett is picky in his clientele. He prefers them rich and headline-making, but every now and then he signs up a less-than-wealthy client if he thinks the case is especially horrifying."

"Pro bono?"

Reynolds snorted. "Hardly, though he will work on a contingency basis, I have heard. How does a miscreant like Jasper Boone come about such funds, or the promise of such thereof?"

"You're hitting the same question I have. You haven't seen any odd transactions in the relic trade, have you?"

He shook his head. Reynolds bought and sold on a higher plane than I did, up in the five-and-six-figure stratosphere. I specialized in tracking down specific single pieces, but he saw extensive collections come up for private auction. And he knew as well as I did that well-moneyed, well-connected racists were often the buyers or sellers. If Jasper had indeed found some white supremacist movement besides the KKK to be his savior, liquidating a few old relics might provide some hard cash.

"I'll send out some feelers come Monday and let you know what I find," he said. He fixed me with a watery, but dead serious eye. "As you know, such organizations as we are speaking of are not charities. Jasper would have to have something to offer them in return besides his undying loyalty."

"That's what I'm afraid of." I adjusted the hang of his scabbard. "There. Once more into the breach. Fingers crossed things turn out differently for you this time, Private Harrington."

He bowed low, sweeping his hat. "Ah, m'dear, I suspect things will play out exactly as they have before. They always do."

◇◇◇

I remembered his words after the melee, when the sun finally set on the battle and the last pick-up trucks growled away, the last picnickers with them. I did most of the clean-up myself while Kenny engaged in the post-battle rundown with his unit. The morning air had been heated into starchy afternoon stillness, but a graying sky and the kick-up of fresh wind meant rain was on the way, so I didn't tarry.

I'd packed the last box when an unfamiliar man stepped up to my counter, bare now of any goods. His khaki shorts and black tee were clean, his pale face unstriped with dirt or grass. He wore his black cap low on his forehead, the brim obscuring his eyes, and there was something off about him. Not a reenactor, not a spectator, not a fellow sutler from one of the other shops.

"Tai Randolph?" he said.

"Yes?"

"Owner and proprietor of Dexter's Guns and More?"

"Yes." I kept my expression blandly professional. "Can I help you with something?"

"Yes, you can." He pushed the cap back, his pale eyes penetrating, uncomfortably so. He got a good long look at me, then handed over a large manila envelope. "You can consider yourself officially served."

I ripped open the envelope and dumped the contents on my table. I started to feel sick to my stomach, and then the nausea ripened into ripping pure anger. Suddenly, I knew where Jasper thought he was going to get the money for his extravagant new defense.

I shoved the envelope and its contents away and looked up. "You can tell that lousy waste of oxygen who sent you that—"

But the man had vanished.

Chapter Eight

I slammed the trunk of the Camaro and put the phone to my ear again. "What the hell is he up to?"

Trey's voice held all the warmth of steel. "He's suing us."

"I know what he's doing, I want to know why he's doing it!"

"Because he wants nine million dollars in damages, most likely to pay for his new defense."

I flung myself behind the wheel and slammed the door. "Yeah, but he's up to something else too. Even he knows there's not a jury in the world gonna award a racist bastard like him that kind of settlement, not for a few well-deserved bullets and a kick to the knee."

"Which is probably why he's serving as his own counsel in this matter. Because he couldn't find a lawyer who'd take the case."

"Because it's ridiculous!"

"Yes, it is. But it's happening nonetheless."

I cranked the engine, yanked the gearshift, and revved my car into a grass-spitting takeoff worthy of an Alabama dirt track. "The creepy son of a bitch who served me disappeared before I could ask any questions."

"Process servers don't answer questions."

"Oh, but this wasn't an official one from the sheriff's department. No, this one knew exactly what he was delivering, and then he hot-footed it out of there before I could yell at him. Jasper hired him personally, I know he did."

"That seems likely as well."

I grumbled some more, gunned the engine. God, I wanted to skewer that arrogant murderous, conniving...

I took a deep breath, blew it out. "What did Marisa say when she got her papers?"

"The same things you did, I imagine. Worse perhaps."

That was the most outrageous part of the suit, Jasper's allegation that when Trey and I defended ourselves, we were acting not as individuals, but as agents of our respective businesses. Which meant that he was technically suing the gun shop for three million, which meant that my co-owner brother was about to get involved, and Phoenix Corporate Security for six million, which meant that Marisa and her platoon of lawyers were already involved.

"So she's mad?"

"Furious. Not at me personally, however, which is a good thing." A pause. "She wants to meet tomorrow morning, as soon as she's done with church. At the office."

"Do you need me to drive you?"

"Yes."

"Because of your shoulder, or because she wants to see me too?"

"Both."

I cursed and banged the steering wheel, accidentally blaring the horn. The guy in the pick-up beside me honked back. I ignored him. Traffic leaving a reenactment event was always a bear. Lots of pedestrians milling about, half of them in circa-1865 garments carrying plastic coolers and talking on their cell phones.

"This is why Garrity's involved," I said, "because they're gonna make him testify about your resignation from the Atlanta PD. They're gonna imply you're damaged goods."

"It was officially a retirement. And I left with a clean record."

"Yes, but Jasper will twist and shred and..." I honked, this time with intent. "Get the hell out of the way!"

"Tai. Hang up and drive."

Trey was right. I needed to concentrate before I ended up with a Confederate soldier as a hood ornament.

"I'll call when I leave the shop," I said. "It shouldn't take long to unpack, and then I'll be on my way."

"I'll be here."

"And hey…" I felt the stubborn blush rising again. "Thanks for the roses."

"You got them?"

"I did."

He didn't speak for a second. "Okay. I'm glad."

And then he hung up abruptly. I stared at the phone until another car honked at me. *Get it in gear, Tai,* I reprimanded myself, and pointed the car toward Kennesaw.

◇◇◇

The almost-full moon cut through the clouds in a wash of light so bright I had to squint against it, illuminating the lot behind my shop. The building was shabby, but still standing, all two stories of it, with the shop on the ground floor, my dinky apartment on the second. I pulled the Camaro into the parking spot beside the back entrance and climbed out into the night, locking the car behind me.

A flicker of movement in the alley stopped me short. I automatically dipped my right hand into my carry bag until I felt the cool metal of my .38.

"Who's there?"

The shadow stepped forward, and the security light flared to illuminate a woman with dark bangs, short hair tucked behind her ears. I wrapped my hand around the grip of the gun and thumbed it free from its holster.

"Hope," I said.

She kept her hands in her pockets. "I was wondering when you'd come dragging in."

"You're supposed to be in jail."

"Early release for good behavior."

I snorted.

She tossed her head. "You can drop the attitude. I know the son of a bitch is in there."

"I have no idea which son of a bitch you mean."

"John. My husband. The one you've been trying to get back ever since he dumped you."

John Wilde. My most infamous ex, the one who'd run off with Hope, returning briefly a year later to drag me into a stew of betrayal and double-dealing and Ku Klux Klan workings. And now here was Hope, fresh from the clink and spoiling for a fight.

I exhaled wearily. "John's not here. I haven't talked to him in five months."

"Then why was your number the last one he called?"

She held up a phone and pressed redial. Sure enough, I heard my voice on the shop's answering machine. "You've reached Tai Randolph at Dexter's Guns and More, please leave—"

She thumbed it off and glared at me. "Care to explain?"

"Beats hell outta me. Ask your husband when you find him. Because he isn't in there."

And then to my utter astonishment, Hope pulled a snub-nosed semi-auto out of her pocket and pointed the muzzle right between my feet.

"I don't think you're taking me seriously," she said.

The gun trembled in her grasp. It was ridiculously tiny and probably less accurate than a slingshot, but she was barely twenty feet away, and shaky hands made for shaky trigger fingers. A year of training with Trey, and I snapped into survival headspace automatically. Unlike Trey, however, my hands trembled almost as badly as hers, especially the one plunged in my carry bag, wrapped around my revolver, heavy on my hip.

Hope waved her gun in that direction. "Get your hand away from that bag and let me in that goddamn shop right now!"

I kept my hand where it was. "Put that piece-of-shit gun away, and we'll talk."

"I don't think so."

I tried to keep my voice neutral. "You may think you did something smart, sneaking over here like this. I know you've spotted the security cameras—you always had an eye for those—and so you're staying in the alley, hunkered down in the blind spot. What you didn't think about, couldn't possibly consider, was the urban in-ground target detector."

She stared at me. The gun didn't drop an inch.

"You're pretending you know what that is, but you don't, so I'll tell you. It's a device set in the ground right about where you're standing now, and it tripped the second you stepped on it. I don't know how it works—I don't even know where Trey finds these things—but as we speak it is pinging his phone with an intruder alert. So I'm guessing you've got anywhere from ten seconds to two minutes before he calls."

She raised the gun higher. "Then you'd better get ready to tell him everything's fine."

I snorted. "Like that'll work. The man's a human lie detector, you know that. If he hears me trying to pull one over on him, he's gonna drive that Ferrari over here like a bat out of hell. But he's gonna call the Kennesaw police first, and then the Cobb County police, and anybody armed and uniformed on his speed dial."

She glared, the gun shaking in her hands.

"So before this phone rings, I suggest you either drop the Calamity Jane routine or get the hell off my property. Your choice."

My phone buzzed, loud enough for her to hear, and she jerked in surprise. That was when I saw behind the bravado. She was shaking, but not from anger. From desperation and fear and probably sheer exhaustion. She wasn't here to shoot me. She wasn't here to shoot anybody, not even John Wilde, wherever the hell he was.

I kept my voice level. "Something's happened, hasn't it? Something worse than your husband sneaking off to be with me?"

She shivered, and the gun dropped a smidgen. The phone rang again, and she hesitated only a second before laying the weapon at her feet. She didn't run, though. She stood there, fierce and resigned.

I pulled my phone out of my pocket and put it to my ear. "Hey boyfriend, I'm just—"

"The IGDT triggered. Someone's—"

"I know. I'm out here now."

"Who is it?"

I hesitated. Despite what I'd told Hope, Trey couldn't detect shit over the phone. He'd either do what I told him, or he'd launch into emergency protocol, and I didn't really want SWAT cops helicoptering into my parking lot. Again.

Trey's voice was insistent. "Tai?"

"It's Hope."

"She's supposed to be in jail."

"Early release, she says."

"You don't know that. I'm calling—"

"No cops."

"But—"

"I'm serious. We're just talking."

Across the lot, Hope stared. The post-adrenalin crash had me buzzed and cranky and a little confused, but I knew one thing—if things got official, Hope would bolt. And I didn't want her doing that until I'd figured out what was going on because there was no way in hell her sudden appearance wasn't a part of the mess Ainsworth Lovett was stirring up.

At Trey's end, I heard murmured conversation, the ding of the elevator. I gripped the phone tighter. "Trey Seaver, do not—"

"I'm coming up there."

"No, you are not. For one, you've only got one good arm. For two, you're hopped up on painkillers, and for three—"

"I'm not driving, Gabriella is."

I felt a cold knot in my stomach. "Gabriella's there?"

"She came to check on me."

I bit back my response. Now was not the time to argue about his way-over-the-line ex. But the time was coming. Like a freight train it was coming.

Trey's voice was steady. "Did Hope come alone?"

"As far as I know."

"Have you checked the car?"

"What car?"

"The one out front. I assume it's hers."

Crap. I'd forgotten to examine all the angles on the security feed.

"I'll do that in a second," I said.

"No, go inside the shop. Take Hope with you and keep her in sight at all times. And keep the surveillance channels open. I'll monitor them on the way in."

"Only if you promise that we'll handle this without official interference. No 911."

"Tai—"

"I'm serious. Promise."

He was being even bossier than usual, and I felt a prickle at the small of my back. Eric had diagnosed this prickle as oppositional defiant disorder. I'd told him to shove it.

Trey exhaled gruffly. "Copy that. I promise. No 911. I'll be there in forty minutes. Don't let her out of sight, understand?"

"I understand. But—"

He hung up. Despite my annoyance, I was relieved to know he was on the way. I was capable of taking care of myself, but Trey was SWAT-trained and situation-ready, and with Hope, I needed all the back-up I could get.

Hope glared. "He's coming up here, isn't he?"

"Of course he is. He saved your life once, and he'll do it again if he needs to, but he will tolerate no nonsense. Neither will I. Are we clear?"

She started to say something, then bit it back. She looked like the only thing keeping her pilot light lit was pure anger, and now that it was burned up, her engine was running dry. I realized then that she'd wanted to find John here. That the alternative was too awful to comprehend.

"What's it gonna be, Hope? Deal with this all by yourself, or come into the shop and tell me what's going on?"

Hope hesitated for two seconds, then shoved past me toward the door. I caught the smell of sweat and stale fast food and knew she was truly desperate. Because out of all the people on the planet, I was the very last person she wanted to ask for help. Which meant she had no other place to go.

I picked up her pistol and followed her inside.

Chapter Nine

I unlocked the door and switched on the lights, keeping one eye on Hope the whole time. She was strangely calm, almost dead-eyed. I examined her gun, a cheap and badly maintained .22 barely bigger than the palm of my hand. It was a classic junk gun, not very powerful or accurate, but quick and dirty and disposable provided it didn't blow up in your hand.

I popped the mag, checked the chamber, then stuck everything in the gun safe under the counter. "What are you doing with a firearm? They'll violate you for that."

Her eyes flashed. "You gonna call my parole officer?"

"Depends on what you say during the next five minutes."

She stood at my counter, scanning the room for exits and cover and security cameras. I'd watched Trey do the exact same thing every time he entered an unfamiliar space.

"It's not mine, it's John's," she said. "I found it in the glove compartment."

"John hates guns."

"I guess he changed his mind."

"Why?"

She didn't answer. In the fluorescents, I could see her more clearly. Jeans, dirty at the knees. Dollar store flip-flops. She wore no make-up, and was thinner than I remembered, skinny now instead of willowy. Her clothes hung on her, and her eyes were red.

"I'll tell you what I know," she said. "But first you have to turn off the interior cameras. There, and there. Audio and video both."

I switched off the two corner cameras while she watched. I didn't look at the deer head mounted behind me. It was fake, but inside its hollow skull was a state-of-the-art covert surveillance system hooked up not only to the screen on the counter, but to a wireless feed. All Trey had to do was tap in the access code at his end, and he could see and hear everything happening in the front room.

We'd had long talks, he and I, about my need for space and privacy. This had been our compromise, that he could access the shop feed whenever he wanted, as long as I knew he was watching. I accomplished this by installing red lights behind the deer's glass eyes that came on whenever he logged in.

I caught a glimpse of the deer head in my peripheral vision. Its eyes glowed demonically.

"There," I said. "Happy now?"

She took a seat at my counter, eyeing the glass cabinets filled with matte black handguns and CSA replica daggers. I sat opposite her, trying to keep every wit I had about me. I'd thought she was out of my life, but now here she was at my gun shop, just like John had been six months ago, and just as desperate.

"You gonna play his message or not?" she said.

I pressed the button on my uncle's ancient answering machine. The first two calls were Kenny, but then John's smoke-cured Alabama drawl drizzled through the line.

"Hey Tai, don't hang up. Long time no see, I know, but something's going on down here and I need to talk to you, soon as possible. Call me back."

He recited his number. The next call was an hour later, and this time he was more agitated, nervous, tension flaying his voice. "I'm serious, Tai, I need to talk to you. I think there's trouble, big trouble, and it's probably headed your way too, so call me."

I turned back to face Hope. "What trouble is he talking about?"

Her eyes skittered to the side. "Somebody's been following me. White pick-up with a camper top. No plates. It started a week ago, right after I got out—showing up at my PO's office, at the trailer, taking off the second I caught them looking. It happened again on Wednesday, and John lost his temper. Said he was gonna take care of it."

"Which meant?"

"He wouldn't say. Said the less I knew, the better, me being on parole and all."

Outside the shop, a car prowled down the street, and her head jerked in that direction. She was nervous to the point of paranoia, her eyes darting and quick, her skin practically crawling.

"Start at the beginning," I said. "When's the last time you saw John?"

"This morning. He was on the way to work, and I had to report to my PO, so he dropped me off. He didn't come get me like he was supposed to, so I called him. No answer. I called Train's shop, but—"

"Wait, wait, wait. Train's shop in Savannah? I thought y'all were in Jacksonville?"

Her eyes hardened. "We lost everything. The house, the pawn shop. John got a mobile home in Savannah so he could be close to me, and Train hired him back at the shop."

Train's tattoo shop was on the west end of River Street, steps from the Savannah River. It was where I'd met John, where I'd gotten my first tattoos—a flaming arrow on my bicep from Train and a sloe-eyed vixen fox in a more private and personal location, this one from John's talented hands. I knew something else too. John had debts in Savannah. Big ones.

Hope raked a hand through her hair. "I know what you're thinking, but he said he and Boone had come to an agreement about the money he owed."

"What kind of agreement?"

"He said the slate was clean, that's all I know."

I found that hard to believe. But we'd all changed over the past five months, for better or worse, and I supposed my uncle had too. Once upon a time Boone would never have forgiven a five-figure debt. But that was before his own son had tried to kill him. Maybe he had different priorities now.

"Okay, so what happened next?"

"I talked to Train, and he told me John had called in and said he couldn't make it, that he had personal business to take care of suddenly. I called everybody I could think of, even back in Jacksonville. Nothing. My PO felt sorry for me and gave me a ride home. I saw the car there, parked in the front yard crazy-like, all catty-cornered. No John. I called again and heard his phone ringing, found it in the car hooked up to the charger. Yours was the last number he dialed."

"That the same car that's out front now?"

"Yeah."

"Was his Harley gone?"

"It's in the shop."

I didn't state the obvious—that if the Harley were missing, it was because John had ridden it out of town. I wanted to tell her John did stuff like this all the time. He'd done it to me, after all. I wanted to tell her this was nothing but payback for something she'd done to him, but I couldn't make my mouth form the words. They felt clichéd, slight, patchwork. Despite their fights and arguments and carrying on, Hope and John found their way back to each other. If John had suddenly vanished without telling her, something had happened. And whatever it was, it was bad.

"Tell me the truth, Hope. Can you think of any reason someone would be following you?"

"You mean besides the obvious one, that some of Jasper's crew are still out there, getting ready to put a bullet in me so I won't testify against him?"

"A fine theory. But it doesn't explain where John is. He's not testifying against anybody."

"Maybe they were coming for me and John got in the way. Maybe I'll be getting a ransom call any second now."

"But why?"

Her voice rose. "I don't know why! I just know he's gone!"

"That doesn't—"

The soft click of the back door shutting interrupted me. Trey. He'd slipped inside without a sound, deactivating the alarm. In the low light, his black workout clothes looked like urban tactical wear. Only the gym bag on his shoulder and the running shoes on his feet revealed him for the civilian he was.

Hope noticed me looking and whipped her head in his direction. Her eyes narrowed. "Well, hoo-fucking-ray. The cavalry has finally arrived."

Chapter Ten

Trey dropped the duffel bag inside the door. Behind him, I saw the swing of headlights—a silver convertible backing out of the lot. Gabriella, choosing for once to stay out of his life.

I took him by the elbow and dragged him into the corner. "Well?"

He didn't take his eyes off Hope. "I heard her story."

"And?"

"It's problematic."

"No kidding." I motioned toward his forehead. "How well does your cranial lie detector function on oxy?"

"I don't know."

"Then we should probably find out."

Trey refocused his attention on me. I was a clever and practiced liar, but I had yet to succeed against his super-sensitive frontal lobes. My brother had explained it using neurology lingo—what Trey had lost in the accident was the white-lie shield that the rest of us used to negotiate social environments. Normal brains could ignore a tiny untruth. Trey's brain couldn't.

I tried to keep my expression blank. "All I had to eat for lunch was a family-size bag of kettle corn and a beer."

He tracked his gaze over my mouth. "True. And foolish. You need protein to—"

"Great. You passed." I spun him around and propelled him toward the front. "Now get in there and...wait a second."

I moved my hand across the small of his back, then pulled his windbreaker open, revealing his old department-issue S&W in a hip carry holster. He'd had to give up side carry after the accident, so when he'd started at Phoenix, he'd traded up to a custom-made shoulder holster, doctor's orders. And yet there he was, side-armed and dangerous again.

I put my hands on my hips. "I thought you weren't supposed to be wearing a holster."

"Gabriella meant the shoulder rig."

"No, she meant—"

He pushed past me into the room. "I know what she meant."

I stifled the urge to snatch him back as he positioned himself right in front of Hope. She regarded him with the feral look of a prey animal about to bolt, and for a second, I wished she would. That would solve most of my problems at the moment. But it would leave the larger problems still lurking.

Her testimony was crucial in the upcoming trial. We had security camera footage from that night, but as Garrity had pointed out, all it had shown was Trey shooting Jasper three times. The necessary background of that encounter—why Hope was in danger, why Jasper was that danger, and why Trey had had to use almost-deadly force to protect her—rested with our various testimonies. But our statements needed context, and Hope—reluctant, wary, and now terrified—was that context.

She held out her wrists toward Trey. "Did you bring the handcuffs? Or maybe you want to frisk me first?"

He ignored her. "Is that your car out front?"

"You know it is."

"Did you come alone?"

"You know I did."

Trey moved closer, about six inches too close for comfort. Hope flinched, then tried to cover it. I sympathized. When Trey put you in his sights, it took a mighty amount of discipline to stay still.

"Tell me what happened," he said. "From the beginning."

Hope retold the tale again, with no variation. Trey asked specific questions—times and places and dates. I could see the cop coming out in him, wanting to get the details down. Despite his time in corporate America, he remained a patrol officer in his heart, with an invisible badge on his chest.

"And you had no contact with John after he dropped you off?" he said.

"No."

"No texts? No phone calls?"

"Do you think I'd be here, in *her* shop, talking to *you*, if I had?"

Trey didn't take his eyes off her face. "Was your husband involved in any illegal activities?"

"No."

"What about you?"

"Five months behind bars was enough. I learned my lesson."

"So no outside contact with known criminals?"

"None."

"No illegal activities or intent to commit illegal activities?"

"None."

He hesitated. Something she'd said was tripping his switch. I knew that look. Technically true but deliberately evasive. She really was hiding something.

Her face was a defiant mask. "You think I'm lying, don't you?"

"I think there's something you're not telling me."

She shook her head. "Nope."

He narrowed his eyes. I knew that look too. The rest of what she said might have been wishy-washy half-truth, but that "nope" was a big fat lie.

He kept his voice non-threatening. "It would be in your best interest—"

"Fuck you." She folded her arms. "You're not a cop. I don't have to tell you anything."

He didn't reply for a good thirty seconds. When he spoke, his voice was composed. "You are correct that I'm not a sworn officer anymore. I am, however, a consultant with the Atlanta Metro Major Offenders Task Force, which is a joint effort between the APD and the FBI. And while you have the right to remain silent, lying to a federal agent in a material investigation is a felony. Section 1001, Title 18 of the federal code. So let me ask you again, as clearly and concisely as I can—what is it that you aren't telling me?"

I tried not to let my astonishment show on my face. He was lying. Well, not lying as much as sticking two pieces of truth together and letting them imply something that wasn't true. It was the oldest trick in my book, one he'd obviously picked up on since even though he was a consultant with AMMO, that did not qualify him as a federal agent, not even close. And quizzing Hope in a gun shop did not count as a material investigation. Even I knew that.

But Hope looked conflicted. She was weighing her options, considering the pros and cons. She didn't trust us, but she damn sure needed us, both of us, and information was a commodity at such times.

She looked up at Trey. "Are you saying I'm a liar?"

"I'm saying that you're lying."

She reached in her pocket and threw him her keys. "There. You don't believe me, search the damn car. Tear it apart. I got nothing to hide. You think I'd still be sitting here, knowing you were on the way, if I did?"

Trey didn't reply, but he pocketed the keys. I could sense the various impulses warring in his brain—kick Hope out and fortify the shop against whatever trouble she'd brought to town, call the authorities to haul her away, interrogate her until she coughed up the details herself—and I knew he couldn't sift through them easily.

He turned and headed for the door. I watched him go, then grabbed a chair, dropped it in front of Hope, and straddled it backwards. "Nice try. Now spill it."

"Spill what?"

"Whatever it is you're keeping from him."

She let a smile flicker at the corner of her mouth. "He'll run after any bone you toss, won't he? So damn predictable. How do you stand it?"

In my peripheral vision, I saw Trey approach the car, a dark blue two-door, dull in the amber streetlight. Even though he had the keys, he didn't touch it. Instead, he pulled a slim pen-light from his pocket and ran it along every inch of the vehicle, starting with the driver's side door.

I shook my head at Hope. "He risked his life to save you once. He did it because he is incapable of anything else. You came in here because you had no place else to go and that hasn't changed, so unless you want me dialing up 911 my own sweet self, you will spit out whatever it is you're still hiding."

She looked like she wanted to argue. I saw defiance in her, but I also saw weariness and a landsliding grief. She was at the end of her rope physically and emotionally, but she had a wild card she wasn't showing.

"You're scared," I said, "and not only because you think something has happened to John. You think you're in danger too. That's why you're putting up with Trey. Because you think you might need him. Again."

Her phone rang. She snatched it up and stood at the same time. Without saying a word, she walked toward the hallway and turned her back on me. Her voice was a low murmur as she answered.

In the parking area, Trey reached the car's trunk. He stopped walking, dropping into a crouch, head cocked. He played the light back and forth across the bumper. Then he pulled a hand-kerchief from his pocket along with his phone. My guts went cold. Handkerchief plus phone could only mean one thing.

He'd found something.

Chapter Eleven

I shoved open the door and joined Trey at the back of the car. He had switched the light to UV and was examining the undercarriage now. He looked up when he saw me.

"Go back inside," he said.

I caught a glimpse of what he'd discovered. I was no CSI, but I knew bullet holes when I saw them. Two of them punctured the trunk, joined by what appeared to be a graze running like a claw mark up the side.

"Back inside, Tai. Now."

He was ice-cold polite, every sentence a command. Voice control, the second step on the use of force continuum. He also had his phone in hand, and I knew what he would be doing the second I went into the shop.

I pointed. "I know what you think is in that trunk."

"Tai—"

"And if you're right, then yes, I'll be calling 911. But open it first."

He shook his head, a warning shot. "You shouldn't—"

"Just open the damn trunk."

He hesitated only a second, then inserted the key. One twist, and the trunk popped open. He lifted it the rest of the way with a handkerchief-covered hand.

It was empty.

I felt a knee-weakening wash of relief. Trey ran his flashlight into every corner of the space, but there was no sign of blood or body or foul play.

I glanced back into the shop. Hope was still on the phone, her eyes on us. Trey had his phone out too. I couldn't watch both of them at the same time. If Hope ran, the alarms would let us know, but she'd make like a rabbit and we'd never catch her. If Trey finished his call, we'd be swarmed with uniforms within minutes.

I put a hand on his elbow. "Listen. I know that every neuron in your cranium is screaming that you need to call this in, but you need to hold off until we've talked to her some more."

"Why?"

"Because she's hiding something, and whatever it is, I am on the verge of getting it out of her. But if the cops come, she'll bolt. Or clam up." I looked him in the eye. "And because you promised me you wouldn't."

His expression changed, a mixture of contrition and determination. "Circumstances often require a change of strategy."

And then I heard it, from several blocks away, the unmistakable growl of a motorcycle. For a wild second I thought it was John's Harley, but then, from the other side of the square, I heard an almost identical rumble. And then several more, from behind the shop.

I glared at Trey. "You son of a bitch. You already called 911, didn't you?"

Something flickered in his expression. "No."

"Then who is that surrounding the place as we speak?"

"The Blue Line."

"The what?"

"It's a law enforcement motorcycle club."

I stared at him. "You called a motorcycle gang to surround my shop?"

"Motorcycle *club*, mostly retired APD. They agreed to provide…non-official protection and support. At least until I could assess the situation."

The night grew quiet again, but in my imagination, I could hear the ticking of cooling engines, smell the bike leathers. I'd seen this particular group of bikers on the news—gray-haired and hard-eyed, lining the roadways during cop funerals. They reminded me of a wolf pack, rangy and silent.

I folded my arms. "And what is your assessment?"

Trey held my gaze. "If John really is missing, then this car is quite likely evidence of a crime. What kind of crime, I'm not certain, but that's not for me to determine. The Line is here to maintain the perimeter until the car can be examined by the proper officials. That might give you the time you need."

"To do what?"

"Convince Hope to go quietly into custody. Because this car has what appears to be bullet holes. Because a man is allegedly missing. Because I have no choice at this point, Tai, I simply don't. And neither do you."

The back door alarms went off inside, but neither of us moved. Hope, making a run for it. Trey was already tapping his phone, one quick text. I heard the roar of more engines behind the shop, saw the white flash of headlights. I heard Hope hit the wall of them. She was screaming at them, cursing. And for the first time since she'd darkened my door, I felt a pang of sympathy.

◇◇◇

It was over pretty quickly after that. Hope got dragged to the station to give a statement, while her car went to the vehicle processing shed and her Saturday night special went into evidence. Cobb County would shove the case down Savannah Metro's way as soon as possible, and then both agencies would play hot potato with it. Nobody wanted to deal with somebody like John vanishing, a man who wouldn't be missed but whose absence would be tough investigating.

In the aftermath, I sat outside on the curb in front of my shop in the glow of the single streetlight. Four had been installed during the fervor of the Kennesaw Revitalization Committee's attempt to class up this particular acre of real estate, but only one of them still worked. Now the dark nestled close, velvety with humidity.

Trey conferred with his Blue Line friends gathered in the square. The leader of the group was a retired APD sergeant named Davis. He was short, barely five-eight, but his body was a rectangle of muscle. He was older than Trey, with gray eyes and a trimmed gray beard. He had a single gold stud in one ear and a tattoo on his forearm, faded now, an eagle clutching a rifle in each talon.

He clapped Trey on the shoulder, and I winced. But Trey didn't throw a Krav Maga block or reach for his firearm. I realized with a start that I was watching my alpha dog boyfriend go beta. Only there was not an ounce of give in it, not a hint of submission. With this man, Trey was one of the pack again, and he fell into his assigned role as easily as breathing.

Eventually he joined me on the curb. The oxycodone had worn off hours ago, so there was a stiffness in his movements as he lowered himself to sit beside me.

"Did they arrest her?" I said.

"No. She's making a voluntary statement."

"Because they would have arrested her otherwise. Or called her PO and got her thrown back in jail."

Trey didn't answer. He was watching the cops in the square, some retired, some active duty, all of them bound by the brotherhood of blue. Davis was tidying things up, getting ready to ride.

"How do you know this Davis guy anyway?

"He was my Field Training Officer. I rode with him my first four months out of the academy, during my probationary period."

So that explained the Trey I was seeing now. He was back in patrol mode, responding to cues like the well-trained sheepdog he was. This wasn't an insult, I'd discovered, among cops. They liked to think of themselves as sheepdogs, protecting the sheep of the world—people like me—from the wolves. As if we weren't all wolves when we got hungry enough.

"Will they put her in Witness Protection?"

He shook his head. "Wit-Sec is only for federally-prosecuted cases. Georgia has no state-run witness protection."

"So what will happen to her?"

"That depends. If Hope has evidence that she's at risk because of her upcoming testimony, she can get protection through the prosecuting attorney. Or from the federal marshals. Depending."

"On what?"

"If something really has happened to John."

Her story was a wild and shaggy one: John's disappearance, his efforts to "make things right" and his phone call that morning warning me of trouble to come, plus the white pick-up stalking her and her own mysterious phone call. A lot of conjecture, very little solid evidence. Except the bullet holes in the trunk. That was pretty solid.

"And how is that story looking officially?"

"We did find one key piece of evidence supporting it." Trey kept his eyes on his friends across the square. "An open box of ammunition under the front seat—.22s—and a receipt dated earlier this morning from a Savannah gun shop."

"Did the bullets in the box match the ones in her gun?"

"We won't know that for a while. The gun had been fired, although I couldn't tell how recently."

Hope hadn't mentioned buying ammo. And since she had no reason to edit that detail from her story, I knew that the purchaser had to have been John. As for the gun itself, Hope had gotten her fingerprints all over it. And then in my haste to secure it, I'd gotten mine on top of that. I'd explained this to the responding Cobb County officer, but not to Trey. I already had a headache. A lecture would have flipped me into the red zone.

"What happens next?" I said.

"Assuming she's not eventually arrested, Davis offered to put her up for the night in a safe house."

"Pffft. Like she'll go for that."

"It would be the smart thing to do."

"Yeah well, we blew our chance at getting her to do the smart thing the second your friends closed in."

We sat there in the dark for fifteen seconds, thirty. I felt a whole tidal wave of things I needed to ask him about, but there was one particularly itchy topic at the top of the list.

"You lied to Hope," I said.

He looked confused. "When?"

"When you trotted out that whole bit about lying to federal officers and section whatever-the-hell."

Now he looked insulted. "I did not. I simply…what's the word, multi-syllabic, starts with C?"

"Lied."

"Everything I told her was the truth. She created the interpretation. That's not lying, it's—"

"Technically true but deliberately insinuating, that's what it is. And that counts as a lie."

He pulled out his phone, didn't reply. He thumbed a quick text, barely paying attention to me. Ever since he'd shown up, he'd been in the cop flow chart—take orders from above, give orders to below. I knew where I ranked in that particular hierarchy.

"I didn't know you could lie. I didn't think your brain would let you."

"Why did you think that?"

"Because the truth tends to fall out of your mouth even when you don't want it to."

He shook his head, eyes still on his phone. "That's not the same thing."

A whistle from across the square interrupted him, and he looked up. Davis was waving him over. Without another word, Trey stood up and trotted back. Acting once again like the cop he absolutely wasn't anymore.

I stood up too, but not to follow him. If Trey wouldn't answer these particular questions, I knew somebody who would. Somebody who'd be downright delighted to pontificate on all matters cognitive-psychological.

Chapter Twelve

It was a little after midnight in Georgia, which made it barely past ten in Colorado, but when Eric answered he was gruff and annoyed nonetheless. I decided to skip the part where he was being sued for a couple of million by our racist criminal cousin and focused on the matter at hand.

He promptly scoffed at my belief that Trey was somehow incapable of lying. "Where did you get that idea?"

"From his prefrontal cortex." I paged through the jargon-dense summary of Eric's long-ago evaluation. "Damage to this area results in reduced ability to suppress verbal expression in response to active questioning, which combined with the damage to the subject's executive function—"

"I know all this, Tai. I wrote the report."

"—means that if you ask him a question, he will answer it. He can't help it. Automatic response." I threw the paper on the counter. "How can somebody like that lie?"

"Because it's only an automatic response if you catch him off guard. His intentional responses remain strong."

I pulled out a fresh piece of nicotine gum. Through the front window, Davis and his motorcycle crew remained gathered in the half-lit street. Even with Trey in their midst, they were hard to distinguish from outlaws.

Eric continued. "Look, it's not as if I can point to a part of the brain and say, this is where lying happens. It's a complicated process involving functions spread out over both cranial hemi-spheres, and while Trey took a hit to some, others remain as healthy as ever. Plus he built his recovery complex around strong countermeasures, which he has sometimes applied to the point of overcorrection."

That part I understood—Trey was textbook overcorrection. Got a brain that makes inconvenient stuff fall out of your mouth? Train yourself to respond to questions with a wall of silence. Judgment a tad unreliable? Get smart people to tell you what to do. Verbal functions wonky? Become an expert in visual data representation. His entire recovery complex was built on maximizing his strengths to cover for his weaknesses.

"But if lying is so complicated, why is he so good at it?"

"He's only good at some lies, like logical strategic ones. Off-the-cuff lies? He should suck at those. Lies about deeply emo-tional matters? Equally sucky. But cool rational lies, especially those that are simply manipulations of the truth? He's probably very *very* good at those."

Which described the play he'd put on Hope perfectly. A care-fully honed truth wielded as skillfully as a rapier.

My brother continued. "Lies are really two-part processes, suppressing the truth, then creating and sustaining the falsehood. He's hit or miss at the former, but the latter? Tai, his whole Italian couture lifestyle is a cleverly constructed, expertly maintained illusion. And don't think for a second he doesn't know it."

Of course Trey was good at lying—his entire life was a lie. A piece of psychological sleight of hand.

"Well, he's out of Armani mode now. As we speak, he's in the square with a bunch of his cop buddies, trading war stories."

"Wait, why are cops there?" Eric's voice held an edge of panic. "What's happened? Are you—"

"I'm fine. But Hope showed up at the shop a couple of hours ago with the news that John Wilde is missing."

"So? He runs off all the time."

"This time it's more complicated. Like bullet holes complicated."

I filled him in on the details. Outside, the cops shook hands and clapped each other on the back. I heard the kick-up of the engines. The crew was calling it a night, which meant that Trey would be back inside soon.

Eric was confused. "What's Trey's part in this again?"

"Nothing official, just his usual routine dialed to eleven. He showed up here with his old S&W on his hip like some Wild West gunslinger, barking orders at me."

"Ah. Enclothed cognition."

"What the hell is that?"

"Short answer? It's the connection between what we wear and how we behave."

I rubbed the headache beginning to throb at my temple. "Are you telling me he straps on the department-issue gun and suddenly he's a cop again?"

"The simple answer is yes. And from what Garrity's told me, he wasn't exactly Officer Friendly, if you catch my drift."

I cursed under my breath. "Crap. So what am I supposed to do?"

"Hard to say. His brain is unique, as are his coping strategies. You should probably…hang on again."

I heard another voice in the background at my brother's end. Muffled, like he'd put his finger over the phone, but definitely female. And then his voice in reply, low and reassuring.

"Eric? Do you have a woman in your hotel room?"

A pause. "We were discussing Trey."

"Now we're discussing the woman I hear in the background."

"No, we are not."

"But—"

"Tai. Is this an emergency or can it wait?"

I sighed. "It can wait. But—"

"Then call me when I get back to Atlanta, okay?"

He hung up. Great, now my brother was avoiding telling me the truth too. Everybody was spinning deceptions, draping them like spider webs.

I stood up as Trey came in, locking the front door behind himself. He flicked his eyes at the roses next to the register, then back at me. I opened the gun safe under the counter and held out my hand. Trey unsnapped the holster and handed it over.

I shoved his weapon inside and held out my hand again. "Now give me your car keys."

"What?"

"Your keys, Trey, so you can't stomp out of here mid-argument when things get uncomfortable."

He folded his arms. "I don't have car keys because I don't have a car."

"Oh right. Because *Gabriella* brought you."

I trilled her name like it was a fancy curse word. And while Trey had frontal lobe damage, he was no fool. He saw exactly where I was headed.

"Now is not the time—"

"It's exactly the time. And when we're done talking about her, we're gonna discuss your attitude tonight, which sucks. And the lying, which also sucks. And then we're gonna talk about how you came barreling down here and sicced your friends on the situation after I asked you not to call the police—"

"Told me."

"What?"

"You *told* me. Not asked. Told." He took a step closer. "You also told me two months ago that I needed to find a way to be in the action again. Your exact words. You said I needed to channel…whatever."

"Well, you know what? I can't work with this particular whatever. Because it's turning you into a complete and utter ass!"

He started to say something, then snapped his mouth shut. We were standing with the counter between us, but he was too close nonetheless, breathing hard and shallow, cheeks flushed, his cool utterly evaporating. He was on the verge of flashpoint, and I felt myself quicken with the knowledge.

Trey rarely got angry, but when he did, it was pyrotechnic. And heaven help me, I liked watching him crumble, liked the power trip that came with unspooling every ounce of willpower he had. We were at that juncture, the point where I could be the agent of his undoing. All I had to do was keep talking. And then, at exactly the right moment, I could reach across the counter and we'd both tumble down to that dark place of instinct and demand and rough pleasure and forget the very real obstacle between us.

I placed both hands deliberately on the counter, palms down. "We have to be very careful right now."

His eyes were burning. "I know."

"We've done this before, tumbled into bed mid-argument. And it's hot, I mean volcano-hot—"

"I know."

"Sweaty, animal, on the floor—"

"Tai!" His voice was sharp. "You're not helping."

"Right. Sorry." I kept the counter between us, like it was some magical force field. "What I'm trying to say is, it's a great distraction. But it doesn't solve anything."

He exhaled in a burst. "No. You're right. It doesn't." He pulled out his phone. "I'll call a cab. You just…stay over there."

And everything broke, like a fever. Without the firearm on his hip, Trey was decidedly less bossy and swagger-y. Suddenly, all I saw was a man trying hard to do the right thing despite the hot-blooded tug-of-war going on between his body and brain.

"Don't," I said.

He looked puzzled. "Don't what?"

"Don't go."

He lowered the phone. "But—"

"Look, I'm exhausted, you're exhausted, and this is one time we definitely need to go to bed mad. So take your meds and go to sleep. I'll be up in an hour or so when you're totally zonked out beyond all responsiveness. We'll discuss this tomorrow. When things aren't so…volatile."

He still wasn't convinced. I used the last weapon in my arsenal.

"Please," I said.

He hesitated, but he went. I watched him go upstairs, the rickety steps creaking. During the argument, I'd glimpsed Fire Trey, moth-to-flame magnetic. But I knew there was another Trey inside—Ice Trey, the professional. Those blue eyes would sheen over and grow opaque, becoming expressionless, unmoved by fear and fury. That Trey was absolute zero all the way to the bone, and I shuddered at the thought of his touch. Not in the good way either.

His voice carried from upstairs. "Tai?"

"Yes?"

"I forgot my bag. Can I come back downstairs and get it? Or should I…what should I do?"

I felt a wash of relief. We were back to Trey-Trey. "It's okay," I called back. "I'll bring it up."

Chapter Thirteen

Sometime during the night, the rain had finally rolled in, leaving the city blowsy with dogwood petals and bright with morning sun. Trey insisted that we go by his apartment on the way to Phoenix. He needed a suit, he said, and I obliged him.

I changed into the closest thing I had to corporate wear—clean khakis and a white button-down—and pulled my hair back into a knot. Marisa definitely wanted something from me, but I wanted something from her too, and if I had to toe the line wardrobe-wise to make that happen, then so be it.

Trey got a call from Davis the second I pulled us into the Phoenix parking garage. His end of the conversation was monosyllabic, but I caught the drift—Hope was gone.

I smacked the steering wheel. "I told you this would happen!"

Trey waved me quiet and kept talking. "Yes, sir. I'd appreciate any further information. Thank you."

He returned his phone to his pocket, and I glimpsed the holster again. It didn't conceal as well as the shoulder rig, but then, concealment wasn't really the point of cop weapons. I wasn't sure what the point was this morning; we were at Phoenix, which was as impenetrable as a moated castle. But a firearm was as much a part of the company dress code as a tie and Brioni lace-ups, even on a Sunday morning.

"Well?" I said.

"Hope declined the offer of a safe house, leaving the station on her own volition, but not alone. She was seen getting into a car with a unidentified woman."

"Unidentified? Didn't they run the plates?"

He kept his eyes out the window. "If they did, they didn't share that information with me."

"Hope got a phone call last night. I bet it's the same person who picked her up."

"An assumption on your part. We have no evidence."

I started to remind him that had I not been trying to manage his obsessive need to call in the authorities, I might have found out who was on the other end of that mysterious call. But I gritted my teeth and kept quiet. He'd started the morning in a reasonably manageable mood, and I didn't want that to change.

He looked annoyed nonetheless. "Hope also declined to fill out a missing persons report, although a police report has been filed on the incident and John's information distributed with a BOLO to Savannah Metro."

"So it's out of her hands now?"

"Yes. And ours."

◇◇◇

Inside Phoenix, the elevator doors opened onto a darkened hall. I'd only been up to the third floor, the field agent offices, a couple of times. It skeeved me a little, to be honest—the carpets that sucked up any sound, the blank gray walls, the office doors that were perpetually closed. I wondered what lay behind them, what electronic eyes were on me, recording and filtering and analyzing.

"Are we the only ones here?" I said.

"Most likely."

I saw Marisa's office at the end of the hallway, the lights on, the door cracked. Trey knocked. When he got no response, he stepped inside. I gritted my teeth and followed him. My mouth was dry. I was gonna get reamed out, I knew it, and I was in no mood for it. I had my own lawsuit to worry about, after all, and Dexter's shop didn't have the deep pockets that Phoenix did, or its own legal team, or—

Trey put a hand on my stomach. "Stop."

I stopped. Marisa's office was deserted. A woman's cardigan hung on the back of the desk chair, pale lilac, an Easter color. A briefcase lay on the desk, closed, along with a cell phone and a key ring. The room smelled strongly of coffee, but I didn't see any. It was as if Marisa had been jerked into another dimension through some space-time portal.

Trey cocked his head, listening. And then he reached under his jacket, switching his hand at the last second to the holster on his hip, moving smoothly from the cross-body draw to a side draw.

"Trey? I don't think—"

"Shhh!"

He held the weapon at low ready and moved into the center of the room. I saw what had caught his attention—a puddle on the carpet, soaked into the dark gray. And beside it, a single high-heeled pump. Lilac, like the cardigan.

Outside in the hallway, I heard the squeak and slam of a door down the hall. Before I could react, Trey shoved me behind the desk. He pivoted, pulled the gun up with both hands, and took a sight line on the doorway. He gave no warning. He just waited, like a tripwire.

Marisa appeared in the door frame. She was shoeless, her stockinged feet silent on the carpet, a coffee-blotched high heel in one hand, a wad of paper towels in the other. She assessed the situation for approximately a millisecond.

"Trey Seaver," she said flatly. "You drop that weapon and drop it now."

Trey slipped the gun back into its holster. "Yes, ma'am. Sorry, ma'am."

And I let out the breath I was holding.

◇◇◇

It took us a minute to get back on track after that. Trey offered to clean up the spilled coffee, but Marisa told him to sit. He refused, preferring to stand in the corner with his back to the wall. I stayed out of the way, behind a chair next to the window.

Marisa wore a shift dress the color of asphalt this morning. Even barefoot, she almost matched Trey's six feet, and she was impressively built, with a bosom like the prow of a warship and hips like an earthworks fortification, with platinum hair forever pulled back in a tight bun. She had a clean pair of pumps on her feet now, back-ups she'd pulled from her desk drawer.

She fumed at Trey as she daubed her shoe with a paper towel. "I should snatch your carry license."

Trey didn't drop his eyes. He didn't respond either.

"Our insurance rep will be the final arbiter on that, however, at the briefing. Tomorrow morning at eleven, right before the McAndrews presentation, which you will also be attending, so don't get any ideas about disappearing into your office." She shoved a stack of file folders in his direction, tapping the top one with her finger. "There's your copy of the civil suit summons and complaint. Tell me what you make of it."

He came out of his corner long enough to pick it up and flip it open to the first page. He read silently, quickly. Then he closed it and put it back on the stack.

"Six million is somewhat excessive," he said, "but still within precedent for a claim of reflex sympathetic dystrophy. He's asking three million of Tai for a much less serious injury."

She switched her stripped-tundra gaze on me. "Ah yes. Tai. Again."

I heard the whisper of Old Charleston in her vowels, a sweet echo of her hometown, only a few miles up the Atlantic coast from my own. She'd practically obliterated the accent from her everyday speech; it only surfaced during periods of intense seethe.

I made myself stand up straighter. "Yes?"

She pointed the shoe at me. "Thanks to you, Phoenix suffered that debacle with the Beaumonts, which forced me to slash our operations and almost cost me my entire enterprise."

I shook my head. "That wasn't my fault. That was—"

"And then you talked me into providing security for some poetry event—pro bono, I might add—that also lurched into debacle in a few short days."

"Yes," I protested, "but you got to meet the mayor, and—"

"And then there was Savannah, and this mess with your criminally murderous cousin, whom we are dealing with yet again."

"Yes, but that one wasn't my idea at all. And I didn't—"

"And then there was the most recent shotgun standoff. In a blizzard."

I folded my arms. "I cannot control Mother Nature. Besides, you weren't involved in that, Trey was. And he—"

"Exactly my point." She pointed her shoe in his direction. "This man used to be my most reliable employee. I could count on him to deliver, in any circumstance, without complaint. But now that you've darkened every doorstep I have, he's up to his neck in complications and conflict." She fixed him with a look. "I can't even count on him to stay fully dressed in the office."

I swallowed my surprise. I thought we'd managed to sneak that incident by her. Trey blushed and shot me a hot I-told-you-so look of epic magnitude, which I ignored. He'd had no complaints at the time, not a single one.

"I'm sorry," I said. "That one really was all my fault."

Marisa's voice rose. "I don't care whose fault it was! That is not the point! The point is that every time my agency has crossed paths with you, it has been to my detriment. And now you're dragging yet another problem in here, this one as fraught with disaster as the previous ones."

"I didn't—"

"I don't care. Deal with it at your end. This is your official notice to keep me and my company out of it." She waved a hand at us. "Now go, both of you. I'm late for brunch."

Neither Trey nor I budged. She raised an eyebrow. "Why are you both still standing here?"

I stepped from behind my chair. "This isn't just about a lawsuit anymore. There's a missing person. And a car shot full of bullet holes."

Trey cleared his throat. "*Alleged* bullet holes."

I waved him quiet. "Fine. *Alleged.* But it's not a coincidence that the same day we all get served with lawsuit papers is the same day that Hope Lyle shows up at my gun shop, full of lies and trouble and rumors. This is a much bigger problem than Jasper's spiteful lawsuits, no matter how many millions are at stake."

Marisa looked at Trey. He nodded. She closed her eyes and rubbed the bridge of her nose. "Explain."

So I did.

Chapter Fourteen

I started with Hope showing up at my shop, described the whole backstory she'd dumped in my lap—missing husband, creepy white stalker truck—then concluded with the Blue Line holding her, the Cobb County PD dragging her off to the station, and her leaving late the previous night with an unidentified woman.

"Anyway, if Hope is right, Jasper is working a scheme bigger than money, and whoever disappeared John—"

"*Allegedly* disappeared John," Marisa said.

I took a calming breath. "Hope thinks whoever *allegedly* did it was really after her, to keep her from testifying. But now she's disappeared too. And we need to find her."

Marisa swiveled in her chair, back and forth. "Has she disappeared? Or has she simply decided to seek protection from somebody other than you?"

"That could be the case. And that person could be Jasper."

Marisa stopped swiveling. She'd connected the same dots I had—that finding Hope was less about protecting her than it was about protecting her testimony. That the only thing Hope had to trade at this point was that testimony, and that if indeed Jasper or his lawyer or his blasted investigator had gotten their hooks into her, we'd lose her in the upcoming criminal trial. And we needed her to verify that Trey's actions had indeed been self-defense. There was, as people kept reminding me, a four-year statute of limitations on aggravated assault. If Trey ended up taking a felony charge for those three bullets, Jasper's multi-million dollar lawsuit would look a lot less frivolous.

She looked at Trey. "You have the 302s?"

He unsnapped his briefcase and pulled out several manila folders, which he handed to Marisa. I recognized my own handiwork peeking from between the covers.

"This is preliminary," he said. "I haven't had a chance to go through LINX yet."

"But you'll do that first thing in the morning."

"Of course. I'll have a report for you before the meeting." His eyes flickered my way. "Tai did the majority of this work."

Marisa read without comment, starting with the file on Ainsworth Lovett. I could see the *New York Times* piece on him, complete with one of the few photographs I'd found. A mousy specimen, nondescript, turning his face from the photographer. For someone who loved notorious cases, the man himself was camera shy.

"This explains the civil suit's astronomical damages," she said. "Lovett does not come cheap."

"He does not."

She tapped her finger against the folder. "Could Jasper be getting some money from other sources? How about his brother, what was his name again?"

"Jefferson."

"Yes. Jefferson is still on the KKK Selectmen Council, isn't he?"

"He is. But this is the new improved family-friendly Klan, the kind that adopts highways, and part of their rebranding is behaving lawfully. Jefferson has completely disavowed Jasper, as has the Klan."

"What about their father?"

"He's disavowed the whole thing. Except for Jefferson. And me." I waved a hand at the materials on her desk. "I don't know how all this connects yet. I haven't talked to Boone or Jefferson since the incident. And Garrity hasn't heard anything from the prosecutor or the detective on the case. But I'm making progress. And when I find something out, I'll let you know."

"Good. Do that." She swiveled some more in her chair, suspicious, assessing. "So what is it you're asking *me* to do?"

"Find Hope. Or John. Or both."

She scoffed. "Phoenix does not offer bounty hunter services."

"Then I'll find them, and when I do, you can offer them executive protection—which Phoenix does offer—until the trial."

Marisa fixed me with a withering stare. "Seriously?"

"Look, I'm not asking for them, or myself." I pointed at Trey. "I'm asking for him. Because despite certain recurring hiccups and regardless of that one—one!—insignificant indiscretion on top of his desk, he's been loyal to you and Phoenix. And you know that if Hope recants, if the trial starts to go sideways, he could get hit with an assault charge, maybe some grievous bodily injury tacked on. And Phoenix legal could probably drag the company out of it, save itself and abandon him to the industrial prison complex. But you're a better woman than that."

Marisa stared. Trey too, with much more discombobulation. I didn't care. He needed all the help that Phoenix could offer, even if he was being an ass, even if I had to convince his own boss, a woman who despised me, to protect the woman I despised most in the world.

I saw Marisa adding up the cost of such a thing, balancing it against the six million Jasper had set his sights on. She'd clawed her way to the top in a field unfriendly to females, and she'd kept the books in the black and the lights burning with a cutthroat pragmatism. But I knew another part of her code was at play. Marisa never left a man behind; she was as unyielding as a Marine about that.

"Find either of them and we'll talk," she said. She turned to Trey. "As for you, you'll be staying as far away from this as possible until the situation cools off, hopefully because John Wilde stumbles back into town."

Trey's eyes were wary. "But—"

"No buts. Go round up your firearms proficiency reports, the most recent ones, and bring them to me."

He hesitated, but then nodded. "Yes, ma'am."

Marisa listened to his footsteps down the hall, then the ding of the elevator. She shook her head. "He's calling me 'ma'am' again. I thought I'd broken him of that."

I shrugged. "Things with Trey are a little…retro right now."

"No kidding. I see he's got his old sidearm again, which does not fill me with optimism." She drummed her fingers on the desk. "What's going on with him?"

"I honestly don't know."

"Is it good or bad?"

"I don't know that either."

She watched the doorway. "This is a piece of nastiness on a Sunday morning. Rumors and revenging, all that Southern Gothic shit." She fixed me with a look. "When do you leave for Savannah?"

I blinked in surprise, but I should have been expecting the question. "Tomorrow morning."

"Without Trey, of course."

I nodded.

"Have you told him yet?"

"No. It's just now becoming clear that this is what I need to do. And that I need to do it without him."

"Good. We agree then." Marisa closed her briefcase. "I suppose you're wanting me to keep him busy at this end?"

"I think it would be in everyone's best interest. He does better when he has a routine."

"That's one way to put it."

She was examining me with all the subtlety of an X-ray. Sometimes I forgot that Marisa was dangerous. I'd only seen her in CEO mode, the smooth hustle of someone who knew how to grease the proper wheels. But she also knew how to break bones with the flick of a wrist and carried a Glock in her fancy handbag.

She stood and reached for her cardigan. "I can deliver at my end. I hope you can deliver at yours."

Chapter Fifteen

Trey didn't speak on the way home. It was a short ride from Phoenix to his complex, and I let him have his silence, hoping it would settle him. It didn't. He was still agitated when we got back in his apartment, even with the door triple-locked behind him. I knew this because he went straight to his computer, holster still on his hips, tie still around his neck.

I sat on the edge of his desk. "Do you want to talk about it?"

"About what?"

"What happened at Phoenix."

"Nothing happened at Phoenix."

"You drew down on your boss. You call that nothing?"

He pulled up a spreadsheet. I recognized it—a statistical summary of the white supremacist organizations currently operating in Georgia, with separate lines for their money trails, including the one that linked the Savannah KKK to the larger relic community.

"My preliminary evaluation of the scene was incorrect," he said. "I adjusted my response accordingly when I had more information. There's nothing to discuss."

His expression was indifferent, words clipped. I knew there was no breaching the wall. My only hope was that a couple of hours mainlining charts like they were tranquilizers would calm him down. Maybe then we could talk. There was only one small problem.

I squared my shoulders. "You're not going to like this, but I'm going to Savannah tomorrow. And I'm going alone."

He didn't look up from the screen. "I know."

"This is not a situation that will respond to top-down management. Savannah is crooked, and weird, and I need to be able to maneuver there, which means…" I froze. "Wait a second, what did you say?"

"I said, I know."

"You're not going to argue about it?"

He started typing. "No. I'm resigned to it at this point."

"But you don't approve."

He kept his eyes on the computer. "Whether I approve or disapprove is immaterial. I have a meeting in the morning with Phoenix legal to discuss the lawsuit, then another meeting with HR, and then another meeting with the new account. Before that, and probably after as well, I'll be in the FBI office putting together a LINX report. Which means that even if I wanted to go to Savannah—which I don't—I can't. So do whatever you need to do, because that's what you do. And I'll stay here and do what needs to be done, because that's what I do."

It was the most words I'd ever heard come out of his mouth at one time, and it left me momentarily thunderstruck. Lots of words, yes, but every single one flat and monotone. Ice Trey surfacing.

I sat on the edge of his desk. "You're mad."

"I'm simply stating the facts."

"Okay then. Here's a fact for you. I was handling this situation just fine until you barged in—unasked—with your motorcycle buddies and scared off the one lead we had. And now Hope's gone, and John's vanished, and the people who trust us have told us everything they know, and the people who don't trust us have clamped shut like snapping turtles!"

"That's what criminals do. You should know this."

"And what does that mean?"

He didn't answer, but the staccato keystrokes hit with the rhythm of gunfire.

I stood up. "Hope came to me, which meant she came to *us*. And she was cooperating until you had us surrounded—"

"She was lying and concealing evidence and manipulating—"

"—and then you started throwing your weight around, which is why she ran, and that, Former Senior Patrol Officer Seaver, is on you."

He kept typing. "If you'd listened to me and followed my instructions, she wouldn't have had a chance to run."

"And if you'd listened to me, you wouldn't have pulled your weapon on your boss when the only threats in the room were an empty shoe and a puddle of coffee!"

Trey stared at me, hard, then shoved his chair back and went into the bedroom, slamming the door behind him. I waited for him to come back. I tapped my foot. Give him time, everyone always said. So I waited. Five whole minutes I waited. Then I went after him.

I found him standing at the bathroom mirror, hands braced on the sink, shirt unbuttoned. He'd peeled off most of the therapy tape and was examining his shoulder, flexing the tendon, testing the recovery. There was an open bottle of oxy on the counter.

"And so now you shut down," I said.

"I'm refusing to argue. There's a difference."

"You're refusing to engage."

He rolled his head to the right, wincing, not looking at me. "What do you want me to do? Tell you I don't want you to go? I don't. Tell you to stay? I would if I thought you'd do it. But you won't. Because once you decide on a course of action, you don't listen to anything that anyone else has to say."

"I took up for you this morning."

"No, that was something else. It had nothing to do with me and everything to do with…whatever it was you were trying to accomplish."

"Is that what this is about? You're mad because I said you deserved to be protected?"

He snatched up the pills and shook two into his palm. "I can take care of myself and will do so until you return. So unless you're going to listen to reason, further discussion is pointless."

I searched his expression. Yep. Ice Trey all the way. Which meant he was right—further discussion was absolutely and utterly pointless, as useless as arguing with an iceberg.

I kicked the door jamb. "Damn it, Trey, why can't you be—"

I bit down on the word that almost flew out of my mouth. Trey didn't take his eyes off the mirror. I stomped out of his apartment, fighting tears. But it wasn't just anger that had the world going swimmy in front of me. It was also the piercing guilt of what I'd almost said.

Normal.

Why can't you be normal?

Chapter Sixteen

I cursed to myself all the way down the elevator, all the way through the doors and into the parking garage. I refused to look at my phone, refused to see if Trey had called. Not that I wanted to talk to him, I only wanted him to call so that I could righteously ignore him. But I wanted…I wanted…

I snatched my keys from my bag. I didn't know what I wanted.

I walked faster, feeling even more solitary as my footsteps echoed against the concrete. My Camaro gleamed like a red beacon across the deck, and I itched to get behind the wheel and put Buckhead behind me. I had to pack, find a place to stay in Savannah. Adjust Kenny's schedule to full-time, redo the research I'd left with Marisa…

And then I stopped.

Parked next to my car was a silver Mercedes convertible, and propped against that was Gabriella. She was dressed as if it were still winter, in black stiletto boots and a light gray tunic, her red curls spilling over the fabric like blood trails.

I stood right in front of her. "I am one hundred percent not in the mood for this right now."

"We need to talk."

"So you lie in wait for me in Trey's parking garage?"

"The cards said you would be here."

I rolled my eyes. "And now begins the woo-woo portion of our evening."

She ignored the insult. "After our little *brouille* the other night, I asked the tarot what I needed to know about the situation with you and Trey. And there it was, in the center. The Tower. And crossing it, Death."

I almost laughed. Even a tarot skeptic like me knew the cards she was referring to—the lightning-struck Tower, crumbling into the sea as its hapless inhabitants tumbled down with it, and Death in all his skeletal glory, complete with pale horse and scythe. I'd seen them when Trey practiced memory work with his own seventy-eight-card deck, one of the brain training exercises she had him do, but there was nothing mystical in those pretty pictures. Gabriella, however, believed otherwise.

"That's why you drove over here?" I said. "To accost me in the parking garage with a tarot reading? Couldn't you at least have waited until there was a thunderstorm brewing? Some rain and wind to spooky things up?"

She glared. "You act as if this is nothing, that death surrounds you. Real death, not the death of metaphor or transformation. Flesh and blood death. This is what you are bringing to Trey's life, and it has to stop."

"For your information, he's up there right now, all alone, totally not dead. So your cards are wrong, and you're wrong. But go on up there and show him all the mortal danger he's avoiding by staying here while I'm in Savannah."

Confusion flitted across her face. "You're going to Savannah? Why?"

"Doesn't matter. The point is, Trey is staying behind in his airless, absurdly secure apartment. So spare me the reckless endangerment lecture."

For a moment she seemed nonplussed, not quite sure of her next move. "Does he know you're leaving?"

"He told me to go. Told me he could take care of himself, his exact words."

"*Non,* I do not believe that. He would never send you away."

I pressed my fingers to my temple, which was starting to throb. On the other side of the lot, I heard footsteps and conversation. A family, headed for the park perhaps, or to get a nice ice cream. Not trapped with a deluded French chick babbling about death and towers as she plotted how to get back in my boyfriend's bed.

"Well, he did," I said. "Maybe you don't know him as well as you think you do."

Her expression hardened. "Trey has built himself a fine tower. And it will come down some day, but it must be dismantled brick by brick, with great care. Not pulled down because it suits your purposes. And if he falls, if he breaks on those rocks…" Her voice cracked, but her eyes stayed fierce. "I will hold you accountable."

My voice was soft, low. "Oh, now that *is* a threat."

"It is, yes. You may count on it. You do not know what I went through those months after the accident, what Trey went through."

"I know enough."

"You know nothing!" Her voice echoed against the concrete. "You weren't there three years ago when he wouldn't even speak, when he did nothing but stare at the wall. He was dying right in front of me, five days dying, but then he crawled back to life, he crawled back to *me*!"

My memory flashed hard and fast to a different night, one five short months previous, in Savannah. Trey, bloody and beaten, lifting his head at the sound of my voice. He'd crawled back then too, on hands and knees. To *me*.

"I know things you haven't got a clue about," I said. "So back off. He's with me now, not you!"

"That is not the point!"

"Damn sure is. Because I'm thinking you realize what a good thing you lost—"

"You don't know my losses!"

"—and maybe you don't feel obliged to limit yourself to one man, but I am giving you fair warning. Hands off Trey!"

She stared at me, her nostrils flaring, eyes crackling with rage. I thought for a second she was going to slap me, and I was ready for it, eager even. Instead, she snatched open her car door.

"Very well. Go to Savannah. I'll be here. And if Trey needs me, he knows where to find me."

She slid behind the wheel, checked her make-up in the mirror. After a hasty reverse that almost ran me over, she peeled out for the exit. I stood there until I couldn't hear her engine anymore, then checked my phone one more time. No calls. No texts. I almost went back up. Almost. But eventually I made myself get into my own car and drive myself back to Kennesaw.

Chapter Seventeen

I sat in my car for a long time before I went in, sucking down the weakest cigarette I'd ever put between my lips. It was the best I could find at the corner store, and it was like smoking a dust bunny, but it eased the jitters and soothed the pounding in my head. I'd kicked the habit once, I would kick it again. Tomorrow. Not today. Today the sky was brilliant blue, the sunlight tart as lemonade, and since I didn't have a blanket I could crawl under, a haze of smoke would have to do.

My phone still hadn't rung. Normally Trey called within five minutes of an argument, sometimes before I'd even exited the lobby. Suddenly going to Savannah felt like a desertion. A necessary one perhaps, but a desertion nonetheless. Rationally, I knew he was better off in Atlanta, that Marisa would keep him in line at least from nine to five, and that he had the apartment and the Ferrari and the suits.

And Gabriella.

I took another drag and thumbed him a quick text: *I'm sorry.* And then I waited. And waited some more. Trey never took more than a minute to text me back—he kept his phone in hand all the time. Unless he was showering or sleeping or…

I checked the phone again. Still nothing. I jammed the pack of cigarettes in the glove compartment, shoved open the car door. I took one final hit, letting the smoke linger in my mouth, then dropped it to the asphalt.

Inside the shop, the only sounds were the humming of the fluorescents and the quiet chirp of the security system. The square was deserted except for Raymond Junior's barbecue joint. He was hosting a birthday celebration for someone in his reenactment group, and I could hear laughter and country music. He'd invited me to come, and I'd declined, but suddenly wandering over and grabbing a beer or two, maybe something stronger, seemed like a fine idea. I opened the front door....

And an envelope fluttered to the mat.

It was cream-colored, rectangular and innocent, my name written on the front in a flowing feminine hand. My heart skipped a beat. It was the same kind of envelope I'd gotten in February at the History Museum. I looked left, then right. The square was empty. I listened hard and heard nothing except the sound of Waylon Jennings across the grass. No retreating footsteps. No car screeching away with squealing tires.

I tore open the envelope. Like before, there was a photograph, only this time it wasn't of me—it was Hope. She looked nervous, her shoulders hunched. Another person was speaking with her, back to the camera, blurred and out of frame. Short brown hair streaked with sunlight, a brown leather jacket. Male? Female? Hard to tell from the half-shoulder. One thing was clear—neither Hope nor the person with her knew they were being photographed.

A single line was written on the back: *She liked what 'ere she looked on, and her looks went everywhere.*

"What in the double hell?" I whispered.

The last envelope had been handed to me by a woman, her black hair cut in a sleek bob. She'd disappeared before Trey could pull to the curb, so I was the only one who'd seen her. And now this, also anonymous...unless.

I scurried behind the counter, sparing a look at the deer head with its covert camera. Its glass-eyed gaze was dull and lifeless. No red light. I suppressed a surge of disappointment and snatched at the keyboard. I typed in my password and logged into the system, then pulled up the archived footage. I scrolled backward until I saw a figure at my door. Someone I recognized, all right, but not from the History Center.

I grabbed my phone. "Raymond, you came over here and stuck an envelope in my front door."

"Yeah?"

I could barely hear him for the noise. I raised my voice. "Who gave it to you?"

"Nobody."

"What do you mean, nobody?"

"I mean, I found it on my car. Had your name on it. I took it over to your place, but you weren't there, and I had this shindig to deal with, so—"

"So you left it."

He hesitated. "Yeah. Was that a bad thing? I swear, I didn't know, I thought it was just one of your customers got the address wrong or something, I didn't—"

"It's okay."

I looked across the square at his ramshackle restaurant, bustling now. Lots of people coming and going, reenactors and spouses and parents and children, noise and commotion.

"Hey, you okay over there?" he said. "This ain't some stalker, is it? I promised your uncle I'd look after you."

"I'm fine. Just let me know if you see anybody unusual over here, especially a woman. Short black hair, slim."

"Pretty?"

"I guess so."

He laughed. "I'll keep an eye out then."

After he hung up, I stared out the window at his party for a while. Then I went upstairs to my bedroom and pulled a plastic storage bin from under the bed. The original photo was right where I'd left it. I shook it free from its matching envelope and held it side by side with the new image. The handwriting was a perfect match. First the New Testament and now poetry of some sort. Vaguely familiar poetry.

I picked up my phone and typed the line into the search box. Bingo. "My Last Duchess" by Robert Browning. It was a short poem, a monologue, and I had no idea what it meant. For the first time, I regretted skipping literature class in high school. But I knew how to fix that. I may have missed most of senior English, but my best friend Rico hadn't.

I sent him a quick text: *Call me, poet man. ASAP.*

And then I waited. But no return texts came from any direction. I thought of going back to the car, getting the rest of the cigarettes from the glove compartment. Instead, I stuck both photographs in my tote bag. Then I went to the closet and got down a cardboard shoe box. I took off the lid, brushed aside the dried wrist corsage from prom and the tassel from my mortarboard.

The photograph was on top, rubber-banded with others from the same afternoon. It was a shot of me on the beach at Tybee Island, denim short-shorts and a halter top barely containing my more illicit parts. I sat on the hood of my Camaro, the chrome glinting and gleaming. I grinned…but not for the camera. For the man beside me.

John. With his stormy eyes and rock star hair and wicked grin. Even in the photo I could see myself preening in his gaze, happy to be looked upon with such ferocious desire. His eyes were like the sun, and when he turned them on me, I felt myself stretching and reaching and growing like a flower. But all suns eventually disappear below the horizon. Night always comes, one way or another.

I thought of Trey, back in his black and white apartment. The man I loved, something I could say in my head even if it didn't trip lightly off my tongue. He loved me too, with a love that was sturdy and deep-rooted. The girl in the photo would have been crushed by it.

I put the photo in my bag next to the ones from my mysterious informant. It was the only picture I had of John, and I knew I'd need something to show people. *Have you seen this man?* When I got back downstairs, I saw the red lights behind the deer's eyes flare to life. My phone vibrated almost simultaneously with an incoming call. I snatched it up.

"Trey?"

"I'm sorry too. Very much."

His voice was calm, but not flat. Back to himself again. I knew the other Treys were there, though, that one or the other was only a swing of the pendulum away.

I hopped up cross-legged on the counter. "It seems like we've been saying sorry a lot recently. Like every day."

"I know. I'm sorry about that too." He hesitated. "Are you still going to Savannah?"

"Yes. But only for one night. Just long enough to check in with a few people who know John, see if they can shed some light on his current absence. See how Hope's story pans out."

Silence at Trey's end. I thought of my latest mysterious delivery, but kept that development to myself. Nothing good could come from throwing such a thing in his lap, not now anyway.

"Besides," I continued, "we're both on edge. Some time apart might be a good thing."

He made a noncommittal noise.

"You know I'm right." I kept my voice nonchalant. "Hey, what did Gabriella want?"

"Gabriella?"

"She was in the parking lot when I left."

"She was? Why?"

I took advantage of the phone connection to concoct a bit of subterfuge. "She wanted to check on you. Didn't she go up?"

"No."

I listened for any deception in that simple response. I heard nothing but puzzlement in his voice, however. And as much as I wanted to quiz him further, spill my guts about my encounter with his angry ex, I decided that particular conversation would keep, along with the rest of the things I wasn't saying. He was calm again, collected. I needed him to stay that way until I could get back to town.

He exhaled softly. "Call me tomorrow night?"

"Of course."

"Thank you. And be careful. Please."

My heart warmed. "I will. You be careful too."

"I will. And Tai?"

"Yes?"

"That indiscretion on my desk? It wasn't insignificant. Not at all."

I flushed at the memory. He'd stretched way out of his comfort zone that night, and he'd done it because I needed him, which was the part that had been out of my comfort zone.

"It wasn't insignificant for me either," I said.

We exchanged good nights, and I felt better as I climbed the stairs to my bedroom. One part of me was satisfied. But another part kept whispering in my ear. Forty-five minutes it took him to call me back.

Forty-five freaking minutes.

Chapter Eighteen

Rico didn't even say good morning. He opened the door, saw me standing there with a dozen Krispy Kremes and two coffees, then turned his back and shuffled toward the kitchen table. I kicked the door closed behind me.

"What? Not even a thank you?"

He flopped himself down at the table, his ebony eyes bleary and bloodshot. "For what? Robbing me of an hour of sleep? You coulda called instead of just showing up."

"You didn't text me back last night."

"I was at a poetry slam. Didn't get in until four."

"Oh. Sorry." I sat opposite him and shoved a coffee his way. "Don't you have to be at work in a little while though? I mean, it's not like you were going to sleep all day."

He grumbled something and stuck his nose in the coffee. His voice was thick with sleep, rough like steel wool, and his skin was lighter than I remembered, more au lait than café. We'd been best friends since middle school, bonding on the margins, and then he'd fled Savannah as soon as he graduated. And while my moving to Atlanta had put us closer in distance, we seemed to have gotten further apart in other ways.

"So you got my text?" I said.

He nodded, pulled his bathrobe tighter around his beefy frame. "Still not sure what you're wanting to know."

"Tell me about the poem."

Rico picked up a doughnut and took a bite. "Your stalker knows the classics. That's Robert Browning, from 'My Last Duchess.'"

"I got that much from Wikipedia. What does it *mean*?"

"It's a confessional monologue from a killer. A murder poem."

I pushed down that sinking feeling. "Oh crap."

"You got that right. The line you quoted refers to the victim, who was free with her looks, who liked things somebody thought she shouldn't like. Cherries, donkeys, flowers. That's what got her killed."

"But what's that got to do with Hope?"

"Knowing Hope? That woman wants to have something in each hand and something else in pocket, you know what I'm saying? And there are people who don't take kindly to that."

"Enough to kill?"

"People die for less every day."

I snagged a doughnut too, still warm, the glaze still oozy. "You know what I think? I think Hope's got herself a helper. And I bet it's that person in the photo with her."

"Shouldn't you be more worried about the person who took the picture? You know, the stalker?"

"I prefer to think of them as a confidential informant."

Rico scoffed. "Yeah? What are they trying to inform you of?"

"That's what I plan to figure out. And I'm starting in Savannah."

The sunlight filtered weak but warm through the drawn blinds, and I heard gentle snoring in the bedroom. A new boyfriend? One night stand? I suddenly realized how very little I knew about Rico's current life. But I was OTP—Outside The Perimeter—and city folk like Rico did not venture into the hinterlands beyond I-285.

He reached for another doughnut. "Savannah, huh? Figured you'd had enough of that town."

"Believe me, I thought so too."

I filled him in on the situation. Outside the window, the Old Fourth Ward was cranking into gear. Vibrant, cultured, Atlanta's crazy quilt of history and renaissance. No wonder he stayed out all hours with his poet friends, his hip hop friends, his cool friends. But Monday morning came for everyone, including spoken word poets with nine-to-five IT jobs.

I toyed with my coffee cup. "I've decided to go right to the source first."

"Which is?"

"Jasper himself."

Rico almost dropped his doughnut. "The hell you say?"

"He's got something to do with John's disappearance, I know he does, and the only way I can figure out how is if I see him face to face. He can't wiggle out of my questions or hide behind his spanking new lawyer then."

"You know you're not supposed to be talking with him. If the prosecutor finds out—"

"She won't. She's got no reason to be checking the visitation list."

"If she gets word you're in town, damn straight she'll check it. Assuming they don't already have you on some 'do not get within ten feet of Jasper Boone' list down at the lock-up."

"I'll deal with that when I get down there."

Rico shook his head. He reminded me of a shaggy bear dragged out of his cave. "Why you gotta do this alone?"

"You know Trey. He can't go off-grid to save his life."

Rico arched a skeptical eyebrow. "Pffft. You don't know what he can do until you give him a chance."

"I know what he's done every single time before, and past behavior is, as Trey himself says, a reliable predictive indicator. Plus he's acting like a cop again, like an entire police unit rolled into one control freak human being."

Rico made a noise.

I put down my coffee. "What did you say?"

"I said, the man may have his issues, but when it comes to control freaking, he ain't got nothing on you."

"What are you talking about?"

"I'm talking 'bout you. You claim to be all flexible and roll-with-it, but that's bullshit. You're about as flexible as a tire iron. You gotta have things your way, and you push until that happens."

"It's called being assertive."

"It's called being a pain in the ass."

"Takes one to know one."

He held up both hands. "Don't kill the messenger, baby girl. And I'll tell you something else. Y'all are arguing, true enough. And Trey may say this is because you're about to do something dumb ass—which you might be—and you may say this is because he's acting like an uptight prick—which he might be—but there's something else going on. There always is with you two."

The alarm clock in the bedroom went off, beeping frantically. I heard a muffled groan, a hand slapping it quiet. Rico looked in that direction, looked back at me. Kept his mouth shut. I refused to ask. If he didn't want to share, I wasn't going to pry it out of him.

"I gotta get a shower," he said. "And you need to get done down there and get back up here so we can sit down and talk. You hear me? I miss you, even if you are a pain in the ass."

"Yeah. I know." I popped him on the shoulder. "Stay where I can reach you until I get back, okay? I have a feeling this isn't the last I've heard from my poetry-spouting confidential informant."

Rico's eyes were solemn. "You are probably right. Which should be bothering you a whole helluva lot more than it is."

Chapter Nineteen

On the outside, the Chatham County Detention Center reminded me of a dictator's headquarters on some small Caribbean island—sand-beige buildings crowned with looping coils of razor wire, minimal windows, and official men milling about in earth-toned uniforms. On the inside, it was bright and sunny, almost cheerful, the concrete block walls and metal folding chairs notwithstanding. My mood, however, was anything but.

I held my paperwork in hand. "What do you mean I can't see him?"

The female guard kept her face impassive. "The inmate in question is unavailable today."

"But he's in Section A, High Risk Seg, and today is visitation for that unit. I looked it up on the website."

"Yes, ma'am. But the inmate in question was moved to Medical this morning."

"Why? What happened?"

The guard shook her head. "I'm not at liberty to discuss that. Come back tomorrow."

"He'll be out then?"

"I don't know. But tomorrow is visiting day for Medical."

"But what if he's back in the regular unit then?"

She gave me the slow patient blink. "Then you'll have to wait until Thursday."

"But I'm here from out of town."

"Then you'll get extra time to visit him, forty-five minutes. On Thursday."

I started to argue, then gave up. I recognized a wall of bureaucratic regulation when I saw one. I clutched my single piece of paper, the fill-in-the-blank half-sheet required for an appointment. Name, inmate, relation to inmate. I'd put my real name, Teresa Ann, just in case Rico was right and Tai Randolph was listed on some "no way no how" list.

"Is there no other way?" I said.

The guard shook her head and returned to her computer screen. "Sorry."

I gave up and headed back to the parking lot. I knew I couldn't kick up a fuss. I did not want Madame Olethea Jones of the Chatham County Prosecutor's Office putting me on her radar, especially if Jasper was off limits until Thursday. She'd be hard to evade for three more days, but if that was what I had to do...

I fished my car keys from my pocket, the only thing besides my license I'd been allowed to bring in, and followed the signs back to visitor's parking. I'd managed to grab a spot in the shade of a frothy white oleander, which had rained blossoms on my windshield in my absence. I started to brush them away when I heard someone clear his throat.

The voice was polite. "Be careful, ma'am, those are poisonous."

I turned. A man stood near my trunk, his navy medical scrubs crisp, his dark hair military short. He had an earbud in one ear and an MP3 player blaring tinny death metal at a hearing-shattering level. I noticed a prison ID clipped to his collar, but I couldn't see his name. I angled my shoulders, moved onto the balls of my feet. I was getting as paranoid as Trey. But then, I was in a mostly deserted parking lot twenty feet from the largest collection of criminals in Chatham County.

"I know all about oleander," I said. "Southern ladies with a disagreeable person to get rid of have made good use of it through the years."

"Is that why you're here? You got somebody to poison?"

"Excuse me?"

He held up both hands, palms forward, and smiled. "Kidding. My sense of humor has gone super morbid since I started working here."

He had a broad face that was an inch short of handsome and tanned skin that disguised a complexion roughened by acne scars. And he was friendly. Way too friendly.

"Can I help you?" I said.

He held the ID card in my direction. "My name's Shane. Shane Cook. I was on my way in, and I couldn't help overhearing you ask for Jasper."

"Are you a guard?"

"No, I'm a physical therapist. I'm here a couple days a week."

"Jasper one of your patients?"

"Maybe yes. Maybe no. Maybe we're not even talking about the same Jasper. But if we are, he'll be available tomorrow. He's going to be in Medical the rest of the week, at a minimum." He twisted his mouth into a rueful smile. "Of course I'm not supposed to be talking to you. They made that clear at orientation."

"That's okay. I'm not supposed to be talking to you either."

His eyes crinkled at the corners. "Then why are you?"

"Because I came here for information, and since I can't talk to Jasper, I guess you'll have to do."

"What kind of information?"

I rummaged in my bag until I found the picture of John and me. I showed it to Shane. "Have you seen this man coming to visit Jasper in the past week or so?"

He examined the photo, then handed it back. "No."

"What about this woman?" I showed him the photo of Hope. "She was an inmate herself until last week."

"Haven't seen her either, not as a patient or inmate. But then, I stay in the medical unit." He looked left and right, and the smile wavered the tiniest bit. "Look, I gotta ask. What's a woman like you doing wasting her time with a low class loser like…well, anybody in there?"

So that was what we had here, a clumsy attempt at a pick-up. A year out of the game, and I'd forgotten how things worked.

"The loser in question is suing me for three million dollars." I smiled evenly. "That's why I'm here."

Shane blinked at me. "You're his cousin Tai."

That caught me off guard. "Jasper told you about me?"

"You're not the only one who's been visiting. His lawyer comes too. They talk. I overhear sometimes. What I'm saying is…uh oh. Act like I'm giving you directions."

He pointed toward the road back to the parkway, still smiling. A pair of sheriff's deputies walked past us, headed for one of the patrol cars. They paid us little attention as they pulled out of the lot and drove off the complex.

Shane's smile vanished. "Jasper Boone was sent to High-Risk Seg because he provoked a fight with one of the resident skinheads. He puts on a good show, especially for the doctors, but I know his type. Sooner kill you as spit on you."

A bus pulled up and delivered a family of three, the woman herding a toddler while trying to unfold an umbrella stroller. The air was thick with diesel fumes and the rising heat. Shane stepped closer, and every instinct I had went singing into overdrive. I didn't back away, but I clutched my keys tighter.

He dropped his voice. "So when the lawyers ask me about his wrist and ankle and knee, and if the damages done warrant a multi-million-dollar settlement, I plan to give them my expert medical opinion. Because that's what they'll need. They can look at charts and X-rays, listen to Jasper himself go on and on. But in the end, it's me that will have to make sense of it. And Jasper knows it."

I examined his features. Open, friendly, salt of the earth. Except something glittered in the eyes.

"Has he tried to bribe you?" I said.

"Not yet. But he will. My time in the Sandbox gave me a real clear sense of good and evil. So you don't have to worry about me. I'll tell them everything they need to know about him." He smiled with charming candor. "If you get my drift."

I tried to keep my expression blank. Was he offering to slant his testimony? And if so, in return for what? If he was telling the truth about testifying in Jasper's civil suit, that same whole-some corn-fed expression could sway a judge or jury any way he wanted the verdict to go. And he knew it.

"The Sandbox. That's Iraq, right?"

"LSA Anaconda outside of Balad, also known as Mortar-itaville. 2nd Brigade Combat Team, 4th Infantry Division. The Wardogs." He grinned and pulled up his shirtsleeve, revealing a tattoo of a slavering black hound. "Lost my leftie in a mortar attack on a convoy back in oh-nine."

"You lost your what?"

"My left foot, right below the ankle. Sheared that sucker right off. So when the days get rough here, I remind myself, sure as hell beats the Box." He gave me a patronizing look. "Look, you seem real nice, so I'm gonna give you some words of wisdom. I'd be careful about talking to Jasper Boone if I were you. The man has friends and enemies in there and out here, and some of them might find you real interesting. And that isn't something you want. Take my advice—stay away."

He smiled again, put in his other earbud, and disappeared into the employee parking area. His left foot moved as naturally as his right, not a hint in his gait of the injury he'd described. I waited until he disappeared into the employee parking area, then brushed the last of the oleander blossoms off my windshield.

I hadn't managed to see Jasper. But Shane the physical thera-pist was an interesting consolation prize. Yes, he was.

Chapter Twenty

I shielded my eyes from the Savannah sun, high now in the powdery blue sky. Despite the downtown crush, I lucked into a parking space on Bay and fed enough quarters into the meter to give me two hours. I took the old stone steps down, steep and narrow and treacherous, then hooked a left into the limestone alley running behind the buildings. A quick turn down another narrow dark passageway, and I stepped onto the cobblestones of River Street, the crazy quilt of shops to my left and right, the rolling Savannah River in front.

The sidewalks were more crowded than usual this Monday, both tourists and locals coming out for a lunchtime breath of spring. The wind off the brackish water smelled like mud and vegetation, and it mingled with cigarette smoke and fried shrimp and stale beer. A Russian freighter cruised by, looking like a condominium complex out for a stroll, the Talmadge Bridge gleaming behind it.

I couldn't help looking over my shoulder, couldn't help examining the faces of every person I passed on the sidewalk. The couple lifting up their trifocals to read a menu, the busker playing eighties sitcom themes on his trumpet, the SCAD students sketching the brick and ballast stone architecture. The usual tapestry. Not a stalker or sniper or no-good-nik among them.

Tai Randolph, I told myself, *you're getting paranoid*. But it was with sweet relief that I finally pushed open the door to Soul Ink Tattoos.

"Hey, Train," I called. "You here?"

I heard a familiar voice from the back. "Be with you in a second."

For ten years, Soul Ink had resided in this same spot on the west end, the funkier section of the waterfront. Its decor was a cross between Episcopalian chapel and post-modern brothel, with dazzling stained glass windows, a golden stamped concrete floor, and squeaky red leather chairs.

Train stepped through the beaded curtain that separated his work space from the private back room. "Tai!"

He was a well-muscled guy, with chestnut hair and a penchant for tight sleeveless tee shirts, the better to show off his intricately inked forearms and biceps, a garden of roses and Celtic crosswork intertwined with Bible verses. He was older than me, but his face read young—full round cheeks above a goatee flecked with silver.

Train took the name of his shop literally. He saw creating body art as a sacred ministry and considered tattoos as prayerful as rosary beads. He was also one of the few people in town willing to provide a job—either at his shop or through his church—for those with tarnished reputations and/or rap sheets, the Lowcountry's second and third-chancers.

"You here to get a new tat?" he said.

"I wish. Unfortunately, I'm looking for John Wilde. Heard he was working here."

"He was, but I haven't seen him since Friday." Train gave me his pastor look. "Why? What's happened?"

"He's disappeared."

"Uh oh. He's not in trouble with the law, is he?"

"I don't know what kind of trouble he's in, but I suspect it's bad."

I sat on one of those red leather couches and filled him in, everything from the new lawyer to the lawsuit to Hope's visit. I left out the part about trying to see Jasper. Train wouldn't have approved of that either.

"What concerns me most," I said, "is that John told Hope he was gonna take care of some things."

"What kind of things?"

"Stalker things. Old debt things. All kinds of powder-keg things. He didn't try to see Jasper, did he?"

"Not that I know of. Steered clear of that whole business." Train rubbed his chin. "He called me Friday morning, said he'd dropped his bike off at a friend's shop to have an oil leak fixed, asked for a ride back. I drove over to the Whitemarsh Walmart and got him."

"What shop?"

Train held his hands up in a "dunno" gesture. "He worked the rest of the day, and I gave him a ride home. That's the last time I saw him. He was supposed to open Saturday morning, but he called in last minute and said he needed the day off. Personal business. I didn't ask why."

I remembered the receipt for the ammunition. Saturday morning.

"Does he skip work a lot?"

"No." Train leveled a look my way. "I know you two had history, and that he has sins aplenty on his tally. But he's trying. Ever since Hope went to jail, he's cleaned his life up. He said they'd both made bad mistakes—"

And Hope's still making them, I thought.

"—but I'll tell you, that mess back in the fall shook him up royally. He is on the straight and narrow now."

"And Hope?"

He shrugged. "She has declined my visits. Has anybody told her he's missing?"

And then I realized—Train didn't know she wasn't in jail anymore.

"She's out. Early release contingent on her testimony in Jasper's upcoming trial."

"Oh. John didn't mention that."

"I think he was trying to keep it on the QT. But now she's disappeared too, and I suspect they've both gotten in over their heads, again."

Train stroked his chin, thoughtful, his dark eyes filling with concern. Not panic. He'd witnessed many recently released cons return to problematic habits, hang with bad crowds, tumble off the wagon. This was familiar ground to him. As I was weighing my options, though, he delivered a question that was a bolt from the blue.

"You don't think he's playing vigilante, do you?"

"What?"

"I mean, you said he said he was going to take care of things. One of the things that bugged him most was Hope getting as much time as she did. He said it was a raw deal, said it was all the fault of your Uncle Boone and company."

I felt the ground I'd been standing on shift a bit. I hadn't considered that John might be off on a solo revenge mission. What if that was what he'd been doing out Whitemarsh way? Not dropping off his bike. Dropping in on Boone, whose estate lay right off Highway 80, barely a mile from the Walmart.

I shook my head. "That doesn't make sense. He's not—"

"What, stubborn? Convinced he can handle things on his own?" Train's eyes were firm and gentle. "Don't even pretend you're not the same way. Isn't that why you're here, after all? Because the law isn't doing what you think needs to be done?"

I wasn't about to argue with him about my motives. But he'd certainly put a new wrinkle on things.

"Are you sure John's disappeared?" he said. "Has anybody actually checked the trailer to see if he's there?"

That startled me. It would be exactly like John to go to ground if necessary. Not without telling Hope—that was weird—but still…

"I don't think so."

"Then here. Take his spare key." Train pulled a cheap penny-colored house key from the register. "He left it with me in case something happened."

"Something like what?"

"He didn't say. I thought he meant the usual things that sometimes happen. But now you've got me worried." He handed it to me, then wrote an address on the back of a business card. "Number 207 in the Shady Grove Mobile Home Community. Let me know what you find."

I slid it into my back pocket. "I will."

"And if it's something suspicious—"

"Right to the authorities. I promise."

"And Tai?"

"Yeah?"

His eyes were solemn, his face composed. "May I pray for you?"

I was hesitant—it had been a long time since anyone had interceded with the Man Upstairs on my behalf—but this was Train's MO, and it was as sincere an offering as any artwork he etched upon skin. I swallowed my discomfort and nodded. He took my hands in his and clasped them together.

He closed his eyes. "Dear Lord, watch over Your daughter, Tai. She's a handful, I know, but You have innumerable miracles in Your pocket. Keep her safe and on the path of righteousness, and bless her seeking, bless her thirst for truth and justice and use it for Your purposes. Amen."

He opened his eyes, but didn't let go of my hands. I wasn't sure if I'd ever set one foot on the path of righteousness, and truth and I were barely speaking some days, but justice? That was as worthy a goal as any, even if chasing it was like chasing a rainbow.

I squeezed his fingers. "Amen."

Chapter Twenty-one

Shady Grove proved to be several trees short of a grove, and the only shade it provided came courtesy of the sheet metal parking structures in almost every driveway. It wasn't particularly shady in a criminal way either, despite what I knew of Hope and John's known associates. There were mostly doublewides, a few singlewides, all of them older models but well-maintained. Some sported flower beds around the borders, fake deer and geese posed artistically next to birdbaths.

It took me a while to find number 207, John and Hope not being the kind of people to put out a mailbox with their names on it, but I finally found what had to be their place, a good half mile from where my phone's GPS put the address. They'd chosen a lot set back from the main stretch, close to the woods, private.

The mobile home itself was tubular and bare, like the fuselage of a jet. No parking structure here. No Harley either. A satellite dish dominated the treeless front yard, but that was it for ornamentation. Despite the lack of greenery, we were close to the marshes here. I could smell them, and I felt a pang of homesickness.

I parked at the edge of the sparse lawn and followed the driveway to wooden steps. The tire tracks in the sand were easy to spot, but hard to interpret. I decided to leave the plaster casting and forensic analysis to the crime scene team and focus instead on the yard.

What would Trey do? I thought.

Trey wouldn't be here, a voice in my head said back.

I ignored the voice and put on my sunglasses, then pulled a pair of rubber gloves from my bag. One thing Trey had taught me was to be prepared. He'd also taught me to observe, get a clear overall picture before moving to specificities. So I walked the perimeter. I walked it first looking at the ground, knowing that my next move would be looking at eye level, then a final time looking up, both clockwise and counterclockwise. I never got that far, however, because I found what I was looking for on my first try—several jagged punctures in the bare baseboards.

Bullet holes.

I knelt, focused my cell phone to take a picture. Bullets went in a straight line. So I traced my steps backwards, cocking my index finger and thumb into a pretend pistol and following the line of sight all the way back to the end of the driveway, keeping an eye on the ground around my feet. If the shooter had used a semi-auto...

It took two minutes of hard looking before I spotted the spent brass in the high weeds of the drainage ditch. I snapped their picture too, but didn't touch them. Not .22s, which meant they hadn't come from the handgun Hope had found. These were .45 ACPs, a massive caliber perfectly capable of making the holes Trey had spotted in the trunk.

I went around back, grateful for the lack of nosy neighbors. The backyard had a new deck, plain and simple and smelling of fresh wood, freckled with rain and pollen. It had a southern exposure, a deck chair for sunbathing, and a shade to keep the sun from the kitchen windows. John was always good with his hands, whether woodworking or wielding the tattoo needle. He'd built this to welcome Hope back, to make this place feel like a home for her.

I pulled open the screen door and inserted the key. Both the regular lock and deadbolt were engaged, no sign of forced entry, and I pulled it closed behind me as I stepped into the kitchen.

The space was small, ill-lighted, with avocado green counters and faux wood laminate, not the kind of kitchen featured in *Southern Living*. I spotted a box of cereal on the counter, a rinsed bowl and spoon in the sink. I opened the refrigerator, which looked like my refrigerator, with only the basics—milk, beer, sandwich meat, condiments. There was a brown circle of gummy tea spilled on one of the shelves under a half-full pitcher, but that was the only mess.

I checked the living room next. The front door was closed, but only the knob lock was engaged, not the deadbolt. The sofa and chairs and coffee table were well-made, but dated and dinged, thrift store finds most likely. John was good at that, picking and poking through trash to find the treasure. A large stain spread in front of the television. I knelt and examined it, breathing a sigh of relief to find only the ghost of a long-ago spill. No blood, no brains.

I flipped the light in the bedroom and stopped short. The room was messy, but not lived-in messy like the rest of the trailer. Random messy. Two drawers on the dresser dangled open, a pair of jeans hanging out. The bedclothes lay on the floor in a pile, the pillows too. A heap of dirty clothes sat next to an empty wicker basket. I picked up a stack of camisoles lying half-folded on the floor and pressed them to my nose. They smelled fresh and clean, like fabric softener.

My knees shook, and I sat on the edge of the bed. The bedroom had been searched. Not the living room, not the kitchen. Which meant that whoever had done the searching had abandoned the search, either because they'd found what they were looking for or because they'd been surprised. And from the ballistic evidence I'd seen in the front yard, I was guessing the latter. Something had happened here. Something that ended in violence.

"He didn't run away," I said out loud.

And then I heard it—the slow roll of tires on sand, the idle of an engine. The slam of a car door followed, and then another. I went to the window, Trey's voice yammering in my head about mobile home construction and bullet caliber as I pulled back the thin cotton curtain.

Cops. Two of them. Not random psychopaths. I felt a surge of relief, followed quickly by a ripple of oh-no. There I was, at a crime scene, on property that belonged to a man gone missing and a woman fresh out of jail.

I saw one of the cops walk around to the back of my car. I cursed again. Running my license plates. So either they were there because the Atlanta PD had drop-kicked John's disappearance down Savannah Metro way, or because somebody else had seen me prowling around and called them to investigate. I couldn't decide which scenario was more problematic.

I pulled out my phone, dialed 911. When the operator answered, I said, "I'd like to report a burglary. I'm at 207…Oh wait, I see you have officers already here. Thank you for your quick and efficient service."

I hung up. Left my carry bag lying on the floor at the foot of the bed. Peeled off the cat-burglar gloves. I opened the front door very slowly using the hem of my tee shirt. The cops looked up as I came onto the front porch, and I saw their elbows dip to touch the butts of the pistols in their holsters. Training, I knew. Double-checking for the weapon. Nothing sinister, but I gulped anyway.

"That was fast," I said.

The young one looked puzzled and checked his orders. "What was fast?"

"You guys getting here since I just this very second called the station to report a burglary."

The older one frowned. "Are you Hope Lyle?"

"No, I'm her friend. Tai Randolph. Real name's Teresa Ann, but everybody calls me Tai." I smiled. "I suppose you've heard that the residents of this trailer are both missing, and that I was checking on them when I found the place like this, which is what prompted me to immediately call the police."

I kept my hands where they could see them, empty and open. The cops looked at each other. The younger was dark and tall, the older one pale and short. They made a pair of suspicious ying-yang bookends.

"Can you verify that you have permission to be on these premises?"

"I can. Not from Hope or John, of course, both of them being, you know, missing. But I got this address and the key from a mutual friend, John's employer."

I gave them Train's business card, making sure they saw the embossed cross on it. One of them took notes, the other kept an eye on the front yard.

"You'll find my sneaker prints in the driveway, and around back on the deck. Other than that, it's exactly the same as when I came in." I smiled bigger. "I date a cop, so I know better than to tamper with evidence."

They had moved from baffled to inquisitive. This wasn't what they'd been expecting, but it wasn't the big bad unexpected. No corpses, no shooting, only little old me. And they were relieved to discover they could handle me easily.

"Do you mind if we come inside?" the shorter one said.

I stepped back from the door. "Oh, please do."

◇◇◇

I sat on the sofa with my knees tucked together, trying to look innocuous while they searched the trailer. They looked mostly bored until my phone rang. Then both their heads swiveled in my direction.

I held up the phone. "Y'all care if I take this?"

The taller one made a "go ahead" gesture. I put it to my ear. "Hey there, Reynolds."

"Good morning, m'dear. How are you this fine day?"

Both cops were pretending to examine the TV stand, but they were really listening to my conversation.

"Oh, same as always. And you?"

"Splendid. I have to be brief, but I thought you might want to know...I did some asking around. As it turns out, there has been a sizeable collection of Confederate memorabilia put up for sale recently, as one grouping. Fine pieces, mostly martial. Extremely reasonable but non-negotiable price."

That meant somebody was looking for a quick sale. "Was it connected to one of the, ah, cultural groups we discussed?"

"Not exactly. It was your cousin Jefferson."

Chapter Twenty-two

The sun was setting by the time I finished with the cops and pointed the car east on Highway 80, the last leg of the Dixie Overland route. The tide had just turned, and the iodine smell of the pluff mud hung thick in the air. A wet breeze blew in from the Atlantic, heavy with deep water, and I rolled the windows down to let it ride along with me.

A stranger would miss the entrance to Boone's place. No sign announced it, no mailbox marked it. A stand of palmetto palms shaded an oyster-shell driveway, which curved out of sight like a trail of breadcrumbs. Boone's private peninsula was a world apart from the sun-bright, beach-happy madness of the highway. A dark, cool country all its own, sovereign unto itself.

I turned down the path. Cat briers and blackberry bushes crowded the lane, morning glory too. Live oaks more than a hundred years old arched overhead in a canopy of gray moss and green leaf. The path had only one destination—Boone's. No way to turn around, no side roads. Boone owned all twenty acres of it, and he and his family were its only occupants.

Five minutes later I turned the last curve, and his house loomed into view. I could see only the very top, however, since everything below the third story was obscured by a tabby stucco wall. A security camera tracked my car as I drove to the main entrance, gated and locked.

I got out. Stood there a minute to let everybody get a good look at me. Then I walked up to the intercom and pushed the button.

A voice answered immediately. "Yeah?"

Definitely female and deep Southern, though more twangy than Lowcountry. "I'm here to see Boone."

"He ain't here."

"Cheyanne? Is that you?"

A barbed silence.

"It's me. Tai. I know we've never met, but—"

"I know who you are."

I knew her too. Cheyanne was Boone's daughter-in-law, married to Jefferson. They had two daughters, but that hadn't mellowed them any. They were both high up in the Klan, the newly sanitized, female-friendly, uber-empowered version. Which made Cheyanne as dangerous as he was.

"I need to talk to y'all," I said.

"About what?"

"Jasper trouble."

A pause. I heard muffled conversation at her end. She was calling someone, either Jefferson or Boone, and asking them what to do. I crossed my fingers it was the latter—Boone had always possessed a soft spot for me, but even more importantly, he trusted me. Jefferson always acted like he preferred me stuffed and mounted.

One minute later, there was a buzzing, and the big gate swung open. I got back in the Camaro and eased it through, squashing down any apprehension as the gate closed behind me.

◇◇◇

Boone's house was shabbier than I remembered, badly in need of a new roof, the gray siding faded and pocked. He'd never been one for landscaping, but now the tangles and brambles had taken over the flower beds, and swaths of Spanish moss choked the branches. It was chaotic and wild, pure tidewater country, and despite my uneasiness, it felt like coming home.

I parked next to Boone's old Thunderbird. Unlike the house, it had held up well. Still a deep blue, shiny in the fenders. Cars, guns, and women—the redneck trinity—the first of those well-represented in the open space beneath the house. Like most Lowcountry homes, Boone's was built with an unfinished first floor, open so that flood water could come and go without wrecking the living areas. I saw at least six vehicles in pieces and parts under there, a couple of watercraft too, including a battered Carolina skiff and a jet ski. Boone hadn't liquidated this collection yet, which surprised me in light of Reynolds' revelation. I knew finances were tight, but why was Jefferson getting rid of prized antiques instead of junk cars?

Cheyanne opened the door before I could knock, wiping her hands on her apron. She was my height, maybe shading into five-seven, but twice as muscled. She'd pulled her fawn-brown hair into a ponytail as thick as my wrist, sun-bleached tendrils curling around her forehead. It created an odd halo effect and matched her deep-set eyes, topaz like a lion's. I caught the pungent odor of fish coming off her, and when I checked her apron, I saw why—it was smeared with blood and scales and slime.

"Jefferson ain't here," she said. "But he said you're welcome to wait."

I followed her inside the massive great room with its two-story windows overlooking the salt marsh. I'd barely shut the door behind myself when two tow-headed girls came screeching around the corner, dip nets and jelly jars clutched in their hands.

The tallest held up a dirty pint of water. "Mama! Guess what we found!"

"Not now." Cheyanne pointed toward the back yard. "Y'all go play."

"But Mama—"

"Git!"

They got. I watched them fly through the patio door and tear down the steps, headed for the cove. The retreating tide would leave treasures of all kinds—silver bait fish, tiny crabs. The playthings of a marsh rat childhood. There were still shotguns behind each door and skinning knives lying as casually as silverware on the counter, but now there were toys scattered on the floor and family portraits hanging alongside the taxidermied deer heads.

One of those featured Cheyanne with her compound bow in hand, a twelve-point buck dead at her feet, its tongue lolling.

I followed her onto the patio to the fish cleaning station just beyond the swimming pool. I couldn't help noticing there were chunks missing from the pavement, and the pool was covered with a thick tarp and puddles of stagnant water. Cheyanne reached into a cooler, pulling out a sea trout. She grabbed it by the tail and slung it on the counter like a potter flinging clay. Then she took her cleaver and chopped the fish's head off in a single slice. She eyed me, watching for some sign of disgust or discomfort. I almost laughed. If she was trying to out-redneck me, she was wasting her time.

"Where's Boone?" I said.

"At the hospital."

I suppressed a twinge of apprehension. "Is he okay?"

She shrugged. "Stable, they say. Another one of his episodes."

"Is Jefferson with him?"

She shook her head. "No, he had to go fetch a gator."

"A gator?"

"Somebody over in the Landings found one on the golf course." She kept her attention on the fish. Chop, slice, chuck the guts in one bucket, heads in the other, cleaned fish in a metal pan. "He does varmint removal. Gators, snakes, bats, whatever. Had to get a water moccasin out of New Life Pentecostal's baptismal pool last weekend."

So that was the business now. The marshlands had plenty of troublesome creatures. Developers bulldozed the swamp, backfilled it, and threw up McMansions at the edge of the wilderness. Then everybody acted surprised at the snake in the whirlpool, the gator in the koi pond.

Cheyanne scraped scales, iridescent in the filtered light. "So what's this trouble you were talking about?"

"You remember the third eyewitness, the one we need to put Jasper away for good?"

"Somebody named Hope."

"Yeah. Hope Lyle. She's missing. Her husband too."

"You think any of us know where they are?"

"This seemed a good enough place to start."

She went back to cleaning the fish. "You can ask Jefferson, but he's been busy taking care of Daddy Boone and chasing varmints. I've been busy with the girls. We ain't had time to mess with nobody. But even if we had, why would we?"

The pop-pop-pop of a BB gun carried over the back yard, followed almost immediately by the crash of glass and girlish shrieks.

Cheyanne's voice went full throttle. "Dixie Lynn and Meredith Lee, I told y'all about shooting up glass! I will tan both your hides and take those rifles away if you do it again, you hear me?"

Guilty silence from the woods. Then two reluctant, drawn-out "yes, ma'am's."

"Get some cans if you wanna shoot. Your daddy put plenty in the recycle." Cheyanne shook her head and went back to the fish. "I swear. You got kids?"

It took me a second to find my voice. "Nope."

"Always into something, kids are. Watch, they'll be setting fires or getting in a fistfight any second now."

About that time, I heard the rolling of tires on the crushed oyster shell. Cheyanne wiped her hands on her apron, the knife too, leaving a smear of blood before she placed it carefully at the edge of the sink. The girls came thundering up from the woods, headed toward the other side of the house, barefoot and hell for leather.

"Y'all keep out of your daddy's way!" she hollered after them. Then she turned to me. "Come on. Jefferson's here."

She headed for the back with the same eagerness as her daughters, and I remembered the many heads and horns mounted on the great room walls. I shot a quick glance at her boots.

Just as I suspected. Alligator hide.

Chapter Twenty-three

We reached the edge of the fishpond as Jefferson climbed down from his pick-up. He was promptly mobbed by the girls. His hair wasn't the platinum blond of his father's—it was the yellow-brown of wheat—but from a distance, he looked like a darker version of the Boone I remembered from my teenage years. Not tall, but lean, with a high forehead and angled Nordic features. Those features were currently hidden under a camouflage hunting cap, the rest of him head-to-toe camo too, even the bibbed hip waders covered in mud.

"It's a little 'un, six feet tops," he said to Cheyanne. "He did put up a nice fight, though."

He steered the bouncing girls toward the back of the truck and pulled down the tailgate. The gator was trussed up like a Thanksgiving turkey and staring at its captors with cold reptilian hatred. Little or not, I wouldn't have wanted to give him a shot at me. Cheyanne helped Jefferson drag the thing out and haul it to the edge of the fishpond, next to the wooden pier. Shallow and muddy, the pond stretched like a boomerang around a hump of soggy land.

I squinted across the stretch of water, glimpsing chain link running around the entire perimeter. "New fence?"

"Yep."

And then I heard the rolling splash of a tail hitting the water. Then another. I shielded my eyes with one hand and stepped up to the edge of the pier. A dozen alligators sunned in the waning light. I'd always heard rumors, that to piss Boone off was a one-way trip to the gator pit with marsh crabs snacking on the leftovers. I'd passed it along myself, laughing in my head because I knew it wasn't true.

Wasn't laughing any more.

Jefferson turned his attention to the beast at the edge of the water, its jaws roped shut. Cheyanne ordered the girls to stay back, and they obeyed wordlessly. She went to help Jefferson, grabbing one end of the critter, her biceps bunching. Together they undid the ropes and heaved the reptile into the water, where it disappeared with a snap and a whip of its tail.

"Lord have mercy," I said. "Y'all turned the fishpond into a gator pit."

Jefferson regarded me for the first time. "Gators are like pigs and goats. They eat anything and turn it into meat pretty fast." He looked at Cheyanne. "Go on and take the girls back to the house. I'll be up in a little bit."

She did as he asked, throwing one final warning glare my way as she gathered her daughters. I slapped at the sand gnats chewing a hole in my neck. Spring brought them out by the billions, tiny specks of teeth as voracious as wolverines.

Jefferson saw my smacking and handed me a dark glass bottle. Lemon eucalyptus oil. I daubed some of it on my neck, rubbed it into my hairline. My eyes watered at the pungent citrus and menthol mixture, but short of DEET or cigarette smoke, it was the only thing that would keep the buggers at bay.

"Cheyanne said Boone was in the hospital."

"Yeah."

I handed the oil back to him. "How bad is it?"

"Bad. He'll come home, though, thank the Lord."

"You see him today?"

"No, he don't talk to nobody when he's in the hospital, not even me. He filed for confidential patient status on account of the people who might still be bearing a grudge for some of his previous activities. The only time I'll hear from him is when they got the discharge papers ready, and he needs a ride back here."

"That makes no sense."

"Daddy's always been a proud man. IPF is hard. It makes for weakness. He don't want anybody to see him like that."

"I'm gonna try anyway."

"Of course you are." He shoved his hat backward, resettled it lower on his forehead. "If you manage to pull it off, tell the old man I said hey."

He pulled out a pack of Red Man, his daddy's chew, and shoved a wad of it in his cheek. Ten years older than me, now he looked decades. Despite his anti-government proclivities, he was cooperating with the investigation. Had to, I knew. They'd dropped some charges in return, softened others, but if he reneged, he'd be in jail with Jasper.

"You coulda called," he said. "We got phones, you know. E-mail and texts, all that new-fangledy stuff."

He delivered the line with deadpan sarcasm. He was wary, distrustful, and didn't like me one bit. But he was smart, in some ways, and knew we were in this together, like it or not. Which is why I knew he'd be willing to help me, up to a point anyway.

"I need to talk to Boone. But I need to talk to you too."

He spat. "So talk."

"John Wilde's disappeared. Hope too."

"So?"

"You know anything about it?"

He shook his head.

"You sure?"

His patience was unraveling. "Why would I have anything to do with that piece of shit?"

"He was threatening to set things straight, and now he's vanished. The last anybody heard from him was a message on my machine."

Jefferson tucked the tobacco back in his pocket. "Man always was an idiot."

"An idiot who still owes you twenty grand. You all forgiving and forgetting now?"

He shrugged. "Every business takes a loss from time to time. I wrote that off as one."

"You can afford to do that?"

"We're getting by."

"Now that you sold Boone's pistol collection. And all his great-granddaddy's Confederate memorabilia."

He didn't deny it, or ask where I'd heard such a thing. He simply watched the sunset-dappled water, following the long shapes riding the surface.

I shook my head. "Thing is, why get rid of that first? Why not all those beater cars and boats under the house?"

He shrugged. "You think I ain't been trying? But the local junk market is over-saturated. As they say."

"So you been keeping your nose clean, just driving around the island in your pick-up, rehabilitating gators."

"Straight and narrow."

He pulled out a sandwich bag full of squashed marshmallows and popped one on top of the water, where it bobbed for a second. A blunt scaly snout rose from the depths, opening and closing on the marshmallow with barely a sound. Across the pond, a half-dozen others slid into the water, headed our way. Gators with a sweet tooth. It made the reptiles seem tame, like scaled and slit-eyed dogs. But a gator was a gator. To see anything else would have been a dangerous mistake.

"You think Jasper's got something to do with any of this?" I said. "He managed to have himself an armed rebellion right under the KKK's nose, and he's still got people out there, I know he does. He could disappear somebody easy, even from jail."

"Maybe so. He does have people. But they ain't my people."

"Ah yes. Your people. Once Jasper started piling up bodies, all your people started hiding and lying and pointing fingers." I let the words trip syllable by syllable off my tongue. "Including you."

He turned hard eyes my way. "Not including me. If you'll remember, I was the one who came to make sure you were okay in the middle of the shitstorm he created." He looked back over the water. "I ain't never tried to hurt you, Tee. You and me are on different sides, true enough. But you're family, and Daddy always says that comes first."

Tee. It had been decades since I'd heard that nickname. A contraction of Tai, which was itself a nickname, dreamed up by a sweetly oddball aunt with a disreputable Vietnamese to English dictionary. And while Jefferson delivered the words calmly, I knew it was a cover. His brother's betrayal had rocked him to the core, and not only the attempted assassination part. Jefferson was a company man. To have his brother, his fellow Klansman, betray not just his family but the entire Aryan nation? That was an abomination beyond forgiveness.

I leaned my arms on the railing. "He's suing me, you know."

Jefferson's head snapped back. "What for?"

"Assault. Suing Trey too."

"How much?"

"Together? Nine million."

Jefferson whistled long and low. "Damn."

Behind him, I could see the back yard, the defunct pool. I could hear the laughter of his girls and it was almost like being a kid again, juicy with delight, ravenous and curious and burning with energy. A final lick of orange light glinted off the Thunderbird, heavy, weighted with memory...

I blinked. From this vantage point, I could see what was parked on the other side of the yard—a 2010 Harley-Davidson Night Rod Special, black on black from fender to fender, its leather and silver chrome piercingly familiar. I could feel the curve of the seat as I straddled it, the vibration of the V-twin engine against my thighs.

I pointed. "Jefferson Forrest Boone, if you haven't seen John Wilde around here, what's his Harley doing parked under your house?"

Chapter Twenty-four

Jefferson's eyes tightened. "Ain't really none of your business."

I felt the caution catch. I'd never backed down from this man in my life, not even when we were kids, and yet I felt the sudden urge to run. I dropped my shoulders, shifted my left foot back six inches. Opened my hands and kept them loose and ready.

"It damn sure is my business," I said. "Now do you want to explain this to me, or to the folks who are gonna come after me?"

"You would, wouldn't you? Call the law on me?"

"Consider it called the second I don't check in with Trey."

Jefferson flinched. I was surprised to see something flash in his eyes that wasn't purely anger. Anger was in there, all right, but it was mingled with affront.

He nodded slowly, coming to terms with it. "Fine. Be like that. I ain't never laid a hand on you, Tee. But it's good to know you think I might. That's mighty fine information right there."

"Stop making this personal. Why is John's—?"

"Because he gave it to me in return for wiping his debt clean. And then he walked out the front gate."

"Walked?"

"Don't believe me? Come on."

He turned and headed for the house, shoving the marshmallows into his pocket. I cursed and followed him back up the path and inside the house. He walked with purpose, shoving open the door without announcing himself, passing Cheyanne in the kitchen with the girls. They giggled and stirred a pot on the stove, their mouths already smeared with chocolate. They didn't see us, but Cheyanne did. Her predator eyes watched us all the way out of the great room.

Jefferson turned left, down the hall leading to the bedrooms. It was hushed in this part of the house, uncomfortably private. I followed, not saying a word. He went to what had been a closet when I was little, but which was now a state-of-the-art safe room, with a bulletproof door and a security console inside. During Jasper's attempted coup, it had been fully stocked with shotguns and pistols and rifles and stacks of ammo, doomsday quantities.

No longer. The room was now stripped to the basics—landline, radio, first aid kit. Crates of water and a stack of blankets.

Jefferson pulled up a chair and sat down at the computer station. He tapped the keys, and a four-plexed screen appeared showing real time footage of the backyard, the dock, the gator pit, and the front gate. He tapped again, and one square expanded to fill the video monitor. Then it went dark. And then it started rolling.

I immediately saw a figure I recognized. "That's John."

Jefferson didn't look my way. "Yep. On the Harley. Now watch this."

I watched as he fast-forwarded past John knocking on the door, disappearing inside, then coming back out. When he left, though, he walked right past the bike until he was out of frame, leaving Jefferson alone.

I turned to the actual Jefferson, standing there fuming with righteous indignation. "Why didn't you tell me this in the first place?"

"Because I don't need any more trouble in this house, and I knew you'd go straight to your cop friends and tell them all about it. I don't know what happened to John, but that was the first time I've seen him in over a year and it was the last time I've seen him since. He was trouble then, and he's trouble now, and I don't need it."

"He's vanished."

"Not because of me."

I tapped my foot. In the kitchen I heard a shriek of joyous laughter. I could smell something baking, something sweet. It was almost dinnertime.

"When was this?"

"Friday morning. He accused me of following him and Hope, told me he didn't want trouble, they were trying to get off to a fresh start. I told him he wanted a fresh start, he needed to wipe his tally sheet clean with me. He said that was what he'd come to do."

Then he'd walked down to the Whitemarsh Island Walmart and called Train.

"So he gave you the bike and you called it square. That's all he took out of here?"

"Yep."

I pointed at the screen. "Then what's that he's sticking in the back of his jeans? A going-away present?"

Jefferson gave me an elaborate shrug. The Boone family might have gotten out of the drugs and tobacco and moonshine dealing, but they carried guns like stray dogs carried fleas.

"Hope found a pistol in the glove compartment, a JA-22 in mighty sad shape. Said she'd never seen it before."

Jefferson didn't drop his eyes. "You don't say."

"John never liked guns and didn't know crap about them, which is why I'm not surprised he'd shove a junk piece like that in his pants. He tell you why he wanted it?"

"Nope. But I guarantee you I wasn't the reason. He walked outta here clean slate. Nothing to fear from me."

I started to argue, but Cheyanne came to the door, wiping her hands on a dishcloth. She looked straight at Jefferson. "There's some sheriff's deputies want to talk to you."

"Where?"

"Out front."

Jefferson shot me a look before he rose to his feet. "This your doing?"

I raised my hands, palms out. "Don't look at me."

He took Cheyanne by the elbow and led her into the hall. I heard muffled conversation, heated, with my name rising up like a bad smell. Eventually, Jefferson headed back into the great room, leaving me alone with Cheyanne.

She filled the doorway, glowering. "We ain't had no problems with the cops until you showed up. Now we got the law on our lawn."

"Well, I didn't put 'em there."

"Like hell you didn't. So you listen up and you listen good—I have worked too long and too hard keeping this family together to let you destroy it." She shoved her sleeves up. "I've got two little girls. And the only thing they've got is me, their daddy, and this land. That's why we have cooperated every step of the way, so that we could keep this house for them, so they'll know what it is to have a home. And now you come, dragging trouble—"

"I'm not dragging a damn thing."

"—like I don't have enough to deal with from…"

She bit back her words. Anger glowed high on her cheekbones, but something else too. Fear, a bright shining wash of it.

"Cheyanne? Who's causing problems besides the law? Jasper?"

"It's nothing I can't handle myself."

She came into the room and planted herself in front of the video monitor. On the screen, the deputies were talking to Jefferson. They stood on the front porch, Jefferson stood inside the door. The conversation went on this way for several minutes, and if I hadn't known the context, it would have seemed friendly, man-to-man stuff. No warrants were produced, no handcuffs either. Eventually Jefferson shut the door and came back inside the safe room.

Cheyanne cut to the chase. "Well?"

"Apparently somebody beat up Jasper, and the law decided I might have had something to do with it."

Cheyanne's jaw dropped. "You? You ain't even been up there."

"Apparently some skinheads got into it with him. Now he's in a hospital bed, saying I sicced them on him." His mouth twisted in disgust. "Like I'd have anything to do with those neo-Nazi sons-a-bitches."

I stayed quiet about my conversation with Shane the PT, but I remembered him saying clearly that Jasper had started the altercation. Had he done it simply so that he could blame Jefferson for the attack? That sounded like something right out of his playbook. He wouldn't cop to that, of course...but his talkative physical therapist might be willing to drop some information if could catch him somewhere besides inside the detention center.

I stood up, shouldered my bag. Cheyanne and Jefferson switched hard looks on me.

"I think it's time I showed myself out," I said.

◇◇◇

Jefferson walked me back to my car, not from courtesy. He didn't speak. Some part of me felt the pull of the blood we shared, but another part despised him, and I couldn't figure out how both parts co-existed simultaneously. Across the water, I heard the bellow of a bull gator staking its territory, marshmallows forgotten. I rolled up my window and started backing out. That was the problem with gators—no matter how many marshmallows they ate, they were still gators.

Chapter Twenty-five

My cousin Billie wasn't convinced that John had fallen upon foul play. "Come on, Tai. Be for real."

"I am for real!"

It was only the two of us around the kitchen table. Billie had the broad shoulders of my mother's people, but where I was freckled and dirty blond, she was pale-skinned and black-haired. She'd been lean as a whippet last time we'd visited. Now her cheeks bloomed full and rosy, her pregnant belly swollen and round. I'd always seen her in mechanic's coveralls, axle grease under her fingernails. She wore maternity jeans now, and one of her husband's blue work shirts with *Travis* embroidered on the pocket.

"You know John, and you know chances are good he's turned tail because he owed somebody money."

"John gave Jefferson his Harley. They called it even."

She waved her hand like she was shooing a fly. "So? The Boone family ain't the only business in town. I bet there's lots of people eager to take out some interest on his hide."

Billie was my cousin in some manner I didn't understand—my family tree had branches that split and converged in unseemly ways that my mother had erased from the official record. She'd rewritten her life when she married my father, setting her sights on some upwardly mobile future far away from Savannah. My father's first and greatest betrayal, the one she'd never forgiven him for, was taking a professor's job in town instead of moving her to North Carolina, where his people rolled around in tobacco money.

"That's probably true," I admitted. "But I can't see him leaving Hope behind."

"She leaves him, he leaves her, you know them two play this game."

"This time it's not a game. I went to their trailer. I'm telling you, something bad happened there."

She sighed and stretched her legs out in front of her. She'd offered to put me up for the night, and I'd gratefully accepted. Her house was modest, but it was fresh-paint and sawdust new, a starter home in one of the more affordable Southside subdivisions.

"Did you see Boone?" she said.

"I tried, but the people at Memorial won't even admit he's in the hospital, much less ring me through. And he doesn't carry a cell phone. He's convinced the NSA has them all bugged."

"Sounds about right."

I spun my cell phone around on her brand new kitchen table. No word from Trey, not even a text. Of course it was Monday, and he'd had a full day. Still.

"Billie?"

"Yeah?"

"Do you think people can change? I mean, in real fundamental ways? Or do you think we're stuck being who we've always been?"

"Jesus, girlfriend, what kind of question is that?"

I rubbed my eyes. "Never mind. I've obviously exhausted myself stupid."

"Then go to bed. That's where I'm headed." She shoved herself up from the table awkwardly. "The baby's room is made up for you. Don't mess with anything. And no smoking anywhere in the house."

"I quit, remember?"

"Right. And if you hear footsteps in the hall, don't shoot, it's just me having to pee again. Travis will be in around ten. Don't shoot him either." She put a hand to the small of her back, regarded me from the doorway. "I'm kidding, you know."

"I know."

She nodded. We had years between us, lots of them.

"'Night," she said.

I watched her waddle her way down the hall, swaying. "'Night."

◇◇◇

The baby's room was decorated in ocean colors, blues like deep water, greens like beach glass. A girl, Billie said, although she and Travis were still arguing over what her name would be.

I started to drop my overnight bag at the foot of the twin bed, but the whisper of a rug looked too delicate. Everything in the room smelled like baby powder, like an invisible infant was already swaddled in the vast white pine crib. I felt lumbering, coarse. When my phone vibrated with an incoming text, I snatched it up.

But it wasn't from Trey. It was an unknown number. I thumbed it open even though I already knew what it was going to be.

Sure enough, it was a photograph, this time of a…I peered closer. Was that an oak tree? Hard to tell from the image, though the English ivy wrapped round the trunk was clear. The words, however, were murky and meaningless.

How closely she twineth, how tight she clings.

I shook my head. I never thought I'd regret skipping English class twice in one week.

◇◇◇

After making sure Billie was in her room, I tiptoed out the back door onto the patio, pulled up one of the plastic chairs, and called Trey. He answered on the first ring.

I tipped my head back and watched the evening clouds scuttle across the sky. "How'd your meeting go today?"

"It was…interesting."

"And the upshot?"

"Still to be determined. Legal will keep me informed."

"And you're okay?"

A pause. "I'm okay."

I told him about visiting Train's shop, checking out the trailer, and filling out a report with the police. I emphasized the part where I kept both gun and cell phone handy at all times, skipped the part about my visit to the prison. He was behaving, and I didn't want him to blow a gasket and come barreling down to Savannah in full guard dog mode.

"What time will you be home tomorrow?" he said.

"Um…about that."

"Tai—"

"I still have to see Boone. I went out there today, but he's in the hospital again." I hesitated. "I did talk to Jefferson, though."

Trey didn't reply, but I felt his hackles rising. He'd decided Boone wasn't a threat, not to me anyway, but he harbored major reservations about Jefferson.

"Stand down, boyfriend. It's not like I went trekking to some Klan outpost in the middle of nowhere. He and his wife and two little girls are staying at the house now."

"Oh. When did that happen?"

"Probably right after the marina got seized. And I know you don't trust him—I don't either—but I'm reasonably sure he didn't have anything to do with John's disappearance."

"Why not?"

"Because John gave him his Harley. Wiped the debt clean. I saw the evidence myself."

Trey didn't interrupt, not even to insert the word "alleged" in there anywhere. I pulled at a tuft of grass, and the crisp green smell hit me with a rush of memory and longing.

"We're still talking foul play, though. If you'd seen that trailer, you'd agree. Plus I suspect Hope is getting some help from somebody on Jasper's side of the fence."

"What makes you think that?"

I took a deep breath. I had to come clean about this part. "I got another insider tip."

Trey's voice hardened. "From whom?"

"Probably from the same source who slipped me the photo outside the History Center. Only this time she left it on my front door. Well, sort of. She actually left it at Raymond Junior's, and he brought it over."

"She? Raymond saw her?"

"No. But it has to be the same person. The handwriting matches and everything."

Trey digested this piece of news. I could feel his frustration through the line. Every time he thought he had the shop's hatches battened down, some mishap revealed new leaks in his system.

I sifted the grass between my fingers, watched it fall back to the ground. "Also, I got another photo, like, fifteen minutes ago. Not in person, though. On my phone."

Silence. One of those heavy, edged silences.

"Trey? Are you freaking out?"

"No. What did it say?"

"This is gonna sound ridiculous, but it's a picture of a tree and a snippet of poetry. A live oak, to be specific. And the poem is something about twining and clinging. I've got a text in to Rico to see if he'll translate poet-speak for me."

"Did you run the geotagging data?"

"The what?"

"Digital images contain data about location. Unless the data profile is deliberately stripped, you can tell where it was taken, when, sometimes even under what conditions and with what kind of camera."

"How do I do that?"

"Rico can do it quite easily."

"Of course. I'll ask him." I dug my toes deeper into the turf. "This is a good thing, right? It means my informant is most likely still in Atlanta. Because this is the first tip that's come by phone and not hand delivery."

Several seconds passed. "A reasonable assumption, if not certain by any means. Rico's analysis should help in that determination."

He didn't use the word "stalking," but I knew he was thinking it. I didn't tell him that was only the half of it. That the more I talked around, the more I understood that something big was winding itself up, getting ready to strike. And whatever it was, it was sneaky and mean and fierce enough to take a chunk out of me.

He stayed quiet. There was expectancy in the silence, and I fought the keen desire to spill the whole of my day, even the prison visit part. He was taking everything more calmly than I'd expected. Maybe Rico was right. Maybe he could maintain that calm better than I'd imagined. I'd opened my mouth, unsure of what might come out, when headlights swung down the driveway, briefly illuminating the backyard. Travis, home from second shift at the docks. Time to get back inside and get ready for the morning.

I cradled the phone between my shoulder and ear. "Trey? Are you really okay?"

He didn't answer, and I felt the first prickle of apprehension. He was doing what he always did when an inconvenient truth threatened to fall out of his mouth—clamming up. My imagination provided a suggestive scenario about what that secret might be, and I gritted my teeth. I would kill Gabriella, I would throttle her with my bare hands.

"Whatever it is you're not telling me, spill it."

A long excruciating pause. "I don't want to talk about it on the phone."

The night was alive around me—crickets, frogs, nocturnal things. The darkness had texture, like it was woven out of black silk, even in Billie's neighborhood, which had been erected on top of a sinkhole and was surrounded with streetlights and yard lights and porch lights, lights of every kind.

"You really are keeping something from me, aren't you?"

A soft exhale. "Yes."

"You're not breaking up with me, are you?"

"What?" His voice was tinged with panic. "Why would you think that?"

"Because you're being all weird and evasive."

"It's something I'd rather discuss in person, that's all."

"But I don't know when I'll be back."

He was quiet for almost fifteen seconds, then exhaled. "It will wait. Call me and let me know how your conversation with Boone goes. Okay?"

"Okay."

"And if you need me, for any reason—"

"I'll call you. Without hesitation."

Another exhale, this one of relief. "Good. Very good."

Chapter Twenty-six

This time around, the detention center accepted my appointment. The same guard I'd seen the day before told me to cover my cleavage, which meant I had to button the shirt all the way past my larynx, but otherwise I was good to go. One of the benefits of video visitation, I supposed. Jasper and I wouldn't actually be face to face—he'd be on a video monitor, like the world's worst reality television show—which made the security procedures much more streamlined. Easier than flying out of Hartsfield, that was for sure.

I took a seat in the waiting area. People fidgeted in the metal chairs, some in work clothes, some in Sunday dresses. Wives twisted wedding bands, bounced babies. *Visiting*, I thought. What a nice polite word. More like tea cookies and front porches than this place, which was as no-nonsense as the DMV.

At every stage of the process, I felt as if I were going to be shut down and frog-marched back to the parking lot. Which would have been the opposite of useful, but damn, did I want out. I couldn't shake the fear that once I got in that separate room, I wasn't coming back out, and I couldn't decide if it was because I hated places of captivity or hated Jasper.

I needed to have questions ready, I knew this. Goals and objectives. Was he threatening Hope? If so, why was John involved? Had he found a new hate group to take him in? Did he really think he was gonna squeeze several million out of Trey and me or was this part of some larger scheme? And why was he picking fights with skinheads after months of "good" behavior?

I knew Jasper wasn't going to cough up answers, especially not with video cameras running. But I also knew that he was one of the smuggest human beings walking the Lowcountry. If he thought his machinations had me in the corner, he wouldn't be able to resist gloating about it. It would shine on his face like a sheen of sweat.

I twisted in my creaky chair and tugged at my collar. The woman seated down the row from me lowered the fashion magazine she was reading.

"You okay?"

I sent a tight smile her way. "I'm fine. Thank you."

She looked like Shirley Temple's disreputable older sister, with piercing china-blue eyes and blond bedhead waves. Her skirt was barely long enough to be within the visitation guidelines, and though she exposed not an inch of cleavage, the bright yellow sweater was tight enough to give anybody with half-assed eyesight plenty of ideas about what was going on underneath it.

She leaned closer. "You're here to see Jasper, aren't you?"

I couldn't hide my astonishment. "Well, I…yes."

"I thought so. They try to keep things like that on the hush-hush, but I heard you say his inmate number."

"I see."

"Yeah. It gets ugly here sometimes, girlfriends and wives showing up at the same time. But I know who you are, I've seen your picture." She tilted her head, assessing. "You're prettier in person."

I turned in my chair and gave her my full attention. "And you are?"

"Ivy Rae Newberry. Jasper's fiancée."

She drew out the final word, exaggerating the syllables. Then she held up her left hand and waggled her fingers, showing off a fat hunk of diamond. Nobody at Boone's place had mentioned a fiancée. But then, I was pretty sure that Jefferson had left out a bunch of things and downright lied about a bunch of others.

And then it hit me—Ivy. *How closely she twineth, how tight she clings.* I didn't need Rico's literary analysis to know I'd been warned about this girl, a piece of information I intended to take seriously.

She kicked her foot up and down. "They won't let me see him again, not this week. They said I caused a disruption last time."

"Oh?"

"I suppose I did. I wore a longer skirt this time, but they still wouldn't let me in."

She folded her hands in her lap on top of the glossy magazine, but the restlessness remained. Jonesing for her phone, I suspected, for the need to check in, text back, look up. Any second she'd start biting her nails in withdrawal.

She adjusted the strap on her shoe. "His lawyer told me to keep a tight lip. He said that I was to treat everyone who worked here as an informant. Is that why you're here? You looking to inform?"

"I'm looking to set some things straight."

"Oh. Right." She nodded sagely. "He told me about the civil suit. Between you and me, though, I don't think he means to follow through. He's had a hard life, and now he's trying to hurt others as he himself has been hurt."

I wanted to shake her. I wanted to tell her, in clear lurid terms, what her fiancé had tried to do to me, had ordered done to Trey, how he'd tried to kill his own father and brother. I wanted to rewind my memories and open up my brain and show her the Jasper I knew, the one with the gun in his hand, soaking wet and burning with psychotic rage. Jasper red in tooth and claw.

I kept my voice neutral, however. "How exactly did you meet Jasper?"

"He answered my Friends Behind Bars ad. We hit it off right away, but we didn't stay friends for long." Her foot kept bobbing. "Does his lawyer know you're here?"

"I have no idea."

Ivy looked over my shoulder into the visitation room and smiled. "He knows now."

I turned. Two people were returning into the waiting area from a far corner cubicle in the visitation room. The man was medium height, medium build, medium coloring, as utterly mid-spectrum an individual as I'd ever seen. Tan suit, ivory shirt, ecru tie, all of it high quality but rumpled. His mouse-brown hair dipped over a pale forehead, almost obscuring his eyes.

The woman at his side matched him in tone. Her slacks and shirt were immaculately pressed, however, and precisely fitted. I'd learned to recognize the hang of properly tailored clothes, and the sharp creases and break of the cuffs revealed the care in hers, especially when contrasted with the lawyer's too-long jacket and wrinkled shirt.

He stuck his hand out when he saw me. "Well, hello there, Ms. Randolph! When my client told me you were on his visitor list, I didn't quite believe him. Ainsworth Lovett, pleased to meet you."

I took his hand. He had soft skin and a firm get-down-to-business grip. The woman slipped the notebook she held into a messenger bag. She didn't extend her hand.

Lovett flipped his hand in her direction. "My investigator, Finn Hudson."

I did a double-take. This was no paunchy middle-aged former G-man. This was an athletic young woman with a peaches-and-cream complexion and spiky terrier hair, her slanting eyes bird-of-prey sharp. I saw humor simmering in her expression, and I knew she knew why I was staring slack-jawed at her.

Lovett's manner was disarming. "I cautioned Jasper this was a bad idea."

Ivy Rae piped up. "I did too."

He acknowledged her with a papery, all-purpose smile. "And yet he insisted." The smile flickered my way. "What's my fine opponent up to, Ms. Randolph?"

"I'm sorry?"

"Madam Olethea. I cannot imagine the circumstance that would have anyone at the prosecutor's office allowing you within fifty feet of my client. But I'm sure there is one. I'm sure it's positively devious."

I folded my arms. "You're the one defending the cold-blooded, racist, murdering—"

"Alleged."

"—lying sack of deviousness that is Jasper Boone."

He wagged a finger at me. "Tut tut, Ms. Randolph. I shouldn't have to remind you that it's people like my client who need the most protection under the law. The court of public opinion would have him swinging in one of those beautiful squares this very afternoon, not because there's any proof he's guilty of his charges, but because he reminds them of every awful thing about humanity that they want to erase. So erase him they would."

"I'm supposed to believe you're in this for truth and justice?"

"I am."

"Then why aren't you doing it pro bono instead of helping Jasper sue me for millions in civil court?"

He sighed extravagantly. "You're speaking of the civil matter, of course. That was Jasper's idea, not mine. I assured him we were working on a contingency basis, that I'd taken him as a client on principal, not for financial gain."

"I don't believe that for one second."

"That is certainly your right. But it changes nothing."

The guard behind the deck stood up. "T. Randolph!"

"I'm coming, I'm coming!" I shook my head at the lawyer. "Look, you can throw your ideals and your money into the toilet if you want, but I don't want to see any more letters from you or your investigator. I am declining to be interviewed, as is Trey, as is Phoenix, as is Detective Garrity, as is everyone. Don't contact any of us anymore."

"Don't worry, those letters were a courtesy which will not be coming your way again. And I'll be counseling my client to have no further contact with you, counseling him firmly. Oh, and one more thing." He stepped closer, dropped his voice, and his eyes went hard as marbles. "If I get even a whiff of your trying to bribe anyone here at this facility into delivering false medical statements, my next call won't be to the prosecutor, it will be to the authorities. That's a federal crime, Ms. Randolph."

I was so mad I could spit. "I'll have you know—"

"T. Randolph, last call!"

I turned my back on Lovett and headed toward the metal detector. He was already walking out the door, but I felt the eyes of his investigator on me. Had she spotted me during my conversation with Shane yesterday and ratted me out to Lovett? Or had Shane been talking to them as well, throwing fuel on the rumor fire? Had he hinted to them as strongly as he had to me that his testimony was for sale?

Ivy joined the two of them, chattering like a blue jay, as they filed out the front door. And it wasn't until that second, until I saw Finn Hudson from the back, her boy-short hair catching in the sunlight, that I recognized her.

She was the woman in the photo with Hope.

Chapter Twenty-seven

I took a seat on the metal stool in my assigned cubicle, pressed my knees together. The long narrow window to my right showed a slice of blue sky, the razor wire gleaming against it. My head felt swimmy-light, almost giddy, and I pressed both hands flat against my belly. I conjured Trey as clearly as I could, not the bossy lecture-y Trey, the solid comforting Trey.

I felt the breath go in, the breath go out.

The screen flared to life, but all I saw was the white-sheeted corner of a hospital bed. I heard voices, a muttered complaint about squeaky wheels. A timer started in the upper right-hand corner—twenty minutes and counting down. The view went shaky as a hand dipped in front of the camera, which then started a slow pan up the bed.

Jasper reclined there. He wore a jumpsuit the color of half-dead leaves. I made myself meet his eyes, which were snake-green, almost metallic. He eased closer to the camera, lean to the point of gauntness, his blond hair dull under the fluorescents. His lower lip was split like a ripe melon, and a shiner the color of a thundercloud darkened his left eye.

He wiggled his fingers at his forehead. "I apologize for my appearance today. The American incarceration experience is brutal at times."

Despite the injuries, he was enjoying himself. He folded his hands over his stomach, a half-smile twisting his mouth. I opened my hands, not remembering when I'd clenched them into fists. On screen, the image jerked to the side, and I saw Shane there, all official in his scrubs. He didn't look my way, not even when he adjusted the camera back on the hospital bed. I knew he was listening, though, collecting every single word.

"I heard you picked that fight yourself," I said. "Practically volunteered to be a human punching bag. That true?"

"Is that why you're here? To ask stupid questions?"

"I'm here to get some answers."

Jasper examined me cannily. "My lawyer says the only reason you're here is that the prosecutor is pulling some strings. Is she pulling your strings, cuz? Like a puppet?"

"Did your lawyer also tell you that there's a police report filed? That we are onto you and whoever you have on the outside threatening Hope Lyle?"

"What makes you think that's any of my doing? If I'd wanted to threaten that woman, I coulda done it while she was over in the women's. Where she made a right nice sitting duck."

"Who's saying you didn't?"

Jasper leaned back, spread his hands behind his head. A bandage wrapped his left forearm, obscuring the Blood Drop Cross tattoo he had there, along with most of the Confederate battle flag. I could barely see the red and blue peeking out from beneath the gauze.

"As much as I'd like to establish my innocence, my lawyer said I shouldn't be answering any of your questions. He said anything I say can be trotted right down to the prosecutor's office, that talking to you will hurt my defense and perhaps prejudice later juries when the civil case comes to trial."

He recited the words fluidly, as if quoting Ainsworth Lovett himself. I edged closer to the screen and folded my hands on the tabletop.

"Oh yes. The civil case. That load of bull puckey."

Jasper looked surprised. "Your boyfriend did with malice aforethought bring his foot down on my wrist, shattering the... what are those bones called?"

"Radius and ulna," Shane supplied off-camera, "with attendant damage to the scaphoid."

"Right. This was after he shot me in the ankle. And I don't even want to talk about what we had to do to fix this shoulder. At least I didn't have to pay for the PT, thanks to the good taxpayers of Georgia."

My hands curled into fists again. "You were reaching for your weapon."

"I was reaching out for mercy, begging him to stop. Haven't you seen the camera surveillance?"

"I have. That's not what it shows."

He shrugged. "My lawyer says the sequence of events is open for interpretation."

"That bullet you sent whizzing by my head was pretty clear."

"All I remember is you suddenly kicking me in the knee and taking off into the woods—damaging my patella, this PT fellow says—and I limped myself after you because I was worried about you, because I'd heard bullets too."

I clenched my jaw. Talk about revisionist history. I wanted to crawl through the camera and shake Jasper until he rattled and then do the same to Shane, who'd obviously picked a side in the upcoming trial.

"I don't care what your best buddy in scrubs there says, you tried to kill me. And then you tried to kill Hope."

He shook his head. "No, I was simply coming to claim what I'd purchased from her. I had a huge investment in that piece of paper she was carrying."

"Hope tells it different."

"The way I hear it, Hope ain't saying shit." He shrugged again, but his eyes glittered. "I mean, I haven't had anything to do with such, of course. Rumors spread like athlete's foot in this godforsaken place."

"Any of those rumors about John?"

"John who?"

"Don't play stupid. Hope's gone, he's gone, and I know you're behind it."

His eyes widened. "Wait a minute, that John? He's missing? Seriously? You want I should get one of these nice correctional officers to call up the law for you?"

I ground my teeth together to keep the expletives in my mouth. The timer in the corner of the screen had counted down to ten minutes. I was supposed to have gotten more time, but I didn't care. I wasn't sure how I was going to manage another second of Jasper's infuriating act, much less thirty more minutes.

"You know damn well John's missing. I want to know why considering John's got zero testimony to offer against you."

He scratched the back of his head, cutting his eyes first at Shane then back at me. "Then why would I be messing with him? Seems if I was that kind of man, I'd start with you and Trey."

My blood went cold. "Is that a threat?"

"What? Lord no! I was just pointing out the inconsistency. Jeez." He shook his head, like this was a big old misunderstanding. "Calm down. Maybe you're a little confused about how things went down that night, but we're family, cuz. And blood is thicker than water, Daddy always says."

"You don't have any family. Your daddy disinherited you. Your brother denounced you. Even the KKK has turned its back on you. You are all alone now except for that pie-eyed lawyer, and he cares more about pissing off his own family than he does your mangy hide."

"Oh, you're wrong about that. Mr. Lovett says he has to champion the cases of people like me—Southern, poor, of limited formal education and with a notorious family." He leaned forward conspiratorially. "I am entirely grateful he stepped up too, let me tell you, considering how Daddy cut me off."

"Considering you tried to kill him too, you're lucky Boone didn't cut you down."

"We both know he's trying. He's still got his fingers on the buttons, especially in here. Him and Jefferson, they got reach and pull. Skinheads, Klan junkies, Nazis. Waiting on a word. You think I picked that fight what put me in this bed? Seriously?" He laughed and looked Shane's way again. "The boys in the medical unit got the betting pool up—when will old Jasper Boone finally catch a shiv? Even Shane here's got skin in that game. Ain't that right, Shane?"

Shane made a noncommittal noise, but Jasper had the look of a man who'd tossed a live grenade and was waiting for it to blow. There was something else too, something I hadn't noticed until I saw him staring at Shane—Jasper was unnerved. Most of what I'd been telling him had been old news, but something had tripped a switch. And I had an idea what it was.

"You really didn't know John was missing, did you?"

"I told you that."

"Yeah, you did. You played it like it was nothing, but it bothered you. Why is that, Jasper? Your information supply line not as thorough as you'd hoped?"

Jasper moved closer, filling the video frame. "Come on, now, this ain't about John, or Hope, or the lawsuit. You're here because you're scared."

"What have I got to be scared of? You? Crippled up in a hospital bed behind bars?"

He shook his head side to side, slowly. "No, not me. Whoever's still out there. Like those men who took Trey the first time. Those men who hurt him so bad, and him SWAT-trained and everything."

"The men you sent, you mean. And they're behind bars. Like you."

"Maybe. But they were the least of their kind. You're desperate to find out what the *real* bad guys are planning, the ones who *didn't* get caught. Desperate enough to come talk to me…even though I had nothing to do with any of it, of course." He cocked his head, his voice soft. "Is that why Trey's not here? You think he's safe back in Atlanta? Like maybe the reach of those very bad men won't stretch all the way up to Buckhead?"

It came with a twinge first, a quiver deep in my gut, and my vision started collapsing at the edges. A panic attack. I tried to fight it down—no, no, no, not now—but I knew that wouldn't work, that resistance was not just futile, it was fuel.

Jasper saw. "That's it, isn't it? You're trying to protect Trey from the evil of this world." He laughed, low and nasty. "That's real sweet, but what makes you think Savannah is the most dangerous place in the South? Atlanta's just as mean, maybe even meaner, especially the folks you hang out with at those reenactments. You never know what kind of criminal could be standing right in front of you up there, looking all innocent."

There was something in the way he said it, and my memory flashed on the process server, the insolence in his eye as he'd slapped me with the lawsuit papers, the dare-me glare. I was right—he'd been one of Jasper's. And he'd been a warning.

Jasper dropped his voice in mock concern. "If I were you, cuz, I'd go check on Trey right now. I'd go as fast as I could. Because you never know what might have happened up there while you were sitting here talking to me."

I imagined Trey's voice. *Breathe, Tai. Breathe with me. On my count. One...two...*

I braced my hands on the table, gripping the wood until my knuckles were white. "I swear to God, Jasper Boone, if something happens to Trey or anyone I love, I will destroy you. I missed one chance to take you down. I won't miss a second."

Jasper smiled, his snake eyes gleaming. The clock in the corner of the screen ticked down to zero, and the screen went black.

Chapter Twenty-eight

I didn't say a single word as I signed myself out. I collected my driver's license and pushed open the double doors, the sunshine hitting me like a shovel to the face. I walked as quickly as I could, thinking that all I had to do was get in my car and I'd be fine. But my legs were rubber, and I couldn't get the key to go into the lock. I had to use both hands to open the door, and when I finally slid behind the wheel, I was shaking so hard my teeth chattered.

I locked the doors. Then I pulled out my phone and called Trey. He answered immediately, and I almost wept in relief.

"Trey! Are you okay?"

"I…what's wrong?"

"Has anything happened? Anything weird?"

A baffled pause. "What do you mean by weird?"

"Stalkings, shootings, breaks-ins. Threats, kidnappings, car bombs."

"Nothing like that." Another pause. "Why? What's happened?"

I let my head fall backwards against the seat. "I don't know."

"What does that mean?"

I closed my eyes. "It means I went to see Jasper. And yes, I know, I shouldn't have done it, but too late now, and…oh, fuck." I fought back tears. "It was too much, way too much."

"What was too much?"

"Talking to him. Seeing him. Remembering…"

What happened to you, I thought, *how close I came to losing you, how much you mean, how much you matter.*

"He threatened you. He suggested he had people in Atlanta, that you were in danger, and that I…I…"

Trey spoke more slowly. "Tai, listen to me. Tell me, very specifically, what you need me to do."

"I need you here. As soon as possible. Get out of Atlanta."

"Are you sure?"

"I've never been more sure in my life. Maybe Savannah is just as dangerous, and maybe I can't protect you here either—maybe no place is safe anymore—but I can sure as hell keep you right beside me until I figure out what to do next."

A hesitation. "Tai?"

"Come. Now. Please?"

His voice was ragged. "Get out of the car. I'm right behind you."

I whirled my head around. It took me ten seconds to find him, stepping out of an unfamiliar brown Toyota. He had on his workout clothes, his phone pressed to his ear. He almost took a step in my direction, but then froze in place.

I threw myself back into the sunshine and went to him. Walking was a good thing. It gave my body something to do. And with every step, I felt my head clearing, my heart beating stronger. I walked faster, not running, even though I wanted to. I wanted to bolt across the pavement at a dead gallop.

Trey started talking before I reached him. "I'm so sorry. I tried to stay away, I really did, and I thought I could do it, I knew I had to try, and I made it until yesterday afternoon, but…"

I covered his mouth with mine and wrapped my arms against him. He let me kiss him, let me hold him, his heart beating too fast against mine.

I pressed my face against his shirt. "Let's both shut up for a little while, okay?"

His arms went around me, cinching me tight. "Okay."

◇◇◇

We sat in Trey's rental, my head on his shoulder. He said nothing, asked nothing, which was as much a comfort as anything. Most importantly, he was solid and real and warm under my hand, the best tonic to Jasper's poison I could imagine.

Closer inspection revealed something terribly amiss, however. His eyes were bleary, hair less then perfectly combed. He'd missed a spot shaving, and he startled at the least noise. There was a sense of unraveling about him, and it unnerved me.

I laced my fingers with his. That was when I noticed the bruises on the knuckles of his right hand. I ran my thumb lightly over the swollen skin, and he pulled his hand from mine.

I sat up. "Trey? What happened?"

He dropped his eyes to the floorboard. "After you left on Sunday, I...didn't do very well."

"Meaning?"

"Meaning I yelled. A lot. And slammed the bathroom door. With my fist." He took a deep breath, trickled it out. "But then I took a very long, very hot shower. And then I saw your text, and I called you, and I was better. And then on Monday morning, I went to work. I went to the meeting. I was fine. But after that, things went...not so well again."

I got a sinking feeling. "What happened at the meeting?"

"I met with the lawyers. We went over the lawsuit. They drafted a response."

"And?"

"And then I left work and drove here."

He was leaving something out of this bare-bones recital, that was for sure. Regardless, he was gonna be in a world of trouble. The one thing Boss Lady had made abundantly clear was that he was supposed to stay away from Savannah.

"Does Marisa know you're here? I mean, surely she's suspicious, what with you AWOL this morning."

"Actually, no. I mean, yes. I mean...Marisa knows I'm here. I told her I was coming. But the reason she's not expecting me at work is because she suspended me."

I knew I was staring at him with my mouth open. I knew I should say something, something girlfriend-wise and comforting, but I was utterly shell-shocked.

"Because of the lawsuit?"

"No."

"Because you pulled your weapon on her?"

"No." He raised his eyes to mine for one second before dropping them again. "That's why she pulled my firearms license. She suspended me because I walked out of a client meeting despite her direct orders."

I remembered our conversation from the previous night. "Is this what you wanted to tell me face to face? That you'd been suspended?"

"That. And...the other thing."

"That you've been following me since, what? Early Monday afternoon?"

He kept his expression neutral. "Correct."

"So last night, during our conversation, you were..."

"Parked in the empty lot across from your cousin's house. The one with the construction equipment."

Excellent concealment, bulldozers and such. I didn't have to ask how he'd found me—my car had an anti-theft tracking system that he had full access to. Of course he'd promised he'd only do so with my permission, or in case of an emergency.

"So the whole time I was telling you everywhere I'd gone, you already knew."

"Correct. Except that you didn't tell me everywhere." He narrowed his eyes. "You left out the detention center."

I winced. "Yeah. I didn't want to worry you." I ran through a quick timeline of yesterday's events. "That was the trigger, wasn't it? At the meeting. You saw that my car was at the detention center and you didn't know why I was there or what was going on."

He didn't say anything; he didn't need to. He pressed his thumb to his temple, closed his eyes. I recognized those symptoms—a headache coming on top of everything else.

"Have you slept?" I said.

"Some."

"How much?"

He frowned. "Four hours. Or five. Four or five hours."

"Have you eaten?"

"Yes."

"Something besides protein bars?"

He hesitated, then shook his head. Suddenly the hornet's nest hanging high in my family tree took a back seat to this new dilemma—my rapidly decompensating boyfriend. And it was a relief, in a way, to backburner that whole mess and deal with the mess right in front of me.

I squeezed his hand. "Trey, listen to me—"

He waved me quiet. "Who's that?"

"Who's who?"

He pointed across the parking lot, and I saw what had him on red alert. Shane the PT guy stood next to my car, peering in the windows. He had his hands shoved in his pockets as he gave the backseat a thorough checking out.

"That's Jasper's physical therapist. And he appears to be casing my car."

Trey put his hand on the door handle, preparing to launch himself like a ballistic missile. I grabbed his arm.

"Hang on a second. Look."

Another car pulled up next to mine, a dark gray Mercedes with Fulton County plates. Shane ambled to it as the passenger side window slid down, then he leaned over to talk to whoever was sitting there. Trey kept his eye on the scene as he scrambled around in the floorboard for pen and paper. He wrote down the tag number just as Shane opened the rear door and got inside. The car sped away, hooking a sharp left past the stand of oleander trees, leaving a flurry of deadly petals in its wake.

I sat back in my seat. "Wanna bet that car belongs to Ainsworth Lovett?"

Trey pulled out his phone. "I'll let you know after I've checked the data base."

"The one you access through Phoenix?"

"Right."

"Will your clearance still work if you're suspended?"

He tapped and swiped and typed. Frowned. Tried again. Frowned deeper.

"Apparently not," he said.

Chapter Twenty-nine

I decided nourishment was our immediate priority, so I took him to the first place I could find, a mom-and-pop sandwich shop at the I-16 junction. Trey sat in the booth across from me, a bland polite cipher. He seemed disconnected, but it wasn't until we tried to order our food and he couldn't even make a decision that I recognized how much he was crumbling.

I flashed on Gabriella's accusations—towers and death, scythes and lightning—and realized his decline was less crash and tumble than she'd predicted. It was a gentle slippage, like a mansion sliding into a sinkhole, but it was definitely slippage. He'd left behind every bit of psychological scaffolding he had—his apartment, his workouts, his nine-to-five, even his gun. And now he was in Savannah, a city as strange to him as Mars. There was one thing, however, I hoped he hadn't abandoned, his most potent touchstone.

"Why aren't you in the Ferrari?" I said.

He took a sip of water. "I couldn't surveil you in the Ferrari. You'd have spotted me instantly."

"So where is it?"

"I had it valet parked. At the Hilton."

"The DeSoto?"

He nodded.

"You got a room there?"

Another nod. Good. He'd at least had the presence of mind to find a place to sleep. When the waitress brought our food, he cut his turkey sandwich into four triangles, then rearranged them on his plate in two squares.

I reached across the table and took his knife away. "Eat. Now."

He dutifully picked up one of the triangles. "Why were you at the detention center? You know you're not allowed—"

"I know. But I risked it because I thought I could pry some information out of Jasper."

"Did you?"

"Yes. But not the information I was expecting."

I explained what I'd seen, how Jasper had batted not one eye at the idea of Hope being threatened, but had been definitely caught off guard by the news of John's disappearance.

"Whatever scheme he's working, it didn't include that," I said. "But I'm betting it does include Shane. That boy's playing both ends against the middle."

Trey took one tiny bite of sandwich. "Have you created a 302 on him?"

"Not yet. But I will be, him and Ivy both."

"Who?"

So I filled him in on the surreal Ivy Rae, on the implausible yet undeniable ring on her finger, and on the rest of my visit, including my confrontation with Ainsworth Lovett and Lovett's definitely-not-some-old-guy investigator. In short, I spilled all of it. He listened without commentary, though I saw him clench his jaw a couple of times.

"You could have told me about all of that," he said.

"You could have told me that you were down here."

He put the sandwich back down. "I know. I'm sorry. And I tried to stay in Atlanta, I really did, but—"

"I know." I reached across the table and took his hands in mine, squeezed tight. "Here's the thing. You and I haven't been the most aboveboard of people lately, but I'm gonna give us some credit. We were trying to protect each other."

"True."

"But it's gotta stop. So let's make a deal. From this point on, we're a team. No secrets, no hidden agendas, no excuses. Deal?"

He nodded solemnly. "Deal."

The waitress came by with more sweet tea just as my phone started ringing. When I saw the name blazing on the display, my stomach plummeted. "Oh hell."

"Who is it?"

"The prosecutor. Madame Olethea Jones herself."

Trey flinched. "Oh."

The phone rang again. Time to face the music.

I put it to my ear. "I can explain."

"Of all the things I thought might go wrong today, getting a phone call from Ainsworth Lovett accusing me of harassing his client was not on the list."

She was not a happy prosecutor. The connection practically sizzled with rage. Dang that stupid self-righteous Lovett. I hadn't expected him to call her this fast.

"There's a situation," I said. "Jasper's suing me for three million, Trey for six."

"So I am learning. But tell me, Ms. Randolph, what do you think this lawsuit is?"

"It's—"

"I'll tell you what it is, it's a ploy to get your attention. To get you in his face. And he succeeded."

"But—"

"We have already been over your testimony. I have made clear the facts to which I am expecting you to testify."

"There's been some other stuff."

She hesitated. "Stuff?"

"You know. Criminal stuff. Stuff like—"

"And you are done talking, Ms. Randolph. I don't want to hear anything coming out of your mouth that I might have to reveal to defense counsel. If you have knowledge of a criminal wrongdoing, or believe that a crime has been committed, then you need to report it to law enforcement in the proper jurisdiction."

"I did."

"Hallelujah. Gold star for you. This means if it's something I need to hear about, I will. Through proper channels. Until that time, I want you to remember what I told you during our first meeting."

I searched my memory banks. "The part about telling the truth?"

"The part about not volunteering anything. If you know of a crime, report it. If you're just supposing there might be a crime, or imagining a crime, then you need to zip it. Now and until the final gavel, the one at Judgment Day. Deal with the civil matter as you must. But as for the rest—"

"I know, I know. Stay out of it."

"Correct. I am putting your name on Jasper Boone's 'no contact' list. If you try to see him again, the captain will sequester you until I get there. There's a lot of lawbreaking and wrongdoing going on, and a lot of room in the Chatham County Detention Center. You want to stay on this side of that line, on the side of the angels. Do we understand each other?"

"Loud and clear."

She hung up on me. I dropped the phone back into my bag, put my head in my hands.

Trey stopped chewing. "What did she say?"

"Exactly what I expected her to say." I sat up, put my shoulders back. "But we'll deal with that later. Right now you need to finish eating. And then we're gonna go back to the hotel and do something that will make us both feel better."

He raised one eyebrow, and I flushed with relief. Coming back to himself, my boyfriend was.

I smiled. "I know what you're thinking. And yes, eventually. But there's something else you need first. Something with a different kind of zoom."

◇◇◇

We drove to the DeSoto, the red brick Grand Dame of Savannah hotels, where I made him lie down for a while. And eventually— freshly showered and shaved and wearing clean gym clothes, with his shoulder newly re-taped—he followed me downstairs to the front entrance, where I had the valet bring round the Ferrari.

He eased into the driver's seat. "Where are we going?"

"Nowhere."

"I don't—"

"Just drive, Trey. Just drive."

He wrapped his fingers around the wheel, double-checked the mirrors. No matter how confusing the rest of his world got, the Ferrari always made sense. Steering and throttle, physics and response, these things he could comprehend. Most importantly, it cared not one whit about anyone's intentions. It did not look out for you, caution you, worry about you, or warn you. It simply responded.

I fastened my seatbelt as Trey revved the engine, releasing that familiar decibel-rich growl. I had a flashback to my first car chase with him, the gleam in his eye as he switchbacked us through the Atlanta streets. I had other flashbacks too, more carnal ones, and felt the blood rush. I'd never driven his most prized possession—yet—but it worked like a steel and leather aphrodisiac regardless.

We took the Talmadge Bridge first, all the way into South Carolina. The river flowed, and the night fell, and the sunset burned a hole in the western sky. And with every mile, I could feel him quickening, returning, coming together again.

I dropped my head to the side, the amber dazzle of Savannah in the rear-view mirror. "Trey?"

"Yes?"

"We've got a lot to do tomorrow."

"I suspected as much."

"But before we get to any of it, I need to see Boone."

"You said he has confidential patient status."

"I know." I rolled my head sideways to look at him, silhouetted against the night. "But I watched you work the rules on Hope, watched you finesse that whole encounter." I reached over and put my hand on his thigh. "I want you to work the rules on the patient coordinator at Memorial Medical Center. Can you do that?"

He didn't look at me, or my hand. He kept his eyes on the road, his own hands on the wheel. But for a second, the speedometer trembled a hair past fifty-five.

"I can do that," he said.

Chapter Thirty

When I got out of the shower the next morning, Trey was ironing. He was barefoot, clad in freshly pressed slacks, his single
dress shirt splayed on the ironing board while he attacked the
cuffs, which the hotel laundry had not crisped to his satisfaction.
There was a freakishly healthy breakfast set up on the side table,
with both tea and coffee, and every scrap of my dirty clothing
had been picked up from the floor and refolded in tidy stacks. I
grinned and plucked my day-old jeans and red La Perla bra out
of the pile. Things were getting back to normal.

I rummaged in his gym bag and found a black cotton tee.
"Can I borrow this?"

"Of course."

"And maybe some underwear?"

He raised his head. "What?"

"I didn't have time to go back to Billie's yesterday and get
my stuff. A pair of your boxer-briefs is the best I can do this
morning."

He waved a hand in acquiescence and returned to his ironing. He was back to the Trey I knew—sharp, capable, mission-
oriented. He had only the suit he'd worn down and the contents
of his gym bag, but he was making do. And making do quite
well. I wondered how much of this had to do with keeping me
in sight, wondered how much of my own renewed equilibrium
was due to his being right beside me. Decided I'd ponder those
things when we didn't have investigating to do.

I pulled on his briefs. "You left early this morning. You didn't try to go for a run, did you?"

"No, I was in the business center."

He pointed toward the desk. A stack of file folders sat on one corner, a stack of yellow legal pads on the other. A concept map covered the middle of the workspace, an intricately linked hierarchy of multiple hubs and clusters, circles and lines. I recognized the names of everyone I'd spoken to over the last three days, even my cousin Billie, their relationships to each other charted and calculated, annotated and footnoted. And in the center…John Wilde.

I paged through the first folder, Shane Cook's 302. It contained only three items, the first a copy of his résumé from an online job hunting site, the second a bit of HR department legalese. The third was an article about him from the detention center newsletter—it included a photo of Shane grinning for the camera, his pants leg hiked, his prosthetic on full display. He'd peeled back the flesh-toned silicone to reveal an impressive piece of engineering under the faux foot, gears and pistons, pneumatics and hydraulics. He could even run with it, the article explained.

"Looks like he was telling the truth about his injury," I said.

Trey shook out the shirt and examined the sleeves. "That much, yes. The rest of his background is unverified. I won't be able to complete it until I can access LINX again. Or until Marisa lifts my suspension and I can get into the Phoenix data bases again."

I ran down the information, which repeated what Shane had revealed in the parking lot—two tours in Iraq before the mortar took off his foot. Physical therapy certification on the GI Bill to supplement his combat medic training, which had focused on the trauma of blast injuries, expertise he now shared with the incarcerated. On paper Shane looked like a hero, practically star-spangled.

Except for one thing.

I held up the second paper, the HR report. "What's an Other Than Honorary Discharge?"

Trey returned the shirt to the ironing board. "It's a service characterization following termination of a military contract. OTH is given when overall performance was satisfactory, yet there was conduct considered problematic. You can find the details in the Uniform Code of Military Justice directives and regulations, but—"

"Just explain why it matters that Shane got one."

Trey put down the iron and gave me his patient face. "That's what I'm trying to do. Because if you'll look at his résumé, you'll see that he eventually received a General Discharge. Any record of the OTH discharge was supposed to have been expunged, but I found the original designation as an addendum to a previous application package."

"So it got changed."

"Apparently so."

"But why was it issued in the first place?"

"Conduct unbecoming. That's all I could find. For now."

That was certainly fodder for further speculation. I put Shane's 302 aside and picked up the second folder, which belonged to Ivy Rae. Her file was considerably thicker. Trey had discovered that in addition to the usual social media presence, Ivy Rae maintained her own webpage—Friends Behind Bars.

"This is the site where she met Jasper! Are you telling me she runs the freaking thing?"

"She does." Trey adjusted the iron, tested the steam. "For non-romantic correspondence only, the website insists. I suspect this disclaimer resulted from the lawsuit."

"What lawsuit?"

"The one against her previous website."

He motioned for me to keep reading. I found the second item, a newspaper article about the case against Hearts Behind Bars, a site devoted to matching inmates with lovelorn free citizens. After her match-ups resulted in a slew of frauds and scams, the entire operation was shut down. Ivy settled the case out of court without ever acknowledging that it had been used as a sophisticated victim pool. But apparently she was at it again. Sort of.

"I don't get it. If registration at this site is free, how does she make any money?"

"Look up the web address."

I tapped it into my phone and figured it out instantly. The website itself was amateurish, but the ads running in the side columns were slick and professional. And every single one featured either buxom young women of various ethnicities eager for a real American boyfriend or shirtless young men longing to "conversate" with special ladies. All of them one phone call away.

"So now she serves as a porn, sex talk, and maybe even soft prostitution portal, with Jasper acting as her word-of-mouth, behind-bars spokesperson for the actual correspondence part of this, which is really just a cover?"

Trey took the iron to an especially stubborn wrinkle. "That is a valid assessment."

I tossed the folder back on the desk. "So is Jasper scamming her? Or is she scamming Jasper?"

"Perhaps both. Perhaps neither."

"Meanwhile Shane the less-than-honorably-discharged is offering medical testimony to the highest bidder."

"We've little evidence of that."

"He made it pretty clear in the parking lot. And we did see him driving off in a car that had to be Ainsworth Lovett and company."

"Allegedly. I haven't been able to run the plate yet." He pulled the shirt from the ironing board and inspected it. "One more thing—Rico called while you were in the shower. He was unable to pull any meta-data from the photograph."

"It had been stripped."

"Yes."

"Damn it. That means we're dealing with a professional, doesn't it?"

"Most likely. Rico said he couldn't help you as much with the second quotation, except that it was from Charles Dickens. I told him you'd figured it out yourself, and he said that was good, and that perhaps for your next trick you could listen to me when I told you to get yourself back to Atlanta."

"Except that you're not telling me that."

"No. I'm not."

"Why not?"

He kept his eyes on the shirt. "Because your original assessment was correct—you need to be here, in Savannah, to resolve this situation. That much is clear. And yes, it may be dangerous, but Atlanta may be dangerous as well, which is why I'm here in Savannah with you. As you said yesterday, we're a team now."

Trey delivered this pronouncement calmly, which made me think he'd overdosed on his medication. Or inhaled too much starch. He'd been incredibly productive while I'd been snoozing away, and I had to admit, he seemed back to his old self. But our investigation was going off-road real fast, and we were going to have to go with it.

I sat on the edge of the bed. "Are you sure you're up for this? Because—"

"I'm okay."

"But—"

"Tai. I'll tell you if I'm not."

He held his cuff links in my direction. I opened my hand and he dropped them into my palm. Up close, I caught the scent of his aftershave, faint but delicious against the smell of starched cotton. His jacket lay at the foot of the bed, his tie next to it. Only one thing was missing—his weapon.

I reached for his wrist. "If you're okay, why is your H&K still in the safe instead of holstered up and ready to go?"

His forehead creased. I knew this wasn't about his injury, wasn't about getting his professional carry permit pulled. He could still ride strapped just about anywhere in the state of Georgia with his retired law enforcement officer permit.

He kept his eyes on his wrist. "After what happened Sunday morning, in Marisa's office…I don't know. It doesn't feel right. Carrying a firearm."

"How?"

"I don't know. It's too…something. Or perhaps I'm too something. Either way, it's not a good idea."

I finished with the cuffs, started on the buttons. "Okay. This is me trusting you to make the right decision. And reminding you that should we need a gun, I've got mine."

He nodded. "Okay. Tell me if we do."

◇◇◇

Savannah rush hour was nothing like Atlanta's smog-choked gridlock, but it came with its own hazards—horse-drawn carriages, one-way streets, tourists lurching into the crosswalks. Despite the usual traffic inanities, I got us to Memorial in a reasonable amount of time. Inside the cool sterile lobby, Trey went straight to the information counter.

"Ms. Anderson?" he said.

The woman looked up. "May I help you?"

"I'm Trey Seaver, formerly with Atlanta PD, currently serving with the FBI Major Offenders Task Force. I'm here concerning a patient placed under confidential admittance, a relative of Ms. Randolph's."

"I've already explained our procedures to her."

Trey nodded in professional commiseration. "So she told me. And of course I'm not asking you to compromise those. As you know, to even acknowledge the presence of said patient in this facility is a violation of the patient's confidentiality and terms for prosecution under HIPPA."

The woman blushed furiously. I suppressed a grin. Trying to out-rule Trey was like trying to out-rule gravity.

"However, hypothetically speaking, should said patient be housed in this facility, said patient needs to be apprised of certain…developments." Trey gave her the serious look. "Developments of an urgent nature that said patient may wish to discuss with me further. Or if not, developments that at minimum need to be discussed with your head of security, whom I will be happy to speak to." He pulled a pen from his pocket and wrote something on the back of his gold-and-navy-embossed

AMMO card. "Pass this along, please, to whomever you deem most appropriate. We'll wait for the response."

She stared at the card. "I'll have to check your credentials."

Trey inclined his head. "Of course. My immediate superior is Detective Dan Garrity. You can call the FBI Field Office in Atlanta and ask to speak to him. He's away from his desk, but if you tell the operator the call is on behalf of Trey Seaver, they'll put you through."

I didn't look his way. Garrity was in Alabama probably covered in preschooler stickiness. But Trey was correct. He'd vouch for him. There would be hell to pay afterward, but he'd vouch nonetheless.

The woman examined the card. "Wait here."

She marched her high-heeled self through a door marked PRIVATE. When she'd disappeared, I turned to Trey. "What did you write on that card?"

"Your phone number."

Ten minutes later, my phone rang. When I answered it, Boone said, "What kind of mess have you gotten yourself into now?"

"Let me come up, and I'll tell you all about it."

A grumbling resignation. "Room 767. And bring me a Dr Pepper and some of them cheese crackers. You know the ones."

Chapter Thirty-one

I plunked the last of my change into the vending machine while Trey fielded a text from Garrity, who, as expected, was demanding to know what was going on. He thumbed a quick reply, then pulled a bottle of herbal relaxants from his pocket and threw two tablets in his mouth, crunching them into powder.

"Uh oh," I said. "That can't be good."

"It's a prophylactic dose. Sometimes hospitals trigger an association response. Those memories can be…difficult."

Five days in a coma difficult, plus six months rehab with tubes and pain and crashing terror difficult. And now the smell of disinfectant and industrial laundry and institutional food, the beeping of monitors, all of it combined to trigger it all over again. He didn't seem on the verge of collapse, though. There was no trace of the Trey of the previous day, the shaky, badly-shaved, hollow-eyed version. This Trey was scimitar sharp.

"So Garrity's cool?"

"He said that I'd better not be aiding and abetting you in some dubious and borderline illegal scheme, because if I were, he would be very pissed off."

"His exact words?"

"Exactly exact."

The elevator opened, and Trey held the door for me. I gathered Boone's snacks and held out my hand.

"Can I have a couple of those herbal thingies? For purely prophylactic purposes?"

He shook two into my hand.

◇◇◇

Boone was on the pulmonary wing, the halls silent save for the hisses and beeps of lung machines, the soft-shoe tread of nurses and therapists. Trey stopped, double-checked the room number. Then he assumed the "post up" position—back against the wall, arms folded—right beside the door.

"You go ahead," he said. "I'll keep watch."

I wiped the sweaty soda can on my jeans and pushed open the door, knocking as I did. Boone lay in bed. He didn't try to get up, just turned his head in my direction. He looked like a ghost, like everything solid about him was collapsing and the only thing holding him together was the outline of who he'd been, the shape of his personality. His breath came shallow and raspy, his silver-shot green eyes fierce above the oxygen mask.

He pulled down the mask and forced a smile. "Hey, girl."

"Hey, old man."

He reached for the pain button and pressed it. "Damn meds make me crazy. Most days I'd rather have the pain than the crazy, but today, the crazy is better." He looked me up and down. "You want I should turn on the TV? 'Bout time for *The Price is Right.*"

"I'd rather talk."

"Ha! When do you ever stop?"

For a second, the old Boone was back. But the effort rattled the thing in his chest awake, and he started coughing. It soundly apocalyptic, a deep pulling cough, as if his lungs were grinding together. It was a cough of Things Gone Very Wrong, and I went to the side of the bed.

"You want me to call the nurse? I can call the nurse."

He shook his head and jabbed a finger at the soda in my hand. I popped the top and stuck a straw in, held it between his lips. Boone took two sips and fell back against the pillow, eyes closed. I suddenly worried that Jefferson had been wrong, that the only way Boone would be leaving this room would be in a hearse.

He waved a hand at the soda, and I put it on his tray table along with the crackers. He swallowed, his voice a whisper. "I can't talk much. Goddamn dragon sitting on my chest."

"I'm sorry."

"You and me both." His eyes were soft, no longer sharpened by pain, the work of whatever was in the IV bag trickling into his veins. "You came here to talk. So talk."

"John Wilde's gone missing."

Boone's forehead wrinkled. "So? That man's cut and run more times than I can count."

"It's different this time."

"How?"

"Even Hope doesn't know where he is. She does know that before he vanished, he was talking about setting things right. With you."

"I am in no way square with that man."

"See, that's what I thought. But then I saw his motorcycle in your garage."

Boone's eyes narrowed. He hadn't known that. "And?"

"And so I finally dragged the story out of Jefferson, that John handed the Harley over to pay off the twenty grand he owed you. Only trouble is, John's still vanished. And before you start telling me why that's not a surprise, you should know that the last thing he did was buy a gun—from Jefferson, by the way—which Hope found in the glove compartment of his empty car, which had bullet holes in the trunk. Trey wasn't too sure about the bullet holes part at the time, but I am now, because I went to John's trailer yesterday, the one he was fixing up real nice for Hope, and found shell casings in his driveway that matched those holes. I also saw that his bedroom had been searched."

Boone turned his eyes away from me, to the blank TV. "Your point?"

"My point is this isn't business as usual."

"Ain't my business at all. Why you gotta drag it to my door?"

"Because that's where it leads. Your door." I crossed my arms. "Did you know that Jefferson has your collection up for sale?

Everything as one lot, from the CSA presentation cane to the Cook & Brother muzzleloader your great-grandfather walked all the way back home from North Carolina after the war, so—"

"So it's worth almost thirty grand, that rifle, which means that yes, I know it's for sale because it was my idea to sell it. We gotta do something to pay the bills. And I would have loved to let you have a crack at selling it, sugar, but you don't run with the big dogs who can afford such."

The speech cost him, and he put the oxygen mask back over his mouth. I waited until his color returned, then pulled the visitor chair over and plopped myself down in it.

"Why?" I said.

"Why what?"

"Why are y'all scrambling for money?"

His eyes flashed, and he pulled the mask down again. "God-damn government, that's why! The tax man, the federal agent man, the po-lice man!"

I slumped back in the chair. "Here we go."

"Those damn drug-sniffing dogs speak German, did you know that? And they cost about ten thousand dollars, so if the po-lice want one, they either gotta get the money from me or get it from the taxpayers. Guess which is more fun?"

"It's all a game, huh?"

"It's the left hand way of doing things, that's all. Ain't nothing but a job once you realize you got a temperament for it." He leaned forward. He smelled like medicine up close, but there was still the odor of Red Man to him. "And you do, girl. So does your fellar out there in the hall, much as I hate to break it to him. He does as much gun-totin' and door-bustin' as any criminal. He just uses his right hand to do it."

I scooted the chair closer, dropped my voice. "Right hand, left hand, I don't care. All I know is John's missing, Hope too. This is very problematic for me, and Trey, considering Jasper's trial is fast approaching. And I know you don't disappear people, but Jasper would. And if that's where this trail leads, back to Jasper and what he was doing while he was under your roof—and I swear to you, I think it does—then this whole piece of trouble is about to come home to roost. To you, to Jefferson, to Cheyanne and your granddaughters. To everyone ever associated with Jasper or who has something to fear from him, because neither the right hand nor the left cares who goes down for his crimes as long as somebody does."

Boone looked sad, angry, sick in his heart. "So what in all the seven hells do you want me to do about it?"

"Talk to me. Tell Jefferson to talk to me."

"I'm not cutting my life open, or my son's, because John Wilde's booked it again. Ain't the first time he vanished. Ain't gonna be the last. You should know as good as anyone how light he can be when the going gets tough."

I shook my head. "This isn't about me and him."

"Sure, it is. He left you when your mama took sick. Didn't hear another word from him until there was his own trouble brewing. Then he called you up again, am I right? Said he needed you. You keep trying to rewrite that script so that you come out on top, so that you're not the one gets left, but that ain't how history works."

I bit my tongue. Literally. Shoved it between my molars and clamped down. Before I could gather my wits, there was a knock at the door. I looked over to see Trey standing there, tentative.

"I'm sorry to interrupt, but…Tai, you need to see this."

"See what?"

"Come into the hall."

I followed him. He pointed toward a television blaring in the room across from Boone's, a news update. The reporter had positioned herself with a white fishing vessel in the background, gulls wheeling, her perfect hair getting a good tossing in the breeze.

Her tone was clipped and singsong. "The body—pulled from the Wilmington River this morning—has not yet been identified, and authorities will not confirm the identity pending notification of next of kin."

"That's Captain Lou's boat, the *Double Down*," I said. "I used to crew for her when I was in high school, during the summers. She found a body?"

"That seems to be the case."

I turned around. "Come on. We gotta say goodbye to Boone."

"Why? Where are we going?"

"To catch the captain before she heads out again, of course."

Trey grumbled something under his breath, then reached in his pocket for the bottle of relaxants.

Chapter Thirty-two

Captain Louise Markowitz was not excited to see me. She didn't even stop dumping ice into the cooler. "Damn it, I told those cops to turn off their flashing lights before they interviewed me. Now I'm on TV. Gonna be overrun by slack-jawed lip flappers."

"Only by people who recognize the *Double Down* from a ten-second prow shot."

Behind her said boat bobbed at the dock. It was a beautiful thirty-foot sport fisher, the star of her fleet. It was as battered and tough as Captain Lou herself, with her wind-hewed wrinkles and sun-bleached hair. I couldn't see the rigs, but it was probably set up for a small group charter, good for tips, which was how I'd made my bread and butter. Old men liked sweet young things in wet tee shirts to bait their hooks.

I put up a hand to shield my eyes from the glare. "What are you after? The temps aren't in the seventies yet, so the whiting should still be running plenty."

She chunked a six pack of water bottles in the ice. "I leave in ten minutes, so stop wasting time showing off. What do you want?"

"I want to ask you about this morning."

"Some other day, I'd be happy to oblige, but I'm already leaving late thanks to the hold-up this morning, and as you know, the tide waits for no woman."

"I can help."

"I don't—"

"Please please please. No charge. Tips go back to you. And you know I can rack up tips."

She squared her feet and looked me up and down, assessing if I still had muscles and sea legs. "Cutting bait and cleaning up too?"

"Whatever you tell me."

She jabbed a chin in Trey's direction. "What about Mr. Suit and Tie over there?"

I looked back at Trey, who was standing in the exact center of the upper dock, peering at the water with a dour expression. He had the haunted, nervous look he always wore when he couldn't glimpse a skyline or feel pavement under his shoes. He pushed aside a branch of a slender water oak, and a lashing of Spanish moss dribbled across his forehead. He smacked it away as if it were a snake.

I sighed. "He's coming too."

"Is he wanting to throw out a line?"

"Absolutely not."

She grinned, her teeth white like a barracuda. "In that case, you got a deal."

She extended her hand, and we shook on it. That was when I heard the screaming. Not the blood-curdling, terror-ridden kind. The high-pitched squealing kind. The door from the restrooms banged open, and a gaggle of Girl Scouts exploded onto the boards, their harried leader barking useless directions behind them.

My heart sank. "A kiddie cruise?"

Lou clapped me on the back. "You got eight minutes. Meet me on deck."

◇◇◇

When I told Trey the news, he folded his arms. "No."

"Trey—"

He shook his head. "I am not going out there. I remember what happened last time I went out on a boat with you."

"Nothing happened."

"You lied. That happened."

I folded my arms too. "I can't believe you're still mad about the sharks."

"You said there weren't any. Now I learn that Wassaw Sound is full of sharks, so full of sharks that it has a place called the Shark Hole."

"Yes, but—"

"You told me you wouldn't let me get into shark-infested water."

"I said I wouldn't let you get into *dangerous* shark-infested water. And you were in no danger that night, none whatsoever."

He wasn't listening. He'd pulled out his phone and was swiping it in a righteous fervor. I peeked at the screen. Oh crap, he'd discovered the OCEARCH app. Even worse, he'd pulled up the real time data showing the tracking patterns of hundreds of sharks off the Southeastern Coast, including…

He flipped the phone around and held it in my face. "Specimen #46374. A great white shark."

"Mary Lee."

"What?"

"Her name is Mary Lee. She's—"

"I don't care what her name is! She's fifteen feet long and weighs three thousand, four hundred pounds. Approximately. And *she's…*" He waved his hand in the general direction of the Atlantic. "Seven miles offshore, out there, right now."

"But we won't be going offshore. We're not even getting in the water, we're casting nets and showing the children the sea critters. Shrimp and seahorses, maybe a blue crab or two. No sharks."

"You could be lying again."

"Look at my face, Trey. No lying."

He focused on my mouth, concentrated hard. "Say it again."

"You are in no danger from sharks, not even great whites, when you are in the boat. And we are *always* going to be in the boat." I drew an X on my chest. "Cross my ever-lovin' heart."

He frowned at the *Double Down*, as seaworthy a vessel as ever rolled out of the Intercoastal. Of course now it was overrun with elementary school girls, their PFDs like bright orange gumballs against their green uniforms.

He shook his head again. "I'm sorry. No."

"You do realize this makes no sense, right? How many times has some human tried to kill you? Dozens at least. You still hang around people. How many times has a shark tried to kill you?" I made a circle with my thumb and index finger. "Zero."

"That's because I don't go in the ocean. Where the sharks are."

I bit my lip to avoid screaming. Or cursing. Across the marina, Lou shot me a pointed look and held up her index finger. One minute. I took a deep breath, made my voice sensible, sweet, understanding.

"Okay then. Don't go. You can stay here, and I'll—"

"No." Panic laced his voice. "You can't do that."

"Trey—"

"Tai. Please. Not out there. I can't get to you out there."

So much for that plan. Being separated from me was a definite trigger. But I knew his refusal to come along wasn't about the psychological whoop-de-doo going on in his head. The not-letting-me-out-of-his-sight part, sure, but the not-getting-on-the-boat part? Pure mulish perversity.

I kept my expression patient. "What will it take?"

"What do you mean?"

"I mean let's make a deal, boyfriend. You give up something, namely this solid ground for approximately two hours, and I give up something." I squared my shoulders. "Name it. I'll do it."

He looked puzzled. This was a new twist, not what he'd been expecting. It was enough to knock him off the path of resistance and into a reckoning frame of mind.

He considered. And then he told me.

I stared. "You're not serious."

"Of course I'm serious."

I stepped closer, dropped my voice. "I said *anything*, Trey. There's a whole smorgasbord of erotic delights on the table, and you want *that*?"

He crossed his arms again. "Yes or no, Tai."

Lou blared the horn. I cursed and headed for the floating dock, grabbing Trey by the elbow and dragging him behind me. "Fine. But I am going to make you pay for this, I swear I am."

Chapter Thirty-three

I spent the next hour knee-deep in seaweed and little girls. Captain Lou's cast net tours were strictly catch-touch-release, but I pitied the poor creatures, dragged up from the depths and subjected to poking and prodding and squealing before being unceremoniously dumped back into the drink. Eventually, we settled the girls on the dolphin-watching part of the trip, and I joined Captain Lou on the flybridge. Trey remained in the cockpit with the first mate, mesmerized by the sonar and GPS system.

Lou chugged down half her water, wiped her forehead with the bottle. "Guess you're wanting the story, huh?"

I leaned on the railing. "I think I've earned it."

"Not much to tell. I was bringing the morning group out, headed for the Intercoastal. I'd just passed the turning basin when I saw a bunch of seagulls all out on the sandbar."

Seagulls. Buzzards of the ocean.

"So I swung it closer. I was expecting the usual, somebody dumped fish guts or something. But right away, I knew this wasn't that simple."

"How?"

"Because I saw shoes. I grabbed the binocs, got a good unhappy eyeful. Then I set anchor and called the Coast Guard."

"Male or female?"

"Couldn't tell. Didn't try. I'd seen enough to know it wasn't a rescue I was calling in, and then I backed off and waited for the patrol to get there." She readjusted her sunglasses, eyes always on the horizon. "I'll tell you one thing, though—whoever done it wasn't a professional. Maybe at killing, but not at disposal."

"Why do you say that?"

"Because they wrapped the body in a tarp, duct taped it, then tied it to a dumbbell."

I wasn't sure I'd heard her correctly. "You mean like you lift weights with?"

"Right. I saw everything bunched up there on the sandbar. Whoever did this didn't come prepared, had to rummage around in their garage for supplies. They probably saw somebody do something like that on TV, but they didn't realize about these tides."

The Lowcountry tide, one of the most powerful on the Eastern Seaboard. People who didn't know the rivers didn't know how they switched up their game every six hours, rising and dropping as much as nine feet.

Lou shook her head. "If they'd known what they were doing, they'd have dumped the body in the water a hair past high tide, let it wash out where the fish could get ahold of it. Bodies gonna bloat, you know. Ain't no twenty-pound weight gonna hold that down forever, especially not one of them vinyl-coated things." She scoffed. "And the tarp may have kept their trunk clean, but it preserved the evidence. Professional woulda put in some cinder blocks, wrapped the whole kit and caboodle in chicken wire, then chucked it in the deep end. Gone baby gone."

We passed the other neck of the river. In the distance I could see the curve of Boone's land, the dock jutting out into the wave-dappled water. The peninsula looked peaceful in the noonday sun, green and welcoming, with no night and shadows.

"Where do you think the body got dumped?"

"Your guess is as good as mine. You know how the tides work. It could have come anywhere from Wassaw to Thunderbolt."

We rounded the bend, and I saw the curve of the boat ramp, the smaller public one just past the bridge. It had an official name, but everybody on the islands called it the turning basin. It was busier than usual for a Wednesday morning. But then I saw the flicker of blue lights, and I saw that the people milling about were wearing the dark blue serge of Savannah Metro. Two officers had the entire shore cordoned off with yellow crime scene tape.

"I think the police have an idea where it came from," I said.

Lou nodded. "They got other ideas too."

"What do you mean?"

She handed me the binoculars and pointed toward Boone's property. I aimed them toward the dock and saw Jefferson standing at the edge, two officers standing with him. They had their feet splayed in the official stance of cops on official business. And I knew that if they'd gotten that far onto the property, it was because they'd had a warrant.

I handed the binoculars back to her. "Shit done hit the fan, Captain."

◇◇◇

Once we rounded the bend, I went looking for Trey. I found him standing where I'd left him, in the exact middle of the boat, surrounded by the crackle of the radio and the LCD glow of Lou's fresh-from-the-factory side-scan sonar. Equipment calmed him the way that an old-fashioned alarm clock calmed a newly weaned puppy. Luckily, it was a calm day too, so he wasn't green around the gills.

I propped myself next to him. "How are you doing?"

"As well as can be expected."

I wrapped my arms around his waist. After a second, his muscles relaxed, but he was only giving an inch. And we had a mile to go.

I tipped my head back so that I could look him right in the eye. "Are you really gonna make me have lunch with Gabriella?"

"You promised you would."

"I'd have promised anything to get you out here."

"I know."

"But why does it have to be that?"

Trey didn't drop his eyes. "I called her Sunday night, when you said you saw her in the parking lot. I asked her why she hadn't come up. She told me the two of you had had…she described it as a difference of opinion."

"That's one way to put it."

"And so I want you two to talk. I know you talk to Garrity, when you have questions about me. And you talk to your brother. But Gabriella knows things too. She can explain."

"I want you to explain."

"I can't. It's too…something. And there are parts I don't remember. But she does. She was there."

"So were you."

He shook his head. "No. I wasn't."

He looked earnest and broken, maybe afraid. Or it could have been queasiness from the waves or a headache from the sun or discombobulation from the squealing and incessant girl chatter. Captain Lou's voice broke through on the loudspeaker with final instructions. We were nearing home, and I was needed to help corral the troops.

"I'll talk with her because I said I would. But you have to figure out how to tell your story yourself. All of it."

"I don't have the words."

"Then think of another way."

"But—"

"No buts. You can do this. I have faith in you."

He considered, then nodded. I relaxed a little and moved closer, hip to hip.

"But speaking of difficult things…"

He tensed. "Yes?"

"Once we get back on land, we need to go to Boone's place. I saw the cops out there as we passed."

"We don't want to disturb an official inquiry."

"I know. That's why I figured we'd park in East Pines and wait for the cops to leave. I already talked to Jefferson once, and while I suspected he wasn't telling me the whole truth, you can actually verify that. Plus you're immune to the kind of redneck crap he throws my way."

He cocked his head. "True. There are other challenges to dealing with Jefferson, but not that one."

"So you're up for it?"

"I am. Are you?"

"I am."

Behind him, the sonar blipped, and a shadow as enormous and sleek as a submarine glided under our boat. I felt my guts go liquid. It was the biggest shadow I'd ever seen, and I knew it for what it was.

What *she* was.

Trey heard the ping and turned his face to look, but I grabbed his chin and pulled him in for a kiss. He complied, and the shadow continued its deep cold journey up the coast.

Chapter Thirty-four

The patrol car came down the road thirty minutes after we parked, moving slowly. I waited until it was on Highway 80 before pulling out of the cul-de-sac and onto Boone's road. I snuck a glance in Trey's direction. He'd already rechecked his seatbelt twice and had a weather eye on the foliage, as if he expected a jaguar to leap on top of the hood.

"We're almost there," I said.

"I know."

"Just hang on."

"I'm not…" He frowned. "Tai? Is that the engine?"

"Is what the engine?"

"That burning smell."

I inhaled deeply and caught the scent. Not strong, but rancid and oily nonetheless. Definitely heavy with gasoline. I checked the dashboard. None of the bad lights were on, and all of the good ones were.

"It's not the car," I said, flipping the air vents closed. "Whatever it is, it's—"

"There," Trey said, pointing toward the gate.

The giant wooden cross was still smoking even though the flames had been extinguished. It lay toppled on its side, charred and peeling, puddles of filthy water all around. Somebody had spray-painted TRAITOR on the wall in dripping slick letters, and the air reeked with chemical fumes.

I drove forward cautiously and parked inside the gate, still open from the cops' departure. Jefferson's truck was parked next to the front door, as was a minivan with its rear door up. I saw suitcases and sleeping bags inside, a red picnic cooler.

Trey faced front again. "Was that what it looked like?"

"It was. The Klan's ultimate calling card." I parked next to the van. "I'm betting this isn't their first warning, though. Last time I was here, Cheyanne mentioned trouble from a source that wasn't the law."

"And you think this is what she was referring to?"

"I do. And it's all the more reason we need to talk to them."

I got out and headed for the front door. Trey didn't look thrilled about this, but he followed me. I rang the bell and soon heard footsteps.

Jefferson answered. He looked from me to Trey and then back to me. "Now's a bad time, Tee."

"So I gather. But seeing as they just this morning hauled a body from the river—"

"I know."

"Then you know we need to talk."

To my astonishment, he stepped back so that we could come in. The house was in that quiet state of purposeful bustle that accompanies bad news. Cheyanne and the girls stood at the kitchen counter, making sandwiches and wrapping them in wax paper. When one of the girls saw me, she smiled and waved, but her sister elbowed her and shook her head.

Jefferson called to them. "Chey, you wanna give us a minute?"

Without a word, she put her hands on the girls' shoulders and steered them down the hallway toward the bedrooms. She glared hot hate at me as I passed, as if whatever had gone down was my fault. I heard a door slam.

Trey stood in the middle of the room, hands open and ready, feet in neutral position. It was the first time he'd seen the inside of the house, and I knew he was analyzing it for escape routes, cover, checking out the placement of concealed cameras. He duly noted the plethora of weapons within Jefferson's reach, including the double-barreled shotgun on the coffee table, broken open for cleaning.

"Chey ain't happy about this," Jefferson said. "She blames you."

"For what?"

"For asking too many questions. Putting us in the crosshairs." He sat on the sofa and went back to cleaning the shotgun. "Daddy called. He said you were in high dudgeon about John, who was still missing, and Hope, who was still missing, and that you lit out when you saw the news about the corpse they dragged outta the river, so apparently you and the cops both think I'm stupid enough to dump a body at the end of my own goddamned dock." He was furious, his cheeks red with indignation. "That why you're here? 'Cause you think I've lost my mind?"

I kept my voice even. "I know that desperate people take desperate measures."

"I ain't that desperate." He dipped the end of a cloth in gun oil, daubed it against the action. "Was it John?"

"I don't know."

"You gotta admit, when there's a missing person and a found body, more often than not, they match up."

The thought gave me a queasy sensation. "You think that's the case?"

"I think I don't care. It don't affect me and mine. Which is exactly what I told those lawmen."

I slid a look Trey's way, raised an eyebrow at him. *Well?* He nodded. Jefferson was being on the up and up.

"Did you show them the security video of John leaving?"

Jefferson's voice was cool. "What security video?"

I shook my head. I should have known he'd destroy it. "What about that other business out front? Your associates come calling?"

Jefferson ran the cleaning cloth over the barrel. "The Brotherhood doesn't want me to testify against Jasper. This was their way of reminding me."

"Why now? You've been cooperating for five months."

"I don't know which muckety-muck got it in his head that now was the time to remind me who I really serve. Don't really matter. My family matters, and so that's what I'm gonna worry about. And that means getting them out of here while the getting's good."

Trey cocked his head. Oh boy, there was that look. He'd pegged something, not a lie, just an…evasion.

"So that's why they burned a cross in the yard of a Selectmen Council member, in broad daylight? Because you're continuing to keep yourself out of jail?"

"It's *lighting* a cross, not burning." Jefferson readjusted his hat. "And yes, as far as I know, it's a misunderstanding, one I aim to clear up as soon as I get my family seen about."

In the back, I heard the scuffle of feet, a plaintive whine from one of the girls and their mother's harsh scolding.

Trey spoke up. "I don't understand why they wouldn't want you to testify. If they've truly cut their allegiance with Jasper, wouldn't they want him to pay for his crimes?"

"They want him free so that they can deal with this their way. Which ain't about him serving time, you know what I mean?"

Trey's eyes narrowed. "No, I don't. Because that's not entirely the truth."

Jefferson cut his eyes at Trey, snapped the gun closed. Trey cut his eyes right back, took one innocent-looking step backward. Lord, if those two started at it, we'd have a ten-by-ten Armageddon.

I stepped between them. "Stop it, both of you. There's something bigger at stake."

After a moment, Trey folded his arms. Jefferson hesitated, then pulled out a wad of tobacco and stuffed it in his cheek.

"I'm getting tired of this," he said. "This is twice now you've come up in my house, accusing me of—"

"The Klan doesn't drop 'reminders' like this lightly. So you need to tell me what's really going on."

"Why? So you can tell the cops?"

"I can't take shit to the cops unless I have it gold-plated. The prosecutor has made that abundantly clear."

He glared at Trey. "He's a cop."

"No, he's not. But he did catch you in a lie. So you have two choices—explain what's really going on, or explain to the cops when they come back again. Because they will be. Because I am certain I'm next on their interview list. And when they ask me what I know about you, and I say, well, he was lying about this, that and the other thing…"

Jefferson muttered a curse and shoved his hat back on his head. No matter which way he turned, there was an obstacle or a trap, an accuser or an adversary. No clear path out of this trouble, and more trouble on his doorstep. Literally. The kind of trouble that burned. I almost felt sorry for him.

He spat into his bottle. "When Jasper formed his little boys' club, he took some stuff from the Brotherhood."

"Stuff like money?"

"Exactly like."

"How much?"

"Rough estimate? Two hundred and fifty thousand or so. And they want it back."

I sat down hard. "Jesus. So that's what that cross is about. They think you have it."

"It has been suggested that I need to cough up those missing funds. But I don't have them, and I don't know where they are. If I had that much money, don't you think I'd be spending it instead of chasing gators and selling family heirlooms?" He skewered Trey with a glare, spat in the bottle again, pointedly. "How'd that read, copper man?"

Trey blinked complacently. "As the truth."

"Good. Then read this. I don't know what Jasper did with the money he took. I do know that the man I used to call my brother is a liar and a violator, an oath-breaker and a thief. I don't care whether he does time or gets strung up from a tall tree, because he will reap his true justice at the hand of the Almighty. Vengeance is mine, sayeth the Lord."

He put the gun back in its case. Trey relaxed a hair, though he remained on a light trigger.

"Who else knows about that money?" I said.

He shrugged. "Beats me. That piece of work he's hooked up with maybe? What's her name?"

"You mean Ivy?"

"Yeah. She came out here once, said she wanted to introduce herself, but she was sniffing around for something else, that was for sure. Cheyanne showed her the way out right quick."

"Have you heard from her since? Or anyone else connected to Jasper?"

"That new lawyer he's got called once. And we got a letter from some private investigator. But I can't imagine Jasper told them about the money. That'd be stupid. And he's a lot of things, but stupid ain't one."

I heard noises from the bedrooms, little girl whining and then Cheyanne's sharp rebuke. I sympathized with them. Inside the house was close and dark—outside the sunshine melted all over the place, and the waterside beckoned.

Jefferson shoved himself up. "Until this blows over, I don't want Chey and the girls here. I'm taking them all to her parents' place up in Kentucky, and then I'm coming back quick as I can. This land is all we got left, and I gotta look after it. And somebody needs to see to Daddy too." He exhaled, pulled off his hat and held it in front of him. "What I'm saying is, Daddy was fine this morning. But if something happens before then, if he needs somebody…"

He didn't finish the sentence. I made myself look at him. His values were not mine. He wanted to see an America that looked like him, thought like him, fought like him, believed like him, a world where everybody was the same color and worshiped the same god and hated the same enemies. Could I stand with him on this single patch of weedy common ground, our love for one complicated old man?

"When will you be back?" I said.

"Tomorrow night."

"All right. If you need me, call me. I'll still be in town."

Relief flickered in his eyes before he covered it. He nodded tersely, shot one final look Trey's way.

"Y'all can let yourselves out," he said.

Chapter Thirty-five

I made Trey drive. He handled the Camaro as well as he did the Ferrari. Already his brain was absorbing the map of the city, the squares and one-ways, the road work and closed lanes. Soon he'd be better at navigating my own hometown than I was.

"Two missing people, one body, and a bunch of clues that make zero sense."

His forehead did that wrinkly-thinky thing. "One clue makes sense."

"And that is?"

"You said that John and Hope's trailer had been searched. Now we have one option as to what the searcher might have been searching for."

"The quarter mil."

"Yes."

"Why would they think Hope or John had it?"

He shook his head, steered us into Billie's driveway. "I don't know. But that's a good question to start with."

Billie's house was dark—Travis was still at work and she was at a baby shower—but she'd told me the code for the garage door. I got out of the car. "Wait here. I'll be quick. And then we can hit the business center at the hotel. We've got a lot more research to do, boyfriend."

Trey got out anyway and took up position in the driveway, right under the yellow-tinged streetlight. I punched in the code and hurried inside. The empty house was thick with silence, broken only by the low hum of the appliances and electronics. Through the front window, I saw Trey standing sentinel. He was an oddly formal presence in the neighborhood, surrounded by the mundane noises and smells of suburbia—the jabber of somebody's television through an open window, the charred smoke of hamburgers on a grill, the hum of a golf cart as two teenagers tooled about. I smiled to myself and pushed open the door to the baby's room.

The figure waiting there shoved me against the wall in the hallway. I didn't have time to get my hands up or regain my balance before the next blow took me to the ground. I landed on my back, hard, and the air rushed out of me in a whoosh.

I tried to scream and couldn't. I rolled to my side, arched my back, trying to work the muscles that would let some breath back into me. It was all instinct, no rational thought. Footsteps pounded down the hall and out the back door. I sucked in a painful hitching breath, then another.

When I finally could, I put my head back and screamed, "Trey!"

◇◇◇

They sent a patrol car to secure the scene. No lights, no siren. No need, my assailant having fled into the dark woods of Billie's backward, disappearing into the subdivision a block over.

Trey refused to budge from my side. He'd already checked me over once, head to toe, and then he'd gone through the whole house, the backyard too, making sure the coast was clear. This was not how one preserved a crime scene, but he didn't give a whomp about that. He was in pitbull mode.

It was not departmental procedure to let him hang out at my elbow, but the cop conducting my interview didn't protest. He wore a body camera, said it was part of a test program. I didn't much like that little lens staring at me, recording me. I felt violated enough.

"Any idea why someone would jump you?" he said.

Trey bristled. "She wasn't jumped, she was assaulted by an unknown perpetrator committing felony trespass. Which means—"

I put a hand on his arm. "S'okay. I got this." I turned to the cop. "I'm pretty sure I interrupted a burglary."

He checked his notes. "You're the same Teresa Ann Randolph who reported a burglary at the home of John Wilde and Hope Lyle on Monday, is that correct?"

"That was me, yes. Though I go by—"

"Tai. Yeah. I see that." He hitched up his belt, adjusted the camera. "Do you think this incident is connected?"

"I don't know what's connected. All I know is that the second I showed up in Savannah, it's been a clusterfu…excuse me. It's been a mess."

By this time, Billie's neighbors were surreptitiously hanging out on their porches and patios, pretending to be engrossed in the moon or the crickets or each other. I let them gawk. Everybody needed something to live for, and this was better than *Dancing with the Stars*. And then I saw the car I'd been dreading most.

Billie. She parked at the curb and came storming my way. The cop intercepted her, but she shook him off.

"What's happened? Are you okay?"

"Everybody's okay," I said.

A tiny precise relief flared in her eyes, quickly smothered with anger. "I don't know what kind of trouble you decided to bring upon my house, but you'd better take it with you when you go!"

The cop stepped between us. "Ma'am, are you the resident?"

"I am."

"Then if you'll kindly step with me to the car, I'll explain."

For a second, I thought Billie wasn't going to comply. She was furious, one hand gripping her pocketbook, the other palming her belly. I'd upset her sanctuary, brought the ugly and the violent into the pastel world she was working so hard to make safe.

The cop went with her, shooting me a pointed look. "I'll be right back. Don't move."

Trey was standing too close now. If a moth had tried to land on me, he would have crushed it into a dusty pulp.

"Trey?"

His eyes were in constant motion around the perimeter. "Yes?"

"Go see about Billie."

"What?"

"She's upset and freaked out, and I don't blame her. She's not accustomed to criminals busting up the peace."

He looked confused. "But I don't know what to say to her."

"Don't say anything. Just stand there and let her unload on you. It's a very calming thing, it really is. Trust me on this."

He did as I asked, reluctantly. Billie lit into him the second he got to her side, but I knew she'd spend her outrage pretty fast. And then he'd answer her questions, make assurances. Sure enough, I watched him cast his protective presence around her. She folded her arms above her swollen belly and cursed a blue streak, but I could see her calming down. Soon she'd be anxious, which was a harder horse to ride than anger, and then she'd be rational. Eventually. She cut a look at me, and it was hard as quartz.

Mea culpa, I thought.

I tried to listen as the officer explained to her what would happen next, just in case there was some new wrinkle. But my head was pounding, and I was exhausted. Which is why I wasn't sure I saw what I saw, not at first. I had to shield my eyes from the police car headlights and squint. But it was her, what was her name, the lawyer's PI, only now she wore a baseball cap and a denim jacket. When she saw me looking, she pulled the cap down lower and ducked behind a garbage can.

I didn't even think. I took off after her.

She bolted, heading for the playground. I bolted too. I heard the cop yelling, Trey and Billie as well, but all I could think was, the bitch did it, and I'm going to catch her, and I'm going to pummel her into the ground until she confesses.

She'd gotten a good head start, though, and by the time I reached the swingsets, she'd vanished. I stopped, sucked in air. Damn it, where'd she gone? To the left was the construction site with the bulldozers and dump bins, to the right another patch of undeveloped woods. I spun a slow circle and listened, but my world was a jumble of the shouting behind me, the stitch in my side, the blurry haze of not enough oxygen.

To the woods, I thought. I spun to my right…

And ran right into Trey. We collided with a wallop, and I scrambled to keep my footing.

"Which way did she go?"

"Who?"

"Finn Hudson! Never mind, you go left, I'll go right."

He stayed planted. I tried to duck around him, but he caught me around the waist and plopped me back in front of him. I ducked the other way, managing to block and evade this time, at which point he snagged me again. I shoved at his chest, but it was like shoving at a wall.

"Let me go, damn it!"

He grabbed my wrists. "Tai! Stop this right now!"

I yanked my wrists free. A side sweep to his calf almost took him down, but he caught his balance and grabbed me as I lunged past. He pulled my back against his chest, then wrapped both arms around me from behind, pinning my arms to my sides. I pulled and wrenched and stomped and screamed. I let fly a donkey kick right at his shins, connecting solidly. He sucked in a sharp breath, tightening his hold, but he didn't let go.

"She's getting away!" I screamed.

"The officer is in pursuit!"

"I don't care, I…I…"

I was out of breath, frenzied, weak. And mad, sizzling mad. I felt it coming like a thunderstorm, riding low, the pressure wave of it building. I tried to control it, but it crushed me, and what came out of my mouth was a gasp, and then a moan, and then my knees went out from under me. I stopped fighting. I was panting, crying, sobbing.

"I can't…I can't…"

My knees collapsed, and I went down, with Trey right behind me. He still held me tight against his chest, but it was no longer a restraint.

"Breathe," he said.

"I don't know how to do this, I don't know what to do, how am I supposed to, how am I—"

"Breathe, Tai. With me. Just breathe."

I heard more shouting behind us, back-up cops on the scene. Lights and sirens now, strobing against the gunmetal sky. I pressed my face into his shirt and cried. Ugly crying, the kind with heaving and mucous and blotches on his white shirt. But he held me. And he told me to breathe. And I did.

Chapter Thirty-six

Next morning, every muscle in my body ached. Trey had warned me about such, explaining that it was a side effect of the adrenalin crash. Before I'd gone to bed, he'd dosed me with ibuprofen and some of Gabriella's anti-inflammatory herbs, which tasted like grass clippings and dirt, then made me soak in Epsom salts. And still I hurt like I'd been beaten with a meat mallet.

I sat on the edge of the bed, utterly spent. If I'd had a white flag, I would have flown it.

Trey came out of the bathroom with a roll of gauze and a tube of antibacterial ointment. He favored his left leg, and I felt heavy with guilt. I'd pulled no punches the night before. Kicks either.

"Give me your hand," he said.

I did. He uncurled my fingers and examined my palm. The scrape flared red, but not as angry as the night before when he'd picked out pieces of gravel. He daubed ointment on the wound, his touch delicate.

I gritted my teeth. "It was her, you know. Finn Hudson. I wasn't hallucinating."

"I know."

"And she was up to something. That cop had no right to yell at me—"

"He had every right. You disobeyed his direct orders. He could have arrested you for that alone."

Trey had managed to talk him out of that, thank goodness. I'd heard the muted conversation, which involved another flashing of his AMMO card.

"Are they going to arrest her?"

"They are going to talk to her."

"Good."

He focused on winding the gauze around my hand. If there was anything he'd learned during a year with me, it was how to apply first aid. Having him wrap a bandage felt as intimate as a goodnight kiss.

"I'm sorry about last night," I said, "especially the part where I kicked you. And elbowed you. And wrenched your shoulder."

"That's okay, I was expecting you to defend." He arched an eyebrow. "I wasn't expecting you to go for a throw, however. That was beyond our training."

"I've been practicing without you."

"Oh."

"A lot."

I tried to meet his eyes, but he fastened them on the bandage. Wrap and tuck, tighten and neaten.

I kept talking. "Garrity's seen more of you than I have lately. So has Marisa. And your trainer. Getting stalked has been the most attention I've gotten from you in a very long time."

Trey flinched, but continued rolling the gauze. "I've been busy."

"Very busy. Busy to the point of perseveration."

"I realize that now and have made the necessary corrections." He taped the gauze in place and examined his handiwork. "I'm not convinced that you have done the same."

"I have. Last night was crash and burn. This morning I'm on my own two feet again."

"But—"

"No buts. You don't like it when I second-guess you about your okay-ness or not-okay-ness. Extend me the same courtesy."

His eyes flicked up to mine. "Point taken. That courtesy, however, does not extend to your smoking cigarettes while I'm in the shower."

Damn it. I should have known I couldn't defeat his nose.

Like a bloodhound, that man. And I'd been so careful, closing the balcony door tight behind me, standing upwind, taking only three delicate puffs before dropping the cigarette half-smoked and sizzling into an old water bottle.

"Momentary lapse. Won't happen again."

"I hope not. Because—"

The buzz of my phone interrupted him. I leaned over and checked the number. Another one I didn't recognize. I shrugged at the question in Trey's eyes and answered it anyway.

The voice at the other end of the line was testy. "I've been blamed for a lot of things, but this is the first time I've been accused of assault."

I sat straight up. "Finn?"

"Yes, Finn. Calling you from the police station, where I have just finished being questioned, thanks to you."

"Don't blame me, you were the one lurking."

An exasperated huff of breath. "I was following you, which is perfectly legal in Georgia, well within the scope of my professional investigation. But I didn't assault you."

"Why should I believe you?"

"You want me to explain? Meet me out front, alone."

"No, you come here. Whatever you've got to say to me, you can—"

"There's no way I'm coming into that hotel and getting my face on the security cameras. If you want to talk, we do it down here, and we do it alone." A pause. "Come to the median in front of the hotel, next to whatever-the-hell monument that is."

"You mean the Rotary wheel?"

"Yeah. That thing. I'll be there for fifteen minutes."

She hung up on me. Trey saw the look on my face. "What's going on? Who was that?"

I shoved myself to my feet. "That was Finn. As for what's going on, I'm about to find out."

◇◇◇

I spotted Finn standing exactly where she said she'd be, next to the bronze sculpture in the median, with Liberty Street traffic flowing on both sides of her. Instead of khaki or denim, she now wore a pale yellow sorority girl frock over black leggings. With her hair clipped to the side in a rhinestone bobby pin and rainbow bangles on her wrist, she looked barely twenty, fresh and glowing and entitled, a carbon copy of every cheerleader I'd gone to high school with.

I jaywalked out to meet her, the low hum of passing cars in my ears. I had to admit, the landscaped strip of grass and foliage made a good meet site—glaringly public, but hard to document with either camera or recorder.

I stood next to her under the low branches of the live oak. "Aren't you the chameleon?"

"Part of the job description."

She sipped at her drink, a slushed up pink thing. On either side of us, people walked the sidewalks, posing for selfies, leaving footprints in the pollen. The sky above us had a bruised, swollen quality. Rain coming, and soon.

"Where's Trey?" she said.

"You told me to come alone."

"Yes, but I know he's watching. He was a sniper once. Watching is what he does best." She jabbed her straw up and down. "Next to sniping, of course."

I was very careful to keep my eyes on her and not flick them to where Trey watched, from the bookstore across the street, which he'd pronounced an adequate surveillance site. Too much straight-on morning sun for his taste, but the clouds had remedied that situation. Most importantly, it was a quick dash across the two lanes if he decided I needed saving.

"Why are you stalking me?" I said.

"Surveilling. Surely Trey taught you the difference."

"Nonetheless. Explain."

She stirred her drink some more. "Look, it's nothing personal. Mr. Lovett asked for background. I'm delivering."

"You delivering him a witness too?"

She shook her head. "Excuse me?"

"I saw Shane Cook getting into Lovett's car on Tuesday. At the detention center."

This was a bluff, but it paid handsomely. Finn shrugged. "We offered you an interview, in writing. You declined. Mr. Cook didn't."

"He offer to sell you his testimony?"

"Heavens, no." She batted her eyes in mock affront. "Did he offer such to you?"

"Let's just say he is free with his charms."

"Such charms are never free. But that's not how Mr. Lovett works."

The valets were doing a brisk business this morning, and constant streams of cars and people flowed around us. I could smell exhaust and coffee and the odor of warm mammal as a horse-drawn carriage clip-clopped down Bull Street, the tour guide telling stories in an exaggerated Southern drawl.

Finn sipped her drink. "You must understand this about Mr. Lovett—he's on a mission."

"Missionaries don't usually pull six figures."

"Mr. Lovett has no trouble saving the world and getting stupid rich at the same time. He sees Jasper Boone's case as the perfect opportunity to exercise his fervent belief in justice for all."

"All the scum of the earth, apparently."

"Mr. Lovett looks to the big picture. In Jasper Boone's case, it's that the entirety of the blame is being laid on him, an uneducated backwater redneck, while the real perpetrators, those rogue cops, are getting lesser sentences."

"So your boss is playing dirty to serve some inflated sense of justice?"

"He's not my boss." There was a flicker of annoyance in her tone, which she immediately smoothed. "And he could no more play dirty than Mother Theresa. He's got big ideals, sometimes too big to see around."

"I'd like to kick him in the ideals."

Finn smiled around her straw. "I understand. That's why I'm

here talking to you, risking my job. His ideals are becoming problematic in this case."

"How so?"

"Jasper Boone is painting bull's eyes everywhere, drawing attention away from whatever it is he doesn't want anyone to see. And I don't know what it is. But I've seen enough to know it's probably mad, bad, and dangerous."

"So why tell me?"

"Because Mr. Lovett's primary goal has always been helping clients avoid mandatory sentencing, not freeing them. But the way this case is shaking out, Jasper could walk. And I know the things he did, the things he will do. That man doesn't need to be breathing free air."

She wouldn't look directly at me when she talked, preferring to stare over my shoulder, at the passing traffic, up at the clouds. Anywhere but in my eyes.

"What did you do with Hope?" I said.

"What makes you think I've—"

"Don't."

Her expression stayed neutral, but I saw a cagey reassessment in her eyes. "Fine. But she's the one who called us, in Atlanta, so don't suggest we're being suddenly nefarious. I promised we'd keep her safe, which we have. And that I'd look for her husband, which I am."

I tried to keep my expression as blank as hers. "Does Lovett know you're hiding the star witness against his client?"

"It was his idea. Like I keep telling you, he's a man of ideals."

"Plus if Hope turned up dead, it would look terrible for his client."

Finn shrugged. "I never said he wasn't strategic."

"Where is she?"

"That's one secret I do need to keep." She looked at me from under her lashes, almost flirtatious. "Are you going to rat me out?"

"To Trey? Of course."

"No, not Trey. Lovett."

"Maybe. Maybe not."

She smiled. "That's what I was hoping you'd say. Because that means we can still help each other."

"How?"

She pulled a flyer from her bag and handed it to me. It was a photocopied announcement from a storage facility in Thunderbolt, right behind the marina.

"Jasper rents a unit there," she said. "He stopped paying for it months ago, so it's being auctioned at noon. If you want to dig through his secrets, I'd get there before some junk hound snaps it up. I would go myself, but Lovett's got me chasing something else." She held out her business card. "And if you're feeling generous, a call letting me know what you found would be appreciated."

I took the card. Couldn't help trying to reconcile the fake image on her website with the woman across from me, a woman who never looked the same twice. A woman I definitely didn't trust.

She inhaled briskly. "Well. It's been lovely, but I have to go. Don't worry, I'll keep in touch."

She waggled her fingers in a little wave, then flip-flopped her way across the street.

Chapter Thirty-seven

The flyer rested in the middle of the bed, untouched. I sat on one side, Trey on the other. He had a mug of vanilla rooibos resting on his knee, I had my third cup of coffee in hand.

"And yet another example of possibly good information from a definitely suspicious source," I said.

Trey examined the flyer like it was a bear trap. "Indeed."

"This is what I meant about things getting weird."

"I know."

"So I entirely understand if you can't—"

"I can. The question is if I should. I mean, if we should."

He'd been assessing the situation since we'd returned to the room, but had reached no clear verdict except that since we had no reason to believe that a crime had been committed, we were entirely within our rights to investigate the unit. If we wanted to.

"Was Finn telling the truth?"

"I don't know. I can't read people at a distance."

"It feels like a set-up."

He took a sip of tea. "It could be."

"Or it could be nothing. A false alarm, a red herring, something to get us out of the way while she wreaks havoc somewhere else."

"Correct."

I grabbed his wrist and checked his watch. "Damn it! We've got an hour before the auction. But what if we show up and there's nothing happening? These places have security cameras.

We'll be forever on video stalking Jasper's old junk, looking suspicious. Or worse, tipping his hand in some way."

"It's a problematic choice."

"Right." I shrugged. "So all things being equal…"

He put his tea on the bedside table and reached for the phone. "I'll have the valet bring your car around."

◇◇◇

The manager of the facility had a deep tan and golf hair and a paunch like he was smuggling a watermelon under his Georgia Bulldogs shirt. He also had two hole-in-one trophies and a stuffed sea bass on the wall of his office. I could barely hear him over the air conditioner in the window, which he had cranked to full blast.

"Y'all the ones called about the unit up for auction?" he said.

I tried to keep my teeth from chattering. "We are."

"You friends with the guy?"

"What guy?"

"The one who rented the unit."

I considered my words carefully. "Jasper's more like family."

"I been trying to get in touch, leaving messages at the number he gave me, but nobody would return my calls. And the back rent's been adding up." He got a squinty look in his eyes. "There's a lot of back rent."

Trey stepped forward, already pulling out his wallet. "We've got that covered."

The manager grinned big. "In that case, done and done! My son in there will take care of the financial matters." He grabbed a clipboard from the table. "Now if one of you will follow me, we'll get the what-not all seen about."

He hoisted a pair of enormous bolt cutters—the tool of all things what-not—but Trey didn't budge. I pointed into the office, where a younger version of the manager sat behind a desk in a matching red golf shirt. Behind him hung a wide-screen array showing a whole buffet of security camera feeds, including every storage unit in the place.

Trey cocked his head, and his forehead uncreased just the slightest. "Oh. Okay."

I patted him on the shoulder. "Join me down there when you're done."

◇◇◇

The manager walked me through the rabbit warren of red-roofed units, most of them climate-controlled. He'd carved his facility out of marshland, strung up some heavy duty chain link around the perimeter to keep out the meth heads and horny teenagers.

He held the door for me at the final building. As I entered, I glanced up and saw the security cameras, one above each entrance, and knew Trey's eyes were behind them. They had a good view of the hallway, but the interiors of the units were in the blind. I'd have to manage my position carefully so that I didn't disappear from his view.

The manager pointed. "That one right there."

Twenty-two DD was a five-by-ten unit, which—to my dismay—was secured with a disc lock. They were excellent for storage units because the slide mechanism was covered with metal, making them almost impossible to cut through. Which made for a lousy afternoon if you needed to do exactly that.

The manager raised his bolt cutters. "Usually the auctioneer does this. Takes a DeWalt cordless grinder to it. That's noisy and dirty, but it'll get you through a mid-grade lock in a few minutes. However, if you know the secret—"

I held out my hand. "Wait!"

I crouched down and took a closer look. Yes, disc locks were almost impenetrable, but that hadn't stopped whoever had tried to penetrate this one.

I pointed out the scratch marks to the manager. "Any idea who did that?"

He looked surprised. "Well, I'll be durn."

"Those security cameras, how long do you keep the footage?"

"I don't know, my boy Jimmy's the one keeps track of all that."

"Can you give Jimmy a call? See if he'll run through the footage for this unit, maybe let us know who might have been trying to break in here?"

He looked uncomfortable. "I could, but that seems like a police matter."

"We'll be glad to pay whatever civilian access fee you think is fair." I let the implication sink in. "I assume that's calculated by the hour?"

The manager caught my meaning. "I believe it is."

"Excellent. Now, can you cut this off without messing up any fingerprints that might be on it?"

He thought about it, hefted the bolt-cutters once again. "Yes, ma'am, I surely can."

It took only one minute. Remembering the possibility of fingerprints, I used the tail of my shirt to roll up the corrugated metal door. The contents were a haphazard mess—shoes, housewares, blankets, sheets, a corduroy armchair with an orange sticker that perfectly matched its burnt orange upholstery. Every single sticker was color-coded and hand-generated, not a bar code in there.

"It's a decoy," I said.

The man looked confused. "A what?"

"A decoy. You get a storage unit, use your real name—which trust me, Jasper would never do if he really had something to hide—then jam it full of crap, in this case, crap he got in one haul from a thrift store. Then you see if the cops show up to take a look. That's how you know they're on your tail about something."

The manager scratched his head. "I've never heard of such a thing."

"See?" I pointed. "He didn't even bother peeling off the price tags."

I heard the door at the end of the hall open and assumed it was Trey. So did the manager. We were both stunned to see Ivy storming down the corridor, the very picture of righteous indignation. With her curls blowing and her breasts heaving, she looked like a Greek harpy, ready to shred some entrails and peck out some eyes.

She jammed her hands on her hips. "What are you doing here?"

I straightened. "Checking out my new stuff."

"That belongs to Jasper."

"Not anymore."

Ivy balled up her fists like she was ready to take a piece out of me. The manager looked nervous. He had not been expecting a catfight, but he was smart enough to avoid getting caught in the middle of it. He got out his phone, pointed it at us.

"I don't want any trouble!" he said.

I ignored him, planting myself between Ivy and the unit. "What's up, Ivy? You come to take a peek at Jasper's junk too?"

"None of your damn business what I'm doing here!"

"Hell, yes, it's my business. You knew this unit was going up for auction, and you were happy to see that because that's the only way you were getting in because Jasper didn't leave you a key."

"That's ridiculous. I lost my key, that's all."

"Uh huh. That why you tried to cut your way in?" I shook my head at her, tsk-tsked. "Why doesn't Jasper trust you, Ivy? Not even with the key to a decoy unit? You ever considered that?"

Ivy bit back whatever bubbled behind her tongue. Glared at me, glared at the manager. She was running her options, but I knew she was straight out of them. She didn't want the cops out there. I didn't want the cops out there either. And the manager certainly didn't want the cops out there because cops had a way of hauling off evidence and not paying for it. Trey was perhaps the only person who wouldn't have minded one bit if they'd shown up—indeed, who may have had them on speed dial as we spoke—but otherwise, it was a three-way standoff.

She threw a hand in the air. "Fine. You want this mess, it's yours. I was trying to be a good fiancée, that's all."

And then she stomped out of the storage building and into the hot damp sunshine just as Trey barreled in the other door.

He was only a little breathless. "Who was that? Where is she? Should I—"

I put my hand on his arm. "That was Ivy, and she's probably screeching tires out of here right this second. She did not like the idea of the police coming down here, not one bit."

He looked at the slamming door, then at the unit, then at the manager, then back at me. "But—"

"Come on." I took him by the elbow. "I wanna show you the boring load of crap we just bought."

◇◇◇

Trey spent the next hour and a half meticulously examining our haul, emptying every drawer, running gloved fingers along joists and seams. He tapped for hidden compartments, slit open cushions, did lots of peering and frowning and professional poking. In the end, he found exactly what I had—nothing.

"Decoy," he pronounced.

"Damn straight."

He dusted off his hands. "And the security footage?"

"The manager's kid showed me—it was Ivy who tried to break in. Otherwise this has been one lonely unit, at least for the past month. No cops, no criminals, no nothing."

I knew Trey was thinking the same thing I was—that since the facility only kept four weeks of archived footage, other people could have scoped out the unit and we'd never know. Of course, Jasper probably had several such units scattered about, some of them with shady managers willing to drop a dime if anyone poked around.

Trey nudged an old mattress with his shoe. "Is any of this valuable?"

"Not a lick. No antiques, no relics, no interesting papers. The furniture is all fiberboard, nothing worth resell. I say we let the manager auction it off after all."

"Agreed." He shucked his gloves. "Do you have a theory as to why Ivy was so anxious to get in here?"

"I have two hundred and fifty thousand theories."

"That sounds valid."

"Yeah. Ivy's a creeper, all right, and she was anxious to creep right in here. But she doesn't have Jasper wrapped as tightly as she thinks, otherwise he'd have given her the key to that lock. Otherwise he'd have told her what this was."

"So he doesn't trust her."

"Not completely. It's one thing to get engaged, after all, quite another to…hang on, my phone's ringing."

I squinted at the display. Another unknown number. I held up a finger to Trey and answered it. "Hey, Finn, thanks for the tip and all, but—"

"Tee, listen to me."

Not Finn. Jefferson. And he was upset.

"What's wrong?"

"They just called me from the hospital. Daddy's gone into PICU—"

"What?"

"Pulmonary intensive care, and they say I've gotta get down there. But I'm eight hours out of town. I need you to go."

Suddenly I felt sick. "What happened?"

"I don't know. They just said to come, and quick."

I started walking toward the exit. "Of course. I'm on my way."

Trey followed right behind, the unit forgotten. "What's happened?"

"Something bad."

He put his hand in the small of my back and steered me forward. "I'll drive."

Chapter Thirty-eight

Jefferson's news evidently qualified as a "life or death" emergency, because Trey broke every rule in the book getting me to Memorial. Red lights ducked through, speed limits scorned.

He dropped me right at the lobby with a screech of brakes. "What do you want me to do?"

"Park and come on up. If it's bad…" I swallowed hard. "Just hurry."

He peeled out toward the parking lot. My stomach growled, but the hunger was no match for the anxiety. I tried to keep my hands from shaking as I got directions to the Pulmonary ICU, which lay behind a set of alarmed doors next to a call-in box. I picked up the receiver, and a male voice answered.

I made my voice as calm as I could. "I'm here to see Beauregard Boone."

"Hold on a second."

A few seconds passed. Then the voice came back. "I'm sorry, we don't have anyone here under that name."

"But you called. You said it was an emergency."

"I have no record of such a call." Another pause. "Perhaps your family member is still on the floor?"

I stood there clutching the phone, baffled. Was I caught in some bureaucratic circle of hell? Or was there something worse going on? Had Boone… I shook off the thought.

"I'll check, thank you."

I hurried back down the hall and took the elevator to Boone's regular room, murmuring to myself, please let him be there, please let him be okay. I walked faster, as if I could outrun the panic, breaking into a jog past the nurses' station. When I got to Boone's room, I skidded to a stop, steeling myself for the worst. Then I pushed open the door.

Boone had the remote in his hand, pointed at the TV. "Jesus Christ, girl, what the hell's chasing you?"

The relief almost knocked me off my feet. "They called Jefferson and said you'd gone to ICU!"

"Well, I haven't!"

"I can see that!"

Now that I'd found him, now that the crisis was averted—heck, had there even been a crisis?—I could catch my breath. Had Jefferson been pulling some kind of con? Or was this some other subterfuge beyond even my own suspicions?

Boone put down the remote. "You look like you seen a ghost."

"I feel like I have."

I saw Trey get off the elevator at the end of the hall. He made a beeline for me, his expression take-no-prisoners serious.

I waved him over, offered a shaky smile. "It's all right. False alarm. Or maybe some more of Finn's shenanigans. Or Jefferson could be—"

"Stop talking." He stood too close, his mouth close to my ear, his voice so low I could barely hear him. "We need to leave. Now."

"What?"

"Please trust me on this."

"But Boone—"

"—is in no danger. You, however, have to leave. Now."

I knew that look. I wasn't about to argue with it. Some part of my brain was sending up signal flares of speculation—was Trey trapped in a hypervigilant hallucination again?—but I decided that no matter what I was dealing with, it was best to deal with it away from Boone. Trey stood in ready position, weight on the balls of his feet. Whatever had him spooked, it was imminent.

I stuck my head inside. "I know this is nuts, but Trey says I gotta go."

Boone nodded. "I'd do what the man says."

"I—"

"Go. I'll be here when you get back."

Trey headed for the elevator at a fast clip, and I had to hurry to keep up. Once the elevator doors closed, I turned to him.

"All right, what's the—"

"Not yet."

His expression remained blank, and he faced straight ahead, as if we were strangers. He kept it up all the way through the lobby, eyes locked in front of him, until we got into my car. He cranked the engine, revved it a couple of times, then took it out of the parking lot with a roar.

I fastened my seatbelt. "You gonna explain?"

"You were being surveilled."

Surveilled, not watched. "There were cops there?"

"Yes. Two of them at the end of the hall, the men in blue work shirts loading the laundry hamper. They were undercover, probably local."

"How do you know?"

"Because there was no laundry in the hamper. And because I could see the outline of their radios. And because they were armed. Also there's a patrol car on Waters as we turned in, supposedly on traffic duty, but it's not. Please don't ask me how I know this, I just do. This entire scenario was a set-up."

"Why me?"

"Not you. Jefferson. I doubt you were the intended target, though you became one quickly." He checked the rear-view mirror. "The call Jefferson got was a pretext. There was no emergency. The authorities were hoping Jefferson would show up because, most probably, they have a warrant for his arrest and can't find him."

"So it was a trap? They got us all worked up for nothing?"

He nodded curtly, his jaw tight. He took the next right at almost full speed, a whiplash maneuver. I grabbed the door handle, braced against the dashboard.

"You're mad," I said.

"I am."

"At me?"

He shot me a look. "Of course not. I'm mad at whoever authorized this. It's unethical, possibly counter-protocol."

Well, well, well. This was a new thing. Trey got pissed off about a lot of things, but this was the first time I'd seen him cut his temper on his fellow boys in blue.

"So this isn't procedure?"

"Of course not."

"You never staked out a funeral, surveilled a wedding?"

A muscle in his jaw ticced. "Those are different situations entirely."

I examined him closely. Yep, mad, but something else too. Violated. Cops weren't supposed to do stuff like this, not to me, because doing it to me was like doing it to him. He was taking this personally.

"Do you think they heard?" I said.

"Heard what?"

"Me talking to Boone."

"Probably. Did you mention Jefferson's whereabouts?"

I thought back. "No."

"Then they'll be waiting for him at Boone's place."

He took the next right at the same breakneck speed, and the Camaro complained. It was made for hauling ass, not agility runs. I rested my hand on his shoulder, an old trick I'd learned from Garrity to bring him down. To my relief, he exhaled in a burst, and the speedometer eased back to legal limits.

I kept my hand on him anyway. "But Jefferson said he had nothing to do with John's disappearance. He was telling the truth. You said so."

"Savannah Metro doesn't know that. And the warrant could be for something else. And it could be valid, regardless of its method of execution."

"That's too many could-be's for my taste."

"Also, I am not infallible. I could be—"

"There you go could-being again."

Trey didn't argue. He flexed his fingers and retook the wheel. I felt the same way, like my anchor line had gotten cut. Why was I so protective of Jefferson suddenly? Not because he'd changed—he was still the racist, fear-mongering redneck he'd always been. So he'd had a cross burned on his lawn? Big deal. That was chickens coming home to roost. So he was freaked about potential violence against his family? More chickens making their way back home. So the legitimate family business was federal property, and he could lose his home, and his daddy was sick, and now there was probably a warrant for his arrest…

"If they find him, he'll go straight to processing at the detention center. Where Jasper is."

Trey's eyes were tight. "Yes. Which is a problematic scenario."

"That's an understatement."

I was torn. Should I let Jefferson know, and perhaps tip off a murderer? Should I keep quiet, and let the unethical pack of cops throw him into the same pit as Jasper, who seemed to have allies in and out and everywhere? Was one way right and one way wrong? Was one way useful?

I flopped back against the seat. "So now what?"

"Now we go back to the hotel."

"And then what?"

He shook his head. "I don't know. I really don't."

Chapter Thirty-nine

Valet parking was full, so Trey parked on the street a few blocks up from the DeSoto. I'd called Jefferson on the way back from the hospital, to tell him that his father wasn't really at death's door, that I'd checked on him myself. He'd immediately figured out the ruse without my having to say a single word about it, which spared me the decision or any debate with Trey. Although judging from Trey's simmer, he might have let me warn Jefferson anyway.

I tugged at his sleeve. "Come on. Let's go upstairs. We can check and see if there really is a warrant out for Jefferson."

Trey made a noise of assent, but still didn't budge. The rain had finally arrived, and was already beating a steady rhythm on the roof of the car. It was soothing, and I wanted to put my seat back and listen to it patter and roar. But that was a luxury I didn't have any longer.

I started gathering my things, clearing out the backseat before we left the car at the meter. It was a riotous mess. I decided to leave the heavy box of shop pamphlets there and started shoving everything else into a plastic bag—my CDs, muddy sneakers, a dirty rolled-up tee shirt.

I frowned as soon as my fingers wrapped around the fabric. A tee shirt shouldn't have been heavy. I unwrapped it, and I felt the blood drain from my head. "Oh fuck."

"What?"

I whipped back around. "There's a gun back there."

"Did you say—"

"Handgun, a .45. Not mine. Wrapped in a dirty tee shirt. Which is mine."

Trey stared at me, then unfastened his seatbelt and leaned into the backseat. He stayed that way for fifteen, twenty seconds. Then he righted himself and put both hands on the steering wheel.

"Told you so," I said.

He turned to me. "Did you—?"

"Touch it? Yep. Plus that shirt is the one I was wearing Friday afternoon, so it's got my skin cells all over it. And now gunshot residue and gun oil and—"

"Did you recognize it?"

"No. But I bet it matches those shells I found at John's trailer. Which means I am being set up."

"When was the last time you looked in the backseat and didn't see the gun?"

I stared at the ceiling, trying to remember. "Last night maybe, when we parked it? But I was a mess last night. Did you check?"

"Not thoroughly. But your backseat is somewhat…"

"I know."

"Have you noticed anyone following you?"

"I didn't even notice you. Did you notice anyone following me? Or tampering with my car?"

"Unfortunately, no." He pulled a piece of paper from his pocket, along with a pen. "Here. Write down as specifically as you can where you went, how long you stayed, and who might have had access to your car since you arrived. I want to check something."

He got out of the car and went around back. I started writing. There was Billie's, the hospital, the trailer, Bay Street. Twice at the detention center, where I'd seen Ivy and Lovett and Finn and Shane. But there were tons of cameras there, plus Trey had been watching my car the second time. What about the mom and pop café where he cut his sandwich into triangles and I worried about his sanity? Maybe. Then I'd parked it with the hotel's valet service while we drove the Ferrari around—the valet lot seemed secure, but it was actually a quick elevator ride from regular parking, not at all protected. Captain Lou's, whose dinky dirt parking afforded ample unsupervised opportunity to slim-jim my doors open and stuff a plant gun in the backseat. And of course Boone's place. It was unlikely an outsider could have gotten through those gates, but anybody on the inside could have. Cheyanne? Jefferson? And then the storage unit, where we knew Ivy had been, and then back to the hospital…

Dammit, there were too many opportunities to narrow it down.

Trey got back in the car, looking even more shell-shocked. "Your bumper has a GPS device attached."

"Somebody's been tracking me. Somebody who's not you."

"Correct."

I kicked at the door, kicked again. "This is all Jasper's doing! He wants me in the detention center! God knows what other evidence he's planted!"

"Tai—"

"There could be a damn body in our hotel room for all we know! Somebody calling 911 right this very second, while we sit here twiddling our thumbs! And you saw those cops at the hospital. They're jonesing for an arrest, and I'll be a silver platter suspect when they see this."

Trey stared straight ahead. He was thinking, hard, but nothing was coming. I knew what he was not saying—that we had to call the police, that we'd be tampering with evidence and setting ourselves up for legal complications down the road if we didn't—and I waited, waited to see if his exquisitely tuned brain could come up with some other way to deal with this.

He shook his head, still not looking at me. "We have to report this."

"Not we. You. And you can call them in a minute. But I'm not going to be here when they arrive."

He looked at me as if I were insane. "No—"

"Listen to me. If this is Jasper's doing—and all the evidence suggests it is—then I'm doomed the second they take me in. They're already suspicious because I showed up at the hospital. But with this?" I jerked my thumb backwards. "They have enough to arrest and charge me. And stick me in a cell. Where I am fair game for whoever he's got on the inside. Where even you can't protect me."

He swallowed hard. "You'll make bail quickly."

"Not before they put me in a holding cell with god-only-knows how many other people."

"You can request—"

"I won't get it."

"Stop it! Stop arguing, stop…just stop!"

He leaned forward and rested his forehead against the steering wheel. He was breathing hard, agitated. I put my hand on his back, and I could feel the rise and fall of his lungs under muscles tight like a snare drum.

"They could be coming any second now. And I can't run from the law, I know that, but I can make myself very hard to find, for a little while anyway. While you figure out what's going on."

He kept his head down, but I felt something ripple through him. Resignation maybe. Anger possibly. His body never lied, and he was at war in there, in his head, in his heart.

His voice was flat. "We have no evidence that a warrant has been taken out for you, or that anyone has reported that you have this weapon."

I shook my head. "That doesn't matter, it's—"

"It matters because if you or I had knowledge of such, then for you to leave now would be evasion of questioning and lawful custody, and it would be grounds for your immediate arrest and detention. Mine as well, for aiding and abetting." He sat up, staring over the dashboard. "But we don't know these things."

I froze in my seat. "Go on."

"You should go to the nearest police station and explain."

I nodded warily. "I should."

"I'm officially telling you to do that while I stay here and watch your car to prevent further tampering." He looked straight ahead, the words coming like a recitation. "You should not attempt to evade law enforcement. They will be talking with everyone you know here in Savannah, including me."

I got a glimmer of where he was going with this. "Except that I might be in Atlanta. Or Jacksonville. You don't know."

"No. I do not. I'll be sure to tell them that when they ask. Because they will."

I suddenly realized why he wasn't looking at me—he didn't want to know if I was lying because he knew he'd have to report exactly what he knew, exactly what I'd said, to whoever showed up when he called. He could only step so far over that line, and lying to the authorities was beyond him.

He continued in a monotone. "Should an officer try to talk with you, do not run. Do not hide. Do not reach for your phone or your bag or your keys. Do not reach into your pockets. Do not go into another room, not even if you need to get a change of clothes. Unless we have a search warrant in addition to the arrest warrant, we're only allowed to search your person and your wingspan."

He'd shifted to "we" and hadn't even noticed. He was aligning himself on the other side of the blue line. Except for the part of him that was telling me how to outwit his own kind.

"What is my wingspan?" I said.

"Fingertip to fingertip. If you have your gun, hold your hands up and away from your body, palms facing forward, and announce to the officer that you are armed, then tell them exactly where you're keeping it. Do not reach for it yourself."

I bit my lip. Damn it, no crying. No throwing up. None of that.

"I got it," I said.

"Should you be detained, say only 'I wish to remain silent. I want a lawyer.' You will probably be wanted for questioning at first, a person of interest BOLO. Should they eventually issue an arrest warrant, however…" His voice cracked, and he looked at me finally, fierce now. "I don't know how to do this, I don't...Tai."

I moved to wrap my arms around him, but he flinched away from my touch. And that almost broke me, almost undid me utterly.

He shook off the emotion, steadying himself again. "If you're going to go, you have to go now, and quickly."

"What are you going to do?"

"I'm going to call this in. And then I'm going to wait here while they file the report. I'll tell them only what you've told me."

He was back to "them" again, on the other side once more. Suddenly I understood exactly what it was like for him to watch me leave, over and over again, right when it was the last thing I wanted to understand. I ached to hold him one more time, assure him I'd be okay, that he'd be okay. But his composure was fragile, and so was mine, and somewhere an invisible clock was ticking.

"I'm gonna be fine," I said. "I promise."

I took a deep breath. Straightened my shoulders. Then I got out, dragged my bag over one shoulder, and left without looking back.

Chapter Forty

I got a rain poncho at the first kiosk I saw and spent the rest of the daylight hours moving from place to place, sticking to venues where people could count on sitting alone and quiet without being disturbed. I walked the side roads and squares with my head ducked and hands shoved in my pockets, one of hundreds of similarly dressed tourists, any second expecting blue lights and the wail of sirens. Nobody stopped me, though, and once night settled in, I made my way down to River Street.

I waited until Train put out the CLOSED sign, then I went around and knocked on his back door. I heard the latch unbolt, and the sharp creaking snap of rain-swollen wood.

Train stuck his head out. "Tai?"

"Yeah. It's me." I lowered the rain hood and shook out my hair. "Any room at the inn?"

◇◇◇

Thirty minutes later, I was warm and dry on Train's sofa, safely ensconced in his secret sanctuary. This ten-by-ten back room served as a combination office, storage closet, and haven of respite for the weary and wounded, for those with no place else to go except back to whatever godforsaken hell they'd managed to escape from.

Taking an inventory was short work since I'd walked away with my bag, my gun, and the clothes on my back. I had twenty-seven dollars in cash and one credit card that I couldn't use, because if the police were tracking me, they'd be looking for that. I'd left my cell phone in my car so no one could trace me that way either.

I picked up my wallet and pulled out the card that had come with the roses, the one with Trey's signature on it. Seeing his name there was a comfort, a connection once removed. I propped it on the side table like a miniature work of art.

Train sat in a desk chair opposite me, his takeout container open on his lap. He'd brought us supper, catfish po' boys from the restaurant two doors down. While he ate, he studied me over his reading glasses, looking for bruises, for track marks, for the bodily evidence of whatever might have brought me to his door. He counseled the battered and abused, the terrified and the lonesome. He saw through facades as if they were transparent plastic curtains.

"Tai—"

"Don't ask. You need deniable plausibility."

He managed a smile. "You mean plausible deniability."

"Whatever. I'm too tired to think straight."

Train took a long pull on his orange soda. "This have anything to do with your cousin Jefferson getting arrested?"

I almost dropped my french fry. "Where did you hear that?"

"I saw it on the news. They found him at his in-laws' house in some little podunk corner of Kentucky. Charged him with some firearms violations and breaking conditions of probation. Currently incarcerated in the county jail there, awaiting transport to the Chatham County Detention Center."

"His wife and kids?"

Train shrugged. "Still there, as far as I know. You said that was the whole reason he went to Kentucky, right? To keep his family out of harm's way?"

"Yeah. But now he's headed to one of the most dangerous places in Chatham County."

"Yeah. Eventually. Once they get transport arranged." Train wiped his mouth, leaned forward. "I know the drill, Tai. So I don't want to know if there's a warrant out for you too. You've got a safe place here, no matter what. But your family has a reputation for dark deeds of a non-Christian nature. And if you are caught up in that—"

"You know better."

"That's not what I mean. I mean, is it the Klan looking for you? A bunch of drug dealers? The cops?"

I put down my sandwich. "All of the above, most likely. Because I am being framed, probably for murder. Jasper's got men on the outside and on the inside, and if I go in, I'm dead meat. There's one body that we know of, plus a quarter million in stolen money, which is probably why John is missing, because either he took it, or somebody took it from him, or somebody thought he had it—"

"That's enough. I get the picture." Train pushed himself to standing, rubbed the small of his back. He shoved his glasses on top of his head and went rummaging in the closet. "I'll bring you the usual—a burner phone, some sunglasses, a cash card. There's a clothing donation box in the hall—find something plain and out-of-character, a dress or church lady skirt in your case. If you need to come here, use the back door, but stay away as much as you can. They'll be asking me questions soon, if they're looking any kinda hard for you, but they don't know about this room. Very few people do. And here, take this. Since you apparently need the full incognito package."

He handed me a box of hair dye. Rich Mink, the label proclaimed.

I looked up at him. "You're way too good at this fugitive thing."

"The wheels of justice sometimes run over the tired and downtrodden." He smiled wearily. "And tonight, you count as one of them."

Chapter Forty-one

The next morning, blue skies returned with a vengeance. I lowered the binoculars, unwrapped another piece of nicotine gum. The eleven o'clock sun made surveillance a pain, but the bookstore was still an excellent perch for keeping an eye on the action at the DeSoto, which for the last two hours had consisted of absolutely nothing.

Trey was a morning person, but he was not a rip-open-the-curtains-and-greet-the-day person. Still, I knew he was in there, probably at his desk surrounded by paperwork. And I knew he'd eventually either come out on the balcony for a bit of surveillance, or come out the front door and have the Ferrari brought around.

I muffled a sneeze into my elbow. The bookstore manager gave me a skeptical look, then went back to her inventory. I put the binoculars up again just in time to see Trey step outside on the balcony.

He looked left and right, checking, assessing. My heart did an odd pitter-patter at the sight of his familiar spit-and-polish self against the red brick. I wondered if he felt the same voyeuristic charge when he watched me unawares, letting his gaze linger on me, light and practiced.

I couldn't fight the tiny smile. *Hey, boyfriend.*

Trey stopped abruptly. Then he raised his chin, like a wolf scenting the wind. And looked right at me.

I froze too, but didn't lower the binoculars. I could see the crinkle at the corners of his eyes, the kink at the side of his mouth. Dang it, how did he know I was there?

"You said you'd call me."

I almost dropped my binoculars as I whirled around. Finn stood next to the Nancy Drew collection. Today she was a middle-aged Savannah tourist complete with cropped cargo pants, off-brand athletic shoes, and a green shamrock tee shirt. A fake ponytail slithered from under a slouchy hat.

Of course, I didn't look like myself either. The hair dye might have billed itself as Rich Mink, but in reality it was the dull brown of old furniture. A navy knit skirt and mousy gray blouse completed my disguise. I still wore my red La Perla lingerie underneath, though, like Superman's S under his Clark Kent button-down.

"Nothing to tell," I said. "It was a decoy unit. Besides, I've been busy being framed. Or haven't you heard?"

Finn stood next to me at the window. Today she had crow's feet and a double chin, hopefully the result of clever make-up. "I know. But not because I put that gun in your car."

"What about the GPS?"

"Guilty as charged. I stuck that on there before you even left Atlanta. But—"

"Yeah yeah, I know. Legal in the state of Georgia, part of your official duties."

She looked around the alcove. "Nice hide sight you got here. But if you're watching to see if the cops come, you're too late. They carted Trey down to the station within an hour of your discovering that gun. Somebody called it in before he did, so they were already on the way. Which I'm sure is no surprise to you." She crossed her arms. "Smooth move, by the way, hightailing it and leaving him to deal with the fallout."

I bristled at her phrasing. "Is he okay?"

"Sure. The man knows how to handle himself under questioning. Told them he didn't know where you were, that you and he often had disagreements about the proper procedure when handling such matters, and that it was entirely in your nature to take off without telling him where you were going, and that if he heard from you, he'd let you know they were looking for you, but that no, he had no information to share except that he would appreciate a call should they locate you."

I recognized the cadence of his voice in her speech and knew she was quoting him word for word. "You talked to him in person."

"I did. At his hotel, last night around ten, as he was coming back from the station. And now I've found you, which was depressingly simple. You must really have it bad for that guy."

"Finn—"

"Which means it will be simple for the cops to find you too, if you stay here. They're starting to look, and hard." She gestured with her chin out the window. "See that undercover car? The blue one with the busted taillight? There's a plainclothes unit in the lobby. Two cops hankering for an easy collar, both of them thinking you're dumb enough to come strutting into the lobby."

I made a noise.

"Exactly." Her expression grew sympathetic. "Talk to me, Tai. You don't want to end up behind bars—that's why you're up here with a BOLO on your back—and I'm here to tell you that you are absolutely correct in staying out of there. Jasper is well-connected. And he's aching to lay teeth into you."

"So?"

"So let me help you."

"Like you helped Hope?"

"Exactly like that."

The bookstore manager peered around the corner at us, her eyes as shushy as a librarian's. The cheerful front-door bell called her back to the register before she could break up our little confab.

I lowered my voice. "I'm not selling my soul to your boss, or my testimony."

"He's helping Hope because he believes she might be in danger."

"From his own client."

"Mr. Lovett has no knowledge of such intentions. And deep down, the strategic part of his brain realizes that if something does happen to Hope, or if something happens to her husband, what's his name—"

"John."

"Right. That guy. Regardless, if either of them becomes the subject of foul play, Mr. Lovett knows Jasper will get the blame. That's his whole defense right there, that a lot of crimes that Jasper didn't commit are getting heaped on his plenty vile and distasteful client. Extra bodies and crimes will not help him, especially not yours."

I felt a flutter of hope. "You said 'if.' So it wasn't John they pulled from the river?"

"There's no ID yet.

Relief washed through me. I liked the idea of John being lazy, John hotfooting it out of trouble, even John trying to wreak some vengeance by stealing Klan money. I did not like the idea of John being murdered.

Finn ran a finger along the dusty edge of an ancient Agatha Christie. "This is my last official task here in Savannah, finding you and offering you protection. I'm off the Jasper Boone case, back to Atlanta. Nonetheless, I can find you a safe house somewhere in the metro area, if you want."

"Out of the goodness of your heart?"

She laughed. "Oh, sure. That's what pays the bills, heart goodness. No, there's a fee attached. But it can be partially ameliorated with information."

"You want information, go talk to Trey again. He's more in the loop than I am."

"I wouldn't mind it, for sure. He's smoking hot and wicked smart, but he's handicapped by that moral rectitude. Unlike you. You have no such limitations. I know this because I've been watching you for months, Tai Randolph. Ever since Lovett took the case."

And then in the crooked slant of dusty light, I recognized her. Her hair had been black and bobbed then, and she'd worn enough make-up for a *Vogue* shoot, but now that I saw it, it was clear as a bell.

"It was you outside the History Center! You're the one who gave me that photograph, the one of me standing at the top of Kennesaw Mountain!"

She smiled in that bewildering way. "Took me five minutes to get that framed properly. You never even turned around."

"But that was before Jasper hired Lovett!"

"You're not getting it. Mr. Lovett chose Jasper, not the other way around. I've been putting together background on you and Trey and your whole family for months now, at his request."

"That's what you call background? Sending me weird photographs with cryptic verses?"

"I have an undergraduate in comparative literature that I rarely get to use." She shrugged. "It was my friendly way of giving you a heads-up. And everything I told you turned out to be correct, didn't it?"

I kept shaking my head. Yes, Hope did fling her looks everywhere, and yes, Ivy turned out to be as clingy and sucking as any parasitic vine.

"But you were in the photo with Hope!"

"Remotely-operated long distance cameras are a PI's best friend."

"But…why?"

"Because I needed your help. I didn't know my way around Savannah, but you connected the dots I gave you, and I followed the picture they made."

"But before that…I get the quotes about Ivy and Hope, but why did you stick a Bible quote on the picture of me? All the kingdoms of the world and their glory?"

"It's from where Satan tempted Jesus. On the mountaintop."

"I know that! I just…what the hell, Finn?"

"It's my way of making you an offer." She pulled out a business card. "Look me up when you get to Atlanta. I could use someone like you, someone adept at crossing lines."

I snorted. "No, thank you. I get caught sticking my toe across the line, there goes my Federal Firearms License, and there goes my shop."

"Like that would be a great loss."

I glared at her. She put up her hands in a conciliatory gesture.

"Sorry. But you gotta admit, you have a taste for risky behavior. Chasing killers, evading cops, sleeping with a former assassin—"

"Trey was a sniper, not an assassin."

She shrugged. "Tomato, tomahto. The point is, you know I'm right. You love working the line. And I'll tell you something else. Sometimes Mr. Lovett represents innocent people. And I do the best that I can for them, but sometimes...Like he always says, it's not about the law, it's about what he can prove."

A strange echo of what the prosecutor had told me during our first interview. If I believed it, then the courtroom was one of the most justice-free places in the entire judicial process. The thing was, I did believe it. Even my ruled-up boyfriend believed it. He'd seen too many guilty people walk free because of this technicality or that rookie goof. And I'd seen too many innocents take a hard fall for a stupid mistake.

Finn waggled the card. "C'mon, Tai. I need a confidential informant. Be mine. Help me do some super-secret good in the world and maybe we won't go to hell after all."

I thought of all the ways I'd stepped over the lines she was talking about. Sometimes leaped over, sometimes snuck over, sometimes erasing the line with my foot. They boxed me in. Safe, yes, but soul-draining.

I accepted the card, dropped it into my bag.

She smiled. "I'll be in touch." She started to leave, then snapped her fingers. "Oh, speaking of confidential informants. A mutual friend of ours is in town and wants to meet with you, say, two this afternoon?"

I got a chill. "Hope's in Savannah? Why?"

"She says she doesn't want to make her parole officer suspicious, but I don't believe a word of that. Regardless, she wants to see you, and I told her I'd offer."

Hope was wanting to talk to me. Which meant she either had a trap to spring or she needed my help.

"Where does she want to meet?"

"Gracie's. I assume you know where that is."

"I do."

Finn gave me a pointed look. "For both your sakes, this Gracie had better not have a big mouth."

I kept my expression blank. "Oh, she doesn't. She's silent as the grave."

Chapter Forty-two

The bus door opened with a wheeze, and a billow of super-cooled air rushed in my face. The driver beamed. "All aboard!"

I dropped a quick glance left and right, then took the steps upward. It had been years since I'd hopped a tour bus. Back then, I'd been the guide, in charge of general goodwill and nonstop yackety-yak. Now, I was a tourist, one of the herd. It felt strange, but since my Camaro was currently under police eyeballs, I needed transportation. And since I was on the lam, I needed cover. A tour bus provided both.

I dropped my enormous sunglasses on my nose and hid behind the trifold map. Transformation complete.

I took a window seat, tuning out the tour guide as she began her spiel. Here was the haunted square, here the haunted rock, here the haunted B&B. The tour bus chugged along, letting me look at my city from its sheltered bubble. Down the green squares, past the fountains of Forsyth Park, up Victory Drive with its columned verandas and arching oaks, finally turning left onto a road I could have followed blindfolded.

The road to Bonaventure Cemetery.

The driver spewed us out at the east end of the cemetery, right on the Wilmington River, with instructions to find the guide. The tourists did as instructed, already snapping selfies as they lumbered toward the center.

I lingered behind. Soon I could hear them only as a distant drone, and the true sounds of Bonaventure rose. Two egrets took flight, their wings beating the saline air. The water lapped low against the edge of the waving fronds of sawgrass and spartina. The sky beyond was the liquid blue of the waves below, the clouds like paint daubed on the horizon. If I stared long enough, I lost track of where the sky stopped and the water began.

I shook off the sensation and continued along the path until I came to the wooden sign that said simply "Gracie." I'd led hundreds of tourists to this spot to gaze on the final resting place of Gracie Watson, who died at the age of six in 1889. A life-size carving of the girl adorned the center of a private garden, protected by a wrought iron fence that reminded me of an ornate cage, as if the statue were a bird that could take wing and fly away. Wind and rain had softened Gracie's features. Tourists could not reach her, or their fingers would have done similar work. They still felt pulled to her, though, and left trinkets at her marker—costume jewelry and marbles and bubble wands.

No sign of Hope, which wasn't a surprise. Gracie was the bull's-eye I was supposed to hit, but she was too public a spot for contact. So I wandered down the curve in the path, behind which the trees formed a shady copse. I waited in that hidden place, up to my knees in faded azaleas.

I wasn't surprised to hear footsteps, but the sound still made me tingle at the base of my spine. The footsteps came closer, and soon I glimpsed a familiar figure at the end of the lane. Hope, going for nondescript in jeans and a tee shirt, her brown hair tousled. She held a cigarette to her lips, the smoke a wreath around her head. She joined me away from the main road, in the tucked away section.

"I wasn't sure you'd come," she said.

She started walking along the river, keeping away from the tourists. I stayed at her side. She didn't comment on the hair or the matronly clothes. She was a chameleon herself and knew the drill. She stopped at one of the wooden benches overlooking the water, a resting place for the living, its boards eroded smooth and gray by the seasons. She didn't sit, though, just stared out over the waves.

"Have they ID'd the body yet?" she said.

"No. But you know it's not John."

She examined the cigarette in her hand, watched the smoke curl off it. "Of course it is."

"Look, John isn't the brightest bulb in the chandelier, but he knows how to stay out of trouble, that kind anyway. Whoever put that body there was an amateur, and whoever they got, it was an even bigger amateur. So, no, not John."

"He'd changed from when you knew him. He trusted people too much. Especially me."

"Meaning?"

"Meaning I told him I wanted to settle down. I told him I wanted a nice easy life, that I would cooperate, testify, all the things they were telling me I had to do. And he took me at my word. But it was all a lie."

She sat down on the bench and extended the pack of cigarettes my way. I slid one from the pack, let her light it for me. These were stronger than my baby puffs back in the Camaro, real smokes. I could feel the head rush from the first inhale.

"You're skipping out," I said.

She shrugged. "They got to me in jail. It was easy enough. They stand too close to you, brush against you. Soon enough somebody tells you what to do, and you do it. That's how you stay alive."

"Jasper's crew?"

She let a trickle of smoke dribble from her mouth. "Nope. The LOTIEs."

Ladies of the Invisible Empire. "You sure it was them?"

"Of course I'm sure. Triple tau on the wrist. God, race, and country on their lips."

"What'd they want?"

"For me to drop my testimony. They want Jasper running around free, where they can get him easy, not sent to some super-max with extra security for high-risk targets."

I took another drag, let the smoke linger in my mouth. A jet-ski came zipping down the river, its high-pitched whine drowning out the bird song and insect hum.

"That's the reason you're still here in Savannah? 'Cause I was betting it was the quarter mil."

She tried to hide her surprise, but I saw it flare in her eyes. "I don't know what—"

"Bullshit, Hope. You're not here being a goody-two-shoes parolee. You're after that money, same as the Klan. Somebody thought you had it—that's why you've been followed, why your place got searched."

She didn't deny the accusation. The unforgiving afternoon light highlighted the circles under her eyes, the bones of her clavicle. Doing time had hardened her, but it had also beaten her.

She stared at the end of her cigarette. "I toyed with idea, true enough. Figure out who had it, find it, then run like hell. Not anymore, though."

"Without your testimony, there's a good chance Jasper will go free."

"The prosecutor has my testimony, signed and sealed. No reason for me to spout it again."

"Trey's boss agreed to provide executive protection—"

"You aren't getting it, are you?" She dropped the cigarette on the ground, crushed it with her heel. "John's dead. And I know you got more riding on Jasper going to prison than most, because Trey's in trouble too, and you'd slice your veins open for that man. Slice anybody's veins open. I understand that part. But I don't have anybody left to love like that. John really believed the straight and narrow was gonna save us, and now he's dead. And he was the next-to-last thing I had to lose."

I shook my head. "You don't know he's dead."

"He would've contacted me."

"There are lots of reasons you can't contact someone, no matter how much you love them."

"John was more heart than head, you know that. That fool would have showed up by now." She looked out over the water. "Look, I'm sorry for what went down with the three of us, back in the day. It was a shitty thing we did. But now it's all said and done, and he said he'd had enough chasing. That little trailer and a job at Train's and that Harley would have been enough for him."

I didn't tell her about the Harley. He'd even given that up for his low-rent American dream.

She stood. "I love that man. And he loved me. I couldn't have cut and run on him, not after all we've been through, but he's gone."

I breathed deep and felt the tug of old scars, where my broken places had mostly healed. I couldn't believe her. John wasn't dead, and I intended to prove it, once I got Trey and me out of the jam we were in.

A splash sounded to my left. An osprey had snagged a fish, a big one, too big to carry. The bird couldn't let go, and its prey was now its captor, two animals entangled in a flapping bloody fight for survival.

I turned back to Hope in time to see her walking away, sunglasses in place, anonymous once more. I knew my bus would be leaving soon, back for downtown and the hidey hole at Train's. I desperately needed a nap, and some food, and a few moments where I wasn't looking over my shoulder. And I needed something else too, something to get me through the rest of what I had to do.

Across the water, the bedraggled osprey dragged itself to the sandbar and the injured fish dove deep to the riverbed, as far from the surface as it could get. The tide would be stronger soon. Irresistible. But until that time, until they had to rise and fight it, both creatures licked their wounds. And waited.

Chapter Forty-three

Train pulled on the black latex gloves. "What brought this on?"

I rolled up my sleeve. "I don't know. Talking with Hope. Sitting by the river. Being alone there, with everything flowing by."

He had the CLOSED sign posted and his tools laid out on the table—the tattoo machine with the needle bar already attached, the round pot of black ink, and most importantly, the stencil of the image I'd given him, duplicated line for line on the thermal copier.

The cops had come by that morning, he said, asking if he'd seen me. He'd lied right to their official faces. They hadn't known to ask about the secret room—they were simply checking my known associates—but he'd have lied about that part too. Train was real clear about his allegiances.

"They'll be back later," he said. "It's Friday night, and they keep a presence. You don't want to be around until things have quieted down."

"I'll find someplace. If there's one thing Savannah doesn't lack, it's dark bars where people don't ask questions."

Train wiped the inside of my wrist with antiseptic, then applied a thin layer of transfer solution. "I don't usually do last-minute ink. I prefer that people sit with their stuff a little while first. But I also know that in times of trouble and chaos, we sometimes need a reminder of what connects us to our Higher Power. We humans are ultimately not in charge of the world. And that's a very good thing."

I flashed back to Rico's words—control freak, he'd called me, as flexible as a tire iron. I didn't know any other way, though. I'd shoved and elbowed my way through my parent's disapproval, through their deaths, through Hope and John's betrayals, countless smaller violations. And then I'd pushed myself into Trey's life…and found something bigger and deeper and realer than I'd imagined possible.

"You ever swim in the ocean?" I said.

Train shook his head. He smoothed the stencil on my skin, then applied pressure with the flat of his hand. The golden cross around his neck glittered in the early evening light.

"The ocean might seem calm on the surface, but riptides can come out of nowhere. Clear blue day and you're dying. You can see everybody on the beach—sunbathing, building sandcastles, picking up shells—and they don't have a clue. People think it's all screaming and arm waving, but it's not. Drowning is the quietest way to go."

"So I've heard." He peeled off the paper and checked the image. "That look okay to you?"

"Perfect."

He blotted away the extra ink and reached for the tattoo machine. I heard the buzz of the needle, felt the first prick, right at the tender spot on the inside of my wrist. He was deep in the process now, like a meditation. I watched the lines blossom black against the canvas of my skin.

"And you can't fight a riptide," I said. "It's relentless. And you can't give in, it'll suck you out to sea. You have to keep swimming parallel to the shore, slow and steady, and eventually it will let you go. You'll toss up on the beach like so much seaweed. But you'll be alive."

Train kept his head bent. "So what is this little squiggle of ink I'm doing for you today? A life preserver in the face of life's riptides?"

I leaned back in the chair, closed my eyes. "It's my reason to keep swimming, which is the closest thing I have to a Higher Power."

◇◇◇

An hour later, I had fresh new ink. Train handed me a tube of the after-care ointment he'd massaged into my traumatized skin, his special proprietary blend. I applied a bandage, which made me resemble a failed suicide, but new tattoos needed cover. I knew it was there, regardless, and that was what mattered.

I stood up to leave as Train's phone rang. He leaned over and squinted at the screen. "Hang on, it's Antonio."

"Who?"

"My cousin down at Coastal. I told him to call me when they had an ID for release."

"Coastal?"

"The ME's office."

I went cold. The body in the river. I watched Train's end of the conversation. It didn't take long, but I knew the news long before he finished talking. The way his face loosened and fell, the way the breath he'd been holding trickled out. The way his voice went low and hushed.

"Yeah man, thanks. I appreciate it."

He put the phone down, his black eyes wet. He put his hand on my shoulder. "Tai."

"Don't say it."

"I'm so sorry."

I sat blinking in the chair. The memories flashed unbidden—John at the beach, John laughing with his head thrown back, John at Hope's arraignment in his secondhand suit and badly knotted cheap tie, John in my bed, John's clothes he'd left behind when he left me behind.

I started rolling down my sleeve. "I have to go."

I went into the back room and started shoving my things in my bag. Train followed right behind me.

"Where?"

"To see Trey."

"Chances are good that BOLO they got on you is about to become a warrant."

"I know. But as soon as he hears this news, he'll try to find me. And if he can't, he might start decompensating again."

I pulled my hair back in a ponytail. The skin inside my wrist stung, and I resisted the urge to rub it. I slipped the hoodie over my blouse. As much as I hated the skirt, it would have to stay. Perhaps it would be camouflage enough.

Train positioned himself between me and the exit. "And how do you plan on getting in the hotel? You know Savannah Metro has somebody watching that place."

"Not 24/7 they don't. They have three hundred active warrants to deal with, plus four shootings this week alone. I'm a tiny fish in a giant pond of felons." I pulled on my shoes. "Besides, there's always a back way in. Wherever employees sneak out to grab a cigarette, I can sneak in. And I still have the key card to Trey's room."

Train frowned. "Do you still have your burner phone?"

"Yes."

"You used it yet?"

"No."

"Good. I have that number in my phone. Stay put for as long as you can at the hotel, and I'll text you when the coast is clear here. It'll be after midnight or so. Use the back door, and keep the lights off."

"I'll try. But as soon as there's a warrant, you can't hide me here anymore. A person who knowingly aids another in escaping from lawful custody—"

"—shall upon conviction be punished by imprisonment for not less than one nor more than five years. I know the statute." He raised his chin, steadied his gaze. "But the laws of the state of Georgia are not the laws I serve."

I straightened my shoulders, scrubbed my eyes clean. God, he was sweet and sincere. And I knew he'd go to jail to protect me. But I couldn't let him do it.

"I gotta hurry," I said.

He put out his hand. "May I send you off with a prayer?"

"A quick one."

He took my hands in his, closed his eyes. But I kept mine wide open.

Chapter Forty-four

Trey was nowhere to be found.

His things were still in the room—stacks of charts and graphs on the desk, gym bag in the corner—but no phone, no wallet, no keys. Had he gotten dragged in for further questioning? Stepped out to meet someone? Gone for ice?

I shook off memories of the last time he'd vanished from his hotel room. There was no violence here, no overturned tables or upended couches, and Trey was not a man who would go without a fight. I pulled out my new phone and dialed his number, but I heard the key card in the door before I could press send.

He came in quietly, shutting the door behind himself, flipping the deadbolt. He stayed near the door, examining me with perplexed frustration. I examined him back. No tie, no jacket, white shirtsleeves rolled to the elbow.

I smiled. "You don't look surprised to see me."

His eyes flicked to the back corner, where I saw absolutely nothing out of the ordinary, just a floor lamp and luggage rack. And yet I knew there was a surveillance camera there, probably one of the test models he got to take home.

I ran a hand through my hair. "Not even a comment about the new color?"

"You're not supposed to be here. If the authorities—"

"Tell me to go and I will."

He opened his mouth, then closed it. He shook his head. I went to him, my fingers trembling as I started unbuttoning his shirt. He didn't stop me, but he didn't respond either.

"Tai—"

"John's dead. It was his body they pulled out of the river. I got the news from Train's friend at the morgue."

He flinched. "Oh. I'm sorry."

"Yeah. Me too." I focused on the buttons, slippery as pearls in my fingers. "I really didn't think it would shake out this way. I don't think I've quite comprehended it yet. It all seems unreal, like a bad dream." I slid my fingers under his shirt. "Not like this. This seems real."

He inhaled sharply, but instead of letting me have my way, he took my hands and held them in his. "You should sit down."

"Why?"

"Just do it. Please."

I let him pull me to the bed, where I sat on the edge. He sat next to me, his eyes roaming my face, trying to read the contents of my head in the curve of my features. But he was getting no traction.

"Why are you here?"

"I had to vacate my former premises for a little while. It was about to be crawling with the Friday night patrol."

"Yes, but why did you come *here*?"

"I was worried you'd hear the news about John and try to find me."

"Tai—"

"We agreed to stop hiding things from each other, not stop showing up. Correct?"

He considered. "Correct. And you're right, I might have… not been okay with this news. But I think I am."

"You think?"

"I think. Being away from you has been…somewhat challenging."

He dropped his gaze to the bedspread between us. I could see the toll our separation had taken in his furrowed brow and tight, clipped words. He was trying, so hard. I put my hand to his jawline, and he turned his face into my palm.

I wanted to tell him, using clear frank language, what I wanted him to do next. And that I wanted him to do it quick and hard, maybe up against the wall, so that I could forget for a few minutes anything but the scent of him, the sensation of skin on skin, the total obliteration he could provide. Before I could reach for him, though, he noticed the bandage on the inside of my wrist.

His frown deepened. "What happened? Are you hurt? Did someone—?"

"No, nothing like that."

I peeled back the bandage and held up my hand so that he could see the fresh tattoo shimmering underneath. He canted his head as he studied the snaking licks of clean black ink. One word. *Trey.* In his own handwriting.

He raised his eyes. "When did you…how?"

"Train made a copy from the card you sent with the roses. And I put it where I could always see it, right on the pulse point. Because no matter what happens in my life—whether I brought it on myself or not—you're there. Because it's not so much that you show up, it's that you never leave. I wanted to make sure I never forgot that. Because I want to be that for you too."

Trey didn't reply, but I saw the emotion flash in his eyes, his armor dropping. I felt the same way, cracked open, untethered. The heavy weight of the past severed now, still present, always present, but sinking down to where I could barely perceive it, at least for a few moments.

I pulled in a shaky breath. "I told you I loved you. It's been harder to let you love me. To accept that you could, that you do. So I decided to trust you. Who you were, who you are, who you will be. All of you, even the parts I don't know because you can't find the words." I moved my hands to his waist, pulled his shirt free of his slacks. "All in, Trey. For better or worse."

The words sounded like a vow, and I realized they were. Trey still hadn't spoken. I could feel the deep desire welling to the surface, the want and need that blurred his circuits and hazed his rational responses, rendering him appetite and longing. I kissed him and felt the succumbing, the yielding and giving way. He smelled of clean sweat and salt musk, and I kissed him deeper, tasting…

I pulled back. "Trey? Why do you taste like bourbon?" I buried my nose in the crook of his neck and inhaled deeply. "And your hair smells like cigarettes, why do you smell like cigarettes?"

He stared at me as if I'd lost my mind. "Because I've been in a bar for the last hour! Drinking bourbon!"

"What? Why?"

"Because you told me to!"

"I did not!"

He looked equal parts annoyed and baffled. "You sent me a text, saying to take a corner table at the Bar Bar, order two Maker's Marks, neat, drink one, and wait for further instructions."

"Why would I do that? Especially not there, you hate places like that, all dank and crowded and…"

And then I figured it out. Apparently I wasn't the only one Finn was playing mind games with.

I smacked the bed. "Damn it! I'm gonna strangle her!"

"Who?"

"Finn!"

He frowned. "The detective?"

"Yes, her. Did you also get bizarre poetry? Maybe a weird Bible quote?"

"No."

"Oh, you will. Wait and see. The woman has *designs*. But you know what?" I slid my arms around his waist. "I don't want to talk about her right now. I don't want to talk about anything out there. I want you."

I kissed him again, running my fingers along the inside of his waistband. His breath caught, but he grabbed my hands when I reached for his belt buckle.

His voice was a whisper, sandpapered with want and need. "Slowly."

I pulled my hands free. "I don't think so."

He seized them again, pinning them between our bodies. Something burned in his eyes, something dark and irresistible and bloodwarm as summer tides. I nibbled the tender spot behind his ear, his never-fail erogenous zone, and he made a soft noise in the back of his throat. But he didn't let go of my hands.

I pulled back. "What is up with you? Is it the bourbon? Because if it is—"

"Not the bourbon."

I tried to slip free again, and he tightened his grip, but that didn't matter. I could win this one if I wanted. I knew his pressure points, how to break him open on his own desire, draw him like an arrow and then loose him. I knew all these things, had learned them at his body as if it were an altar.

But he was asking something of me, not with words, and my body was answering in kind. He interlaced his fingers with mine, easing me backwards until I lay beneath him. He held my gaze as he released one hand, waited to see if I'd move. When I didn't, he unbuttoned my blouse, the fabric falling open at his touch. He was breathing harder, the blue of his eyes crystallizing, all edge. And I knew the edge for what it was, the line between. I'd seen it on the training mat, seen it behind the wheel of the Ferrari, seen it when he said he loved me. It was the line of total and irreversible commitment—no backtracking, no side roads, no detours.

His voice against my ear was rich and dusky and intoxicating. "You say you want me to be more…this. But you take control every time I try. You could take it now, if you want. You know I won't resist. But I am asking you…I'm asking…"

He exhaled slowly, not finding the words, but still sure of what he was trying to say. He trailed kisses down my neck, his entire body against me, all of him, so that I could know how much he wanted me, that it wasn't hesitation or uncertainty holding him back. That he was waiting for my permission, he submitted himself to that, and that alone.

"You said you were all in, Tai. Did you mean it?"

I could barely make my tongue work. "Yes."

"Okay. Good. Because there's something…and I can't explain it, no matter how hard I try. I can't tell you. But I can show you. If you'll let me."

And I knew what he was asking for, and it made me dizzy to think of giving it to him. I'd always been the one to do the undoing, not him. This was new territory, unexplored. But if there was one thing Trey knew how to work, it was fear, and he worked it expertly, channeling the chemicals sluicing through my blood, through his, into sensation and response.

He slid his hand along my jaw, his fingers tangling into my newly darkened hair. "Will you let me? Please?"

The skin at my wrist beat with every thrum of my pulse, and I stopped resisting, stopped fighting him for the reins, stepped right off that ledge into pure exhilarating freefall. I arched my head back against the pillow, letting him at my throat.

"Yes," I said.

Chapter Forty-five

I rested on my side, sated, breathless. Through the window, swaths of moonlight pearled the gathering clouds, gossamer against the black sky. Rain on the way in. Or out. Always one or the other during the springtime.

My phone buzzed with an incoming text. I rolled over and checked the readout. Train, wondering where I was. I sent him a quick reply, told him to go ahead and close up, that I'd be there soon.

"My safe place is safe again." I rolled back and faced Trey. "Which means I have to go."

He flinched only the slightest. "I know."

I took his hand, pressed his knuckles to my mouth. "Are you going to be okay?"

"I am." He sounded like he meant it. "Are you?"

"Yes."

I couldn't take my eyes off him. There was a word for the kind of art he was, a charcoal sketch. Sharp lines and angles with artistic blurring here and there to suggest movement or secrets.

"I'm sorry Finn sent you on a wild goose chase. I'm sure she has her reasons, but—"

"It wasn't a goose chase."

"It wasn't?"

He shook his head. "No. That's what I was trying to tell you before you…Anyway, I couldn't figure out why you'd send me to a bar unless there was a reason you couldn't show up yourself. So I went. And I stayed. And I saw Ivy."

I suddenly understood. Score another point for Finn. Ivy would have spotted me in an instant, but she'd never seen Trey. He, however, had gotten a good eyeful of her on the surveillance camera at the storage unit.

"So what did you find out?"

"That you were correct—she has at least one secret she's keeping from Jasper."

"And that is?"

"She's having an affair."

I sat up, the sheet falling away from my chest. "Seriously?"

"Seriously."

He rolled over and fetched his own phone from the bedside table. He scrolled down before turning the screen around so that I could see it.

Sure enough, it was Ivy. I'd have recognized those cupid-bow lips and jazz-babe curls anywhere, even in the blurry, neon-tinged photos. She was seated in a corner booth, across from a rugged guy with his back to the camera. Buzz cut dark hair, tank top showing off gym-rat muscles. And he was locked lip to lip with Ivy.

"So not platonic," I said.

Trey leaned back against the headboard. "No."

"What were they talking about?"

"I couldn't hear. The bar was too loud."

"Yeah, all that brick reverberates. It's probably why they picked that spot. Dang, I knew she was hiding something." I stabbed the phone with my finger. "This guy. If Jasper knew about this, he'd pluck out this guy's heart and eat it unsalted."

Trey looked puzzled. "Don't you recognize him?"

I scrolled through the shots. With his back to the camera, he was another anonymous bar crawler. But when he and Ivy stopped sucking face, I pegged him immediately.

"Holy hell, it's Shane Cook!"

I examined the photo closer. Something wasn't quite right. I zoomed in on Ivy's face, on Shane's face, finally zeroing in on the tattoo on his upper arm.

"That's not the same tattoo he had in the parking lot. That one was a dog's head, an army mascot. This one is…I can't make it out."

"That makes no sense. How can you change a tattoo?"

"Temporarily? Ink-based stencils are the best way. Train made one from your signature to use as a guide. But in Shane's case, I suspect he's using it to hide something, probably something related to his less-than-honorable discharge. He expunged his record—"

"Attempted to."

"Yes. And now he's attempting to expunge whatever is under that dog-head on his bicep. But only temporarily. It's a disguise, not a change of heart."

I leaned back against the padded headboard, and Trey draped his arm around my shoulders. I wanted to stay, very much. Too much. My safety was an illusion in that soothing cocoon of a room, and we both knew it. The first law of being on the lam—stay on the move.

"What do you think we should do with this information?" I said. "Tell the police?"

"She's not committing a crime by having an affair."

"What about Shane? I doubt his job description includes sexing up a prisoner's fiancée."

"No. And it may be cause for his dismissal, but it's not illegal."

I forced myself up, abandoning the clean sheets and firm mattress and Trey's naked body. He let me go without a fight. I sat on the edge of the bed and searched the floor for my bra and panties. They were easy to spot, a flaming red puddle of satin and lace on the beige carpet.

I wiggled into the panties. "We could confront Ivy, threaten to tell Jasper unless she spills whatever she's up to, which I am betting has something to do with that missing two hundred and fifty thousand. Or do the same with Shane. Threaten to tell the warden if he doesn't cough up some information."

Trey shot me another look. "That would be extortion."

"So that's a no?"

"Yes. I mean, yes, that's a no."

I found my other clothes next to the armchair. Trey watched me dress. I couldn't imagine the matronly blouse and skirt did anything for him, but he'd picked out the lingerie himself. So I took my time with the bra, a wickedly structured creation with enough push-up to distract an army.

"Oh, one more thing. I saw Hope today—long story, Finn-related, the details aren't important—but she confirmed what I suspected, that she's being coerced into dropping her testimony."

"From Jasper?"

"No. The KKK. They're putting the screws to her just like they did Jefferson, only they got to her in the detention center. She agreed with Jefferson, though, that they want Jasper walking around and breathing free air so they can take him down on their own terms, which will include poking him with hot sticks until he takes them to their missing money."

"Is that who's been following her? In the white truck? The Klan?"

"That scenario makes the most sense. But we have no proof."

I reached behind myself to fasten the bra, but Trey sat up. "Here. Let me do that."

He leaned forward, then reached around me and engaged the hook and eye closure. Then he adjusted the straps, first the right, and then the left. He took his time, sliding his hands along the curved padding, the Venetian lace décolletage, until he had everything tucked and hoisted to his satisfaction.

"So, what now?" I said. "Wait on Finn to drop another clue? Accost Ivy? Pay a visit to the detention center and catch Shane in the parking lot? Talk to Boone again?"

He gave the brassiere a final adjustment. "I don't know. But I should be doing it, not you. You should stay out of sight as much as possible."

I sighed. "Yeah. I left you the number of my new burner phone, so you can find me if you need to. But it will only be good for one call, and then I'll have to dump it and get a new one." I handed him my blouse, and he held it so that I could slip my arms into the sleeves. "You spotted me watching you earlier, didn't you?"

"I did."

"How?"

He started on the buttons, his fingers nimble and efficient. "I saw the glare from the binoculars. The bookstore makes a good hide site except—"

"—for the fact that it faces the sun, should have remembered that. How did you know I wasn't some cop?"

"Because I'd already spotted the unmarked car outside. And even though you're wanted for questioning, I couldn't imagine they would sent an additional counter-sniper surveillance unit. So I considered all of the other people who might have been inexpertly surveilling me, and I decided it had to be you."

I put my hand to his face, and he pressed a kiss into my palm. He was close to cracking my resolve, which would be a dangerous thing for both of us.

"So what are we—I mean, you—doing next?" I said.

"I'll chart this new information in the matrix and see what connects. But after that, I don't know. I'll find a way to let you know, if I can. And I do have one thing for you. Before you go."

He gestured toward the bedside table. A pair of car keys lay next to a folded wad of cash.

"It's the rental. I never returned it. It's still parked in the garage at the corner. The money is for you too."

I smiled down at him. "That's definitely aiding and abetting."

"I know. I'm less concerned with that than I am with keeping you out of the detention center."

"So you have a plan?"

The corner of his mouth twitched. "I have several plans. But I can't tell you about them. Telling you about them makes it easier to tell other people about them. And we don't want that."

I didn't argue. He knew his brain, and how to subvert it, better than anyone else. His eyes were tired, and I missed him, even though I was standing barely twelve inches from him. His fingers brushed my skin as he returned me to order and properness, a process almost as sexy as being undressed. He was calm, collected. Not veering into either shutdown or breakdown, his Tower fully intact even if a bit lightning-singed.

I smoothed his hair from his forehead. "You're turning out to be a natural at the underhanded arts."

"Your brother says atypical cognitive presentations are a part of my recovery complex."

I pulled his face up so that I could see his eyes. "And the interlude before that? Was that part of your recovery complex too? Or was that the bourbon?"

He finished buttoning the blouse. "Not the bourbon."

"Good." I kissed him then, kissed him good, enough to last the rest of the night. "Still, I'll be keeping a bottle of Maker's Mark at your place from now on. Just in case."

I gathered the keys and cash and started for the door, but he held me in place, his hands on my hips. He had the hem of my blouse crumpled tight in both fists, and I thought, this is it, this is where we both fall apart.

I took his hands in mine. "I have to go."

"I know."

He didn't resist when I slipped free from his hold. I saw the same look in his eyes as when I'd left him in the car, and I realized he was exerting every ounce of willpower he had to let me leave him again, and that something was breaking inside even as something else was growing stronger.

His eyes were serious, searching. "Tai? Are you really okay?"

I almost nodded, almost tried to pretend. But then I shook my head. "No. I'm not. But I have to act as if I am, until we're finished with this mess. And then I plan on falling to pieces."

He inhaled, let it out slow. "I understand."

Chapter Forty-six

The Friday night crowds ran thick up and down Abercorn, noisy with beer-fueled cheer. In simpler times, this would have been my life, my last tour ended and the pub crawl just beginning, my whole existence a glass waiting to be filled. Now it ran over with trouble and ruin, complication and consequence.

I lit my last cigarette, blew a plume of smoke behind me. Maybe Trey would end up with something useful, a graph or a circle map or a Venn diagram. Something with an arrow pointing clearly to a next step. As things stood, there were too many wild cards at play for me to figure anything out.

Ivy was cheating on Jasper, which meant that her whole lovestruck routine was a cover for some other motive for being with him, most likely the missing money. She'd probably thought it was in the storage unit, but couldn't figure out a way to get into it without causing too much attention to herself. Had she charmed Shane with a Bonnie and Clyde tale of grabbing the loot and hitting the road?

Was Jasper onto her? Or Shane? Using them? Being used? I'd been warned over and over that he was planning something. I'd assumed it had involved me. But what if he were toying with me just for the hell of it, as a distraction from his real agenda—getting revenge on Ivy.

I sucked in a long slow drag and kept walking. God, I'd missed nicotine, the sweet pacifying smack of it.

I had Finn's card in my bag. She'd obviously been suspicious enough to send Trey to spy on Ivy and Shane—had that been a good hunch or a lucky guess? I'd trusted her so far, and she hadn't let me down, but I didn't like being the target of hit-and-run information if I wasn't privy to the agenda.

And then there was Hope. She adjusted her loyalties like sails, her primary objective staying alive. She'd lied to John, let him believe they'd had some kind of life here, which might have been why he'd made the decisions he had. And now she'd fled the scene, the Klan on her tail.

A Savannah Metro car rolled by, and I dropped my head, kept my eyes on the sidewalk. *Look innocent*, I said to myself, *look preoccupied and harmless and innocent.* Another followed right on its bumper, plainsclothes officers behind the wheel, both of them moving purposefully, heading south toward Liberty. Not the routine patrol. These cars had mission and purpose.

I kept them in my sight as I stepped off the sidewalk and under one of the spreading magnolias. I sent a quick text to Trey—Two patrols prowling your way?—and waited. No lights, no sirens. Not that they would engage either for serving a warrant, a stealth move of the first order.

When nothing happened, I continued walking, threading my way through the flowing crowds toward the river. I still hadn't figured out Jefferson's role either. My sympathy for him was knee jerk, like watching a rattlesnake get hit by a car. Cheyanne was just as bad, maybe more so. But those little girls broke my heart, as firecracker-wild as I'd been at their age. I knew their parents would eventually turn them into people just as fiercely deluded as themselves, baby rattlesnakes with the same deadly venom.

And of course, at the center of it, Boone. Dying now, a word that hurt to think, even though there was hope in that frail old package. He'd somehow changed his mind, changed his heart. He was still reckless and stubborn and unreconstructed in every way, but he'd hacked off a huge malignant part of his identity and survived. And that was a miracle, but it had happened. The soul had the same plasticity as the brain perhaps. A recovery complex all its own.

I took the steps down to River Street, the fat slice of moon half-revealing, half-concealing the cobblestones. The dark tunnels that led to the back of Train's shop were quieter this time of night, so there would be no one to harass me about polluting the fine Savannah night with my cigarette.

I exhaled, watched the smoke cloud the darkness. I had my hand on the door of the shop, my key in the lock, when my phone buzzed. Not a text. A call. I examined the number, an Atlanta extension.

I pressed the button. Didn't say anything.

"Tai? Are you there?"

I almost dropped my cigarette. "Gabriella?"

"Yes. Trey just called and gave me this number. He said that two detectives are in the lobby with a warrant, and that you must surrender to lawful custody at this time."

"Damn it!"

"*Oui.*"

I dropped my cigarette to the cobblestones, ground it out with a twist of my shoe. "So now what?"

Gabriella's voice was firm and calm. "He stressed that you were not—I repeat, not—to surrender to Chatham County authorities. You are to take the rental car to the Statesboro Police Department, out of Chatham County jurisdiction. A lawyer will meet you there, as will Trey, as soon as he can. You'll be interviewed there, and then processed and bonded out without ever setting foot in the Savannah jail."

So this was Trey's secret plan. As plans went, it was pretty genius. At Gabriella's end, I could hear noise in the background, voices and music. Bar sounds. I pushed my way inside, the creaking door splintering the silence. I instinctively reached for a light switch, but then remembered Train's warning to keep the shop dark. I was getting used to the dark.

Gabriella kept talking. "I've called Garrity—he is on his way back—and your brother, who is on the next flight. We will keep you out of the hands of that fucking monster, I promise." She delivered the words with real malice. "Do not call back on this number. I borrowed it from an anonymous young man. He is smiling at me, and I am smiling back. He will not connect us."

I saw Trey's method in the madness of having Gabriella as our go-between. If for some reason the cops checked Trey's phone records, they would see her number, but if anyone checked her records, they'd find no calls to me. They'd have to find the unnamed guy at the unnamed bar, who had lent his phone without hesitation to an attractive damsel in distress, and then they'd have to recognize that number as my burner phone. It was a needle in a sea of haystacks.

I relaxed just the slightest. We had a plan. It was going to work. I could stop running.

"Thank you," I said.

"*De rien*." She hesitated. "I am sorry for our previous contretemps. Trey says you and I have to work things out."

"He told me the same thing."

"Of course. And you have to go now, but I must explain this first—I read the cards wrong. They weren't about Trey, they were about you. There is death, yes, all around you. And your world is crumbling, dissolving, moving in shape and form. You have no choice in this, it is not a process you can control. All you can do is keep your head above water."

I remembered the Tower card, the hapless figures tumbling into the raging sea, the structure collapsing around them. I'd never put much stock in Gabriella's predictions, but suddenly, that card made perfect sense.

"I wish I could do more," she said. "Because you matter to me too. Truly. And I am sorry—"

"We'll figure it out. When we talk."

"*Bien*. Now be careful. Your main concern is getting out of Savannah. Do not talk to anyone until you do, not even Trey. Understood?"

"Completely and utterly."

The line went dead. I stared at the phone. Yes, Trey had a plan, but it was one that meant dragging myself back into the night. I dropped the phone into my bag, not wanting to think about it, not wanting to move, bone-weary.

"Train?" I called. "Are you in here?"

The attack came from behind, a thickly muscled forearm tightening around my neck. I instinctively turned my head into the crook of my attacker's arm and saw the blurry black tattoo. Not a dog. A black and twisted cross with drops of blood.

I bit and kicked and twisted, jerked and tried to scream. I tried to go for a throw, tried hard, but the pressure at my throat wasn't stopping. I kicked behind me and connected with meat and bone, but then the color washed from my vision. I felt a prick and burn at my neck, and a black curtain closed off the world.

Chapter Forty-seven

I woke up with a splitting headache and a splintering pain in my throat, duct tape over my mouth, hands and feet bound with the same. I smelled rubber and dust, saw only darkness. I blinked into it, heard the rumble of tires, felt the sway and lurch.

I was trapped in a trunk.

I cursed in my head. The green glow-in-the-dark child safety switch was faint but still visible. How long did it take that thing to go dark? The trunk was hot and close, and every time I turned my head, nausea roiled through me. I closed my eyes and willed down the heaves. I was being hauled to some secondary crime scene, the place where all the bad shit happened. This was not good.

My thoughts flashed on Train, but the panic that rose almost undid me. I breathed a silent prayer that his Higher Power had indeed kept him safe, and forced myself calm. I had two things going for me. One, they hadn't killed me, and they could have, which meant there was still something they wanted from me, which meant that two, I had leverage.

I heard voices from the front seat, Ivy Rae and Shane. The radio thump-thump-thumped—goddamn country music twang—but they'd jammed me with my head right up against the back seat so I could hear their voices too.

Ivy's voice was annoyed. "We should have killed that guy."

Shane made a noise of annoyance. "So the cops could hear the gunshot and come running? That would have been stupid. We'll be long gone by the time they find him, so stop worrying."

"You could have given him some of that stuff you gave her."

"I needed it for her, Ivy."

"I'm just saying." The radio skipped down the dial from static to gospel then back to the country station. "At least Jasper was right about where she'd be."

"Jasper said the tattoo shop guy would know where she was, not that she'd be there. I had to text her to get her to come back."

"It worked, though, didn't it?"

"Because of me, not Jasper. He's not as smart as you think he is."

"I know exactly how smart he is. He doesn't have a clue how smart I am though—how smart *we* are—and that's the important thing."

The car shimmied over a bump and my hipbone drove up hard against the spare tire, so hard I had to clench my teeth to keep from screaming. I was a mass of bumps and bruises, my throat felt like someone had crushed it with a sledgehammer, and the dizziness and nausea were worse than any seasickness I'd ever had. They'd shot me full of something, who knew what, and that thought was almost as terrifying as being trapped in the trunk.

The radio switched to hard rock, and the speakers buzzed with the bass overload. "I still don't know why we had to get her," Shane said.

"Because we still don't know where the money is, and until we do, we gotta keep up the act and do what he says. So like it or not, that means bringing her."

"She knows where the money is?"

"Why bring her if she doesn't?"

Oh, triple crap. There was a ton of money floating around, every last cent of it ill-gotten and dirty and vanished, but I didn't have a clue where any of it was. If that was the only reason they were keeping me alive, I was doomed. I had nothing to barter except whatever half-cracked story I could drum up, hopefully one that would last until I could think of something better.

"Jasper's the one who hid the money," Shane continued. "Why do we need her?"

"If he says we need her, we need her. At least until we can be done with both of them."

"What you gonna do after that, dump 'em in the river? That worked real good with the last guy. I told you those weights wouldn't—"

"Did you come up with something better? No. So stop blaming me for it. What's done is done. And like you said, we'll be long gone by the time anybody finds them."

I got sick again, and started shaking. John. They were talking about John. They were the ones he'd surprised at the trailer, and they'd killed him and dumped him in the river for the fish and crabs, and I was next, and…I blinked back more tears, the litany of obscenities running in my head.

Shane's voice was barely intelligible. "You let me handle this next part then, all right? We can't make any mistakes, not with Jasper. He's not like that guy at the trailer. And neither is this one in the trunk."

"Her? She's just some cousin from Atlanta."

"She took a hunk out of my arm, then about knocked my knee sideways, the whole time scrambling for that gun. She ain't going easy."

Damn straight, I thought. But I wasn't in my car, which meant Trey couldn't track that, and I didn't have my regular phone, so he couldn't track that either. When I got out of this alive—because I sure as hell was going to—I was going to beg his forgiveness and have a GPS chip installed under my skin.

Ivy laughed. "Easy or hard, she's going eventually. So is Jasper. And then we're home free. You and me, baby."

Shane laughed too, and I felt like throwing up. He was a KKK plant, that much was clear, the mark of the Blood Drop Cross as telling as a rap sheet. It was also clear he'd been deliberately placed in the prison infirmary, his record expunged, all as a ploy to get close to Jasper and find out where he'd stashed the missing money. It sounded like he'd ditched that plan, though, in favor of taking Jasper's money *and* his girl and hitting the road.

But until then, he was still following Jasper's orders. Which made no sense to me, none at all. Why follow the orders of a man you were leaving behind? A man in a jail cell?

The car slowed, and I heard a familiar crunching underneath the tires. Oyster shells. The car dropped to cruising speed, then stopped.

"I'll get the emergency override," Shane said. "You drive through."

I heard him get out, and then a couple of minutes passed as the car idled. Eventually I heard the screeching of a gate opening. The car rolled forward to a grinding stop, and I heard the front door open and then shut.

Five seconds later, Ivy banged on the trunk. "I am about to open this up! I have a four-ten sawed-off pointed at you, and I will blow you in half if you give me trouble. You hear me?"

She cracked the trunk. I blinked into a floodlight, Ivy silhouetted against the glare. She stepped back, and a massive form filled my vision. Shane. He was blurry and indistinct, and he dragged me out with more roughness than necessary. I fought to keep my balance as he dumped me on my feet.

He grabbed my hair and twisted my face up. "I gave you enough methohexital to knock you out, but not keep you out. That's so you can walk, because I don't feel like hauling your ass around. But you give me trouble, I'll shoot you full of something that will take you down hard. Then I'll drag you up those steps. You understand?"

I nodded. I'd had enough of unconscious. So I let him haul me upright and slice the tape binding my ankles. We were in a nondescript four-door car, yellow-looking under the amber bug lights. But we were parked next to a white pick-up with a camper top, just like the one Hope had spotted tailing her. She hadn't been paranoid. But it hadn't been the KKK after her, not exactly.

Ivy stuck the muzzle of the shotgun into my stomach. "Move it."

I turned around. Boone's house loomed in the silver moonlight.

I managed to stagger down the path and onto the porch, Ivy right behind, Shane ahead. I noticed with some satisfaction that he had a bandage on his forearm where I'd bitten him. My only hope was that he'd bring some fleshy part close enough for another go.

He stopped at the front door. It was closed, but not locked, the strike plate a mess of ripped metal and splintered wood, the calling card of a battering ram. Shane snatched down the piece of paper stuck to the front door, official notice of search and seizure.

He pushed the door open with his boot. The house was dark inside, and silent. No little girl noises, no fish cooking in the kitchen. The ghostly animal heads loomed, but I didn't see a single weapon lying around, not a knife, not a gun, not even a baseball bat. Either Jefferson had taken everything with him, or the cops had confiscated it all. Either way, I was out of luck.

Ivy looked panicked. "You think the cops found the money?"

"No. Jasper isn't stupid enough to leave it where they could. Besides, they would have been bragging about it on the news. Taking selfies with it on Twitter."

Ivy poked the couch with the end of her shotgun. "You sure it's cops? Could have been the Klan."

"Klan wouldn't use fingerprint powder. Come on."

They hustled me down the darkened hallway to the safe room. The door here was an even bigger disaster, completely blown off its hinges and propped against the wall.

Shane examined the scene. "Det cord. Good job with it too. Most cops don't know shit about explosive breaching."

He kicked aside a pile of shredded paper and shoved me inside. Here was the most obvious evidence of searching—provisions scattered, the first aid kit jumbled up, the safe cut open with the door left dangling. The cops had been thorough and hadn't cared one bit about cleaning up. Shane pushed me down into a desk chair and rummaged through the safe.

Ivy stood beside him. "You sure they didn't take the money?"

"I'm sure. This is just legal stuff, bunch of paperwork."

He'd let me see his face, and Ivy's. These were not good indicators of their eventual plans for me. What would the cops do when they got here? It would be a hostage situation, that was for sure. They'd send in the negotiation team, form a perimeter, then set a sniper up in the trees, somebody looking for a clean shot to the T-zone. My best bet was to stay small, stay down, and stay out of the gunfire.

Shane stood in front of me and peeled the edge of the tape up. "An overdose of methohexital sodium comes with nasty complications. Cardiac arrest, respiratory failure. You scream, and I put you out again, and this time you maybe don't wake up, you got it?"

I nodded. There wasn't any use screaming anyway. We were in the middle of twenty acres, in the middle of a house in a safe room with walls a foot thick, reinforced with concrete, designed to withstand automatic gunfire. I could scream until my tonsils bled and nobody would hear a thing.

He ripped the tape off in one brutal swipe, and I bit my tongue to keep from crying out.

"Where's the money?" he said.

I tried to talk, but dissolved in a coughing fit. He watched me hack, arms folded, his real tattoo shimmering black and red. He wore camo, army fatigues and combat boots. A man used to warfare, trained in it. His résumé detailed every deadly talent he possessed.

"I don't know anything about any money," I said.

"Jasper thinks you do."

"He's wrong."

"Then what's he want you here for?"

"Don't know that either." I looked him in the eye. "You say that like he's on his way. That's a nice trick for a man behind bars."

Shane laughed. He started toward the door, pointing at me as he left. "Ivy Rae, you start with her kneecaps if she acts up."

Ivy wrapped her fingers around the shotgun and took up position in front of me. She wanted to hurt me. She had a taste for hurting, I could tell, like a sweet tooth gone rotten. My head swam with all the hurt I wanted to put on her in return.

When Shane came back, he'd changed. His medical scrubs were dark blue and starched perfect, his tattoo once again the mascot of his platoon. He looked All-American scrubbed and sane, a real good guy. He smiled, a nice clean smile. His eyes crinkled. He knew how to fake it, knew how to fake a lot of things.

He sat opposite me and retrieved a prosthetic foot from his gym bag. It was covered with pale rubbery skin, unlike the futuristic biomedical blade he'd been wearing in the newsletter photo. He switched the new foot out with the identical one he currently wore and slid it into his sneaker.

He smiled as he laced his shoe, then fastened his prison ID to his shirt. "You girls be good 'til me and Jasper get back, you hear?"

Chapter Forty-eight

Ivy held the shotgun with no prowess, but shotguns at close range required zero prowess. I wasn't going anywhere, and the helplessness was beginning to eat away at me. I couldn't stop thinking, plotting, looking for places to get a toehold. But it was just me and Ivy and the infernal silent house.

I licked my lips. "If you're counting on Jasper, you may as well hang it up. He's in it for himself, not you."

She smiled. "He's in it for me, don't you worry. I could tell from his first letter. Very courtly, gentlemanly, but hungry underneath."

"Then why did he never tell you about the money?"

"Because that's men's work." She pronounced it with a sarcastic edge, the smile twisting bitter at the corners. "Him and Shane, buddy-buddy all the way. They share a white man's understanding of the world, you know."

"That what got him his OTH discharge?"

"That was part of it. Mostly it was the fact that he liked hurting people." She readjusted her grip on the shotgun, kept her finger on the trigger. "The army doesn't actually approve of that, strangely enough. Not anymore anyway." She narrowed her eyes. "How did you know about the OTH?"

"I looked it up."

"That was supposed to be expunged. He got lawyers to do it."

I hesitated. How much to reveal, how much to conceal? If she knew I knew about her and Shane, or about Shane's true reason for being in the detention center, she'd plug me before Jasper ever set foot in the place.

"I was convinced Shane was selling his professional opinion," I said, "so I got Trey to look it up. He has access to stuff like that."

Ivy burned with curiosity. She really *really* wanted to figure out where that money was before Shane got back, and keeping me talking probably looked like her best tactic. But she couldn't let me know that she and Shane were planning on betraying Jasper, and I wasn't about to let her know that I'd already figured that out. We were both in the same dilemma—trying to get information without giving too much away.

"So what's going to happen?" I said. "Shane gonna sneak Jasper out in the trunk of his car?"

Ivy smiled, then went back to searching through the papers. Suddenly, I wasn't sure who she was playing, Jasper or Shane. Maybe even both. Maybe she wanted to be Thelma and Louise all rolled into one so that she didn't have to go out in a blaze of glory. No, she'd go out with all the money and none of the hassles that a hanger-on man might bring. It was a plan I could approve of…except I was a hassle that needed leaving behind too.

"Shane works in medical," I said. "No wonder Jasper's been complaining about his ankle, provoking fights. He needed face time with his accomplice."

She'd moved to upending drawers, riffling through stacks of papers, running her fingers around inside the safe. Obviously taking advantage of her time without Shane or Jasper to look for the money herself. But Shane was right. No way Jasper would leave it in an office, especially not a safe room. If she knew Jasper, she knew this too. But she wasn't taking any chances.

Eventually, she gave up on the search and pulled a chair face to face with me. Her voice was pleasant, cajoling. "If you'd just tell me where it is, we could avoid all this."

"I don't know where the money is."

"You sure? It's here somewhere. That's why Jasper said to meet here. Well, one of the reasons anyway." She leaned forward. She smelled of the same floral cologne my mother wore, almost syrupy. "But we don't have to wait for him. You tell me where it is, and I'll get it and let you go."

"I told you, I don't know."

"Fine." She stood. "Suit yourself. He'll get it outta you one way or another."

Ivy upended the box of blankets with her foot. I tried to think. Jefferson hadn't known where the money was or he'd have given it back to the KKK. Plus Trey said he'd been telling the truth. That meant Jasper had to have hidden it so well his own think-alike brother hadn't found it. And it had to be someplace Jefferson would never accidentally stumble on it. It would be simple to retrieve, but hard to find. I doubted it was in the house, but I wasn't about to tell Ivy that. Let her trash the place. It would keep her busy.

I pulled at my hands, the skin raw under the duct tape. Tugging wasn't particularly useful, and yet I couldn't help it. It was that or scream or cry or give up. Jasper knew I had no clue where the money was, which meant that despite what he'd told Ivy and Shane, he wanted me there for some other reason. I got sick at the thought of what that might be.

What I wouldn't have given for Trey to pull one of his stalker cards out of the hat and show up in full-on assassin mode, eyes like ice, perfect and deadly and ruthless. But no, he was headed for Statesboro, where he was expecting to meet me. That was my one ace in the hole, that when I didn't show, he'd come looking. But how would he find me? How would anyone?

Frying pans and fires, all of it.

I tried to keep my voice calm. "Whose idea was it to plant the gun on me?"

She pulled out a drawer and dumped its contents on the floor, poked through it with her toe. "Mine. Shane's the one actually did it, though. Popped the lock in ten seconds. He said you learn a lot of things hanging out with criminals all day."

"When?"

"At the storage unit place. Shane had wanted to throw the

gun in the river, but I told him we could use it, that people would believe you killed that guy, y'all having history and all."

History. That was one word.

"It was Shane who attacked me at Billie's too, wasn't it?"

"Attacked you? You surprised him and he ran, that's all." She shook her head and kicked at the mess on the floor, half-hearted now. "I told Shane that was a dumb idea, breaking in there, but does he listen? No. I told him you didn't have the money, and that even if you did, you wouldn't stash it there. I was right, yet again."

"How'd you get Train's phone?"

"Took it. Amazing what people will hand right over at gunpoint." She smiled. "Oh, don't make that face. We taped him up good and locked him in that little hidey hole at the tattoo parlor, that's all. He's fine. You can be fine too. If you'll tell me where the money is."

"Fine like John?" I said.

Ivy's eyes went hard. "That was different. The trailer was supposed to be empty because he was supposed to be at work. But Shane had only been in there ten minutes, and here that guy comes, barreling up in the yard with a gun."

"So Shane shot him. No questions, just—"

"No, honey, I shot him. I was lookout, parked on the road. But I didn't want to kill him. Wouldn't have if I hadn't had to. Remember that."

I tried to say something, but I couldn't. She'd just confessed to homicide, which meant no matter what she'd just said, she knew I wasn't long for this world.

"Why'd you think he had the money?"

"Not him. His wife. She'd been seen talking to the Klanswomen at the—" Ivy stopped talking, recalculated. "But you know all about that, just like you know all about the money. You could save us both a whole lot of grief if you'd just tell me where it is."

"I would if I could. Believe me."

She sighed. Her phone rang once, then twice. Then silence. She checked the number. "That would be the good news. Let's turn on the TV and see."

She switched on the dinky television in the corner. It was bad reception, obviously supported by some equally decrepit rooftop antenna. Despite the static, the breaking news report was clear.

The reporter was breathless, high spots of color on her cheeks, beautiful and perfect in front of smoke and strobing red and blue lights. Suspected gas leak at the detention center, followed by an explosion in the infirmary. Mass evacuation. Two dead, dozens injured. They didn't have a tally yet on the inmates and staff—how many were still under the rubble, how many slumped dazed and bloody in the parking lot, how many had fled to the surrounding woods.

The screen flashed with mug shots, including Jasper's. Prisoners unaccounted for, presumed at large. BOLOs for the general area. Already the news was pinging across social media, and the good citizens of Savannah were locking their doors, loading their own shotguns. Already every law enforcement officer in the Coastal Empire was being called in to help close the roads and blockade the area around the center.

Ivy watched the report, her face gleaming, positively patriotic. "Damn if it didn't work."

I tried to sound calm. "Shane smuggled it all in, didn't he? Who's gonna check a prosthetic foot for det cord and blasting caps?"

But she kept shaking her head, smiling at the screen, her expression glazed with pride. Then she cocked her head, listening. A car coming through the gates. The panic was instantaneous. I'd had a chance with Ivy, maybe even her and Shane together, but not Jasper. I breathed it down. He wanted me alive for some reason, that was my leverage. I heard the door open, heavy boots on the wooden floor. *Breathe*, I told myself. *Stay calm. Work what you've got.*

And then he was standing in the door—hiking boots, jeans, a dark gray long-sleeved shirt. Jasper. He looked untouched by the flames, undusted by ash.

He smiled, and a hank of blond hair tumbled over his still-bruised face. "Hey, cuz. Long time no see."

Chapter Forty-nine

He clomped into the room, the boots heavy on the hardwood. Limping now, which gave his stride an awkward lurch. He moved closer until he was right in front of me, dropped into a crouch. He smelled singed up close, despite the clean clothes, which he'd topped with a ballistic-proof vest.

He looked at me with Boone's eyes, frostbit green. "Cat got your tongue?"

I strained at the tape. "Fuck you."

He slapped me. Then he pulled my face up, mashing his thumb into the tender flesh of my jaw. Pain went singing through my head, and my eyes watered. I tasted blood.

"That's enough outta you," he said.

Ivy stood beside him. "She wouldn't talk. I figured I'd let you make her."

"Aren't you sweet?"

She cast a nervous glance behind her to the empty doorway. "Where's Shane?"

"He's in the car."

Ivy froze. Something had gone wrong, and she was desperately trying to figure out what it was without tipping her hand. She kept the shotgun, held it by the barrel. She was wishing she'd had it by the stock, finger on the trigger, so that she could level it at Jasper now.

Instead she smiled. "Let's don't make him wait, baby. Let's get the money, pay him off, and be on our way."

She was seductive, coaxing. Ripe for the taking. And yes, Jasper was hungry for her. But not the way she thought.

He stepped closer, gathered her face in his hands. I saw the flicker in her eyes—relief? fear? uncertainty? Things weren't going as planned. But he ran his fingers through her baby doll curls and kissed her, slow and deep. And I watched, sick to my stomach, because I knew what was coming.

"You think I don't know?" he said.

The flicker again. "Know what, baby?"

He took her shotgun before she knew it, wrenching it from her fingers. She started to say something else, but Jasper spun her around and shoved her toward the door.

"Come on," he said. "Let's go see Shane."

She started begging as he dragged her down the hallway. She didn't stop talking—rapid-fire, pleading, desperate. I heard a scuffle, then a scream. Then two shots, one after the other. And then it was quiet, just kicking, scrabbling noises, followed by the heavy thud of a body hitting the floor.

When Jasper reappeared in the doorway, he was breathing hard, eyes bright. Blood flecked his hands and stained the vest. "That was unfortunate. She would've been fun for a little while. Now Shane, that's a different story. Hurt like hell to put him down. Like a brother, he seemed to be. Of like mind and heart." He shook his head. "I counted on them to work together, and instead they go behind my back, killing people for no good reason, looking to take my money—mine—like I was too stupid to figure it out."

On the television, the screen filled with a different image. Shane. In his uniform. Among the missing, presumed kidnapped. And then Jasper's mug shot. Among the escaped, presumed dangerous.

Jasper sighed. "You're all the family I got, cuz. And I thank you for telling me that John Wilde was missing. That's what made me figure out that those two were up to something. After I confronted him, Shane confessed that things had gone off-plan. A snafu, he said. He was sorry they hadn't told me, he said. But I figured out what they were really up to there, him and Ivy. And it wasn't much from there to figure out who'd really sent him."

I licked my swollen lips. "You know where the money is. Go get it and hit the road."

"You and I got some business to attend to first." He crouched down behind me, stroked the blade lightly against the back of my ankle. "Now, I'm gonna cut off this tape. And as long as you behave, the only thing I'm cuttin' is tape. You hear me? Say you hear me."

"I hear you."

He sliced my ankles free. Then he slashed the tape that held me in the chair. He grabbed me by the collar and hauled me upright, the knife at my throat.

"Let me explain my choices here, because I have thought them out. As much as I'd like to flay you alive, I don't have the time. And as much as I'd like to do it in front of Trey Seaver, then fill him full of buckshot, he's too much of a complication to work easily into this scenario." He tsk-tsked. "Dangerous man you're shacking up with, and I know one when I see one. He's no doubt up now and frantic, calling your phone and getting no answer and imagining all kinds of awfulness happening to you, no way to find you. Which makes me all warm and fuzzy inside. It's second best, but it will do."

He marched me to the hall. "Now, I do get some delight at the thought of him finding you dead. But again, ain't no cause for that. Maybe I'll just break you. That'll eat him for the rest of his life, which will be good enough. That okay with you? Alive but broken?"

He was lying. He was gonna kill me. After he used me as a hostage. Or a human shield. And he might be quick to flee afterward, or he might be mean enough to stalk Trey down too. He was dangling survival like bait, and I wanted to grab it with both hands, do whatever he said to walk out alive. It was a deadly temptation, and I resisted it.

Jasper's eyes narrowed. "I asked you a question. Deal?"

I tried to keep my voice steady. "Deal."

"Good. Then let's go."

"Go where?"

He pushed me into the living room. I averted my eyes from the heap that was Ivy, tried to stay focused even though my head pounded and my legs shook. Jasper stuck the knife in his boot and hoisted a rifle standing beside the front door. He double-checked to make sure it was loaded, then held it up where I could see.

"Shane had nice taste in hunting rifles. Remington Model 700. Drill a hole through a buck's skull at three hundred yards. He fitted it with laser sights and everything. Military grade."

He aimed it at me, and I saw the green light blossom in front of my heart. I almost dropped to my knees.

"Head for the dock," he said. "I'm right behind you."

I walked through the doors, stronger but too unsteady to run. Jasper followed behind me at a nice safe distance, the mounted light on his rifle illuminating my path and blinding me every time I looked back. In the dark, the night dense around us, I couldn't fight the memories that rose, the last time Jasper and I had stalked each other around that dock. I'd detailed that night for the prosecution over and over, but being back in this place on another moon-washed night fired up the fear in a way that telling the story never had.

I saw that the backyard had been hastily evacuated. The girl's toys remained where they'd left them, the dip nets and jars, shovels and soccer balls. The BB-pocked cans they'd used for target practice were scattered at the edge of the clearing, right next to the canoes, which had been hauled up from the dock. A one-person kayak lay flipped over next to the shed, the paddle beside it.

Jasper played the light over it. "Get that and drag it over."

I stumbled forward. Was he going to try for an escape? It was certainly possible. The river was mostly empty this time of night, and a kayak could slip into the night like a ghost, avoiding whatever road barricades the cops were surely setting up. I'd let him go, not stand in his way one second.

I bent over to grab the tow rope. The kayak was old and bat-tered, waterlogged too, heavy as hell when I hoisted one end… and saw the glint in Jasper's light. I pretended to adjust my grip and looked closer. It was a piece of broken glass, brown, long as my hand and sharp like a dagger. A remnant of the girls' illicit BB shooting.

Jasper noticed my dawdling. "Hurry up. The thing can't be that heavy."

"It's full of water."

"So dump it out, idiot."

I dragged the kayak forward until my right foot rested next to the glass. Then I knelt and tilted the kayak, the water pour-ing out, the hull obscuring my hand as I grabbed the glass and slipped it up my sleeve, where it rested against the inside of my wrist. I righted the kayak and started to haul it toward the dock.

Jasper interrupted me. "Not thataway."

"Where then?"

"Where do you think?"

And then I knew the kayak wasn't for him. I knew he wasn't trying for an escape, not yet. He still had his money to get, and I realized with fresh horror where he'd hidden it. And why I was still alive.

Chapter Fifty

I gaped at him. "You hid it in the gator pit?"

Jasper shrugged. "Was a fish pond when I put it there. I gotta tell you, when Ivy told me what Jefferson had done, I was ready to string him up. That little fishing hole had been the perfect hiding spot, easy as pie to get to, nobody gonna be looking there. And then he had to go and stick gators in it. Now it ain't that easy. Lucky for me, I got you. Now get on."

I couldn't move, couldn't think. I had a sliver of broken glass, all but useless at a distance. Running was futile—Jasper could pick me off in a hot second before I made the woods or the water.

He spoke louder. "I said, move."

I picked up the kayak and started dragging. He stayed behind me all the way back to the house and down the path to the edge of the pit, which lay silent and dark beyond the pier, surrounded by the chain link fence.

I stared into the water. "You never were going to take Ivy anywhere. She was supposed to be the one wading up in alligators while you and Shane watched."

"Yeah. She was gonna be useful. And I swear, I thought me and Shane..." He shook his head mournfully. "Ah well, he ain't the first man swayed by a piece of tail, won't be the last. And he turned out to be useful too. For a while."

I heard splashes, the roar of a bull. The spring fever surged in them, and they rutted and fought and chomped in the frenzy.

The males charged anything—logs, canoes—and the females hunkered down near their nests on shore and sunk their teeth into whatever stumbled close.

Jasper marched me down to the edge of the water, right beside the pier. It was concrete around the edges, good for supporting the chain link fence, but soft sand at the banks. The kayak scraped until I got it deep enough to float.

"Bad timing to be rummaging around in a gator pit, I know. But I didn't pick it. Damn Klan breathing down my neck, Ivy and Shane plotting. It made the timeline for getting out a little… what's that fancy word? Compressed. Thank goodness that dang lawyer showed up and gave everybody something else to think about." He grinned. "Threaten to take a couple million, and people get distracted. Even people like you who don't have a million to take."

I wanted to kill him. I wanted to slice some bleedy part open and shove him on top of the gators and watch the churning. Revulsion mixed with fury, burned bright. As long as I didn't let the fear overflow, I could ride those. They'd make fine fuel. I was more worried about the dizziness and the nausea, my shaky body and unsteady feet. Whatever Shane had popped me with, it came with damnable aftereffects.

Jasper swung the rifle up, once again pinning me in the light. "Get in. I'll tell you what to do."

I took a quick inventory. My sneakers were already soaked, the sucking mud pulling at them. My skirt would be a soggy bundle of uselessness. The blouse would offer some protection from sharp rocks and pointy branches, but not gator teeth.

I pointed. "There's a pair of waders in the dock box. Throw them to me."

"What?"

I dropped the tow rope and shucked the skirt. "You want me messing around in there, you gotta give me some protection."

Jasper hesitated. "This better not be a trick."

"You want me to get your damn money or not? If not, shoot me now and wade in yourself!"

He stared at me. I could see the jangly burnt-wire part of him that wanted to do it, and I saw it smoothed over by the efficient no-nonsense part. He needed me swift and successful. Then he could shoot me.

He trained the gun on me as he worked the top of the dock box, feeling around inside until he dragged out Jefferson's hip waders. He chucked them to the edge of the water, where they slapped like a gator tail.

"There. Now get to it. And if you make one sly move—"

"I know, I know."

I dragged on the heavy rubber. Yes, some protection, but mostly stalling for time. The water was shallow, deepest in the middle around the aerator, maybe ten feet. The waders were too big, but they would keep my shoes on my feet. And I was going to need those shoes. I was gonna need to run, as soon as I got a half-chance. I flexed my fingers and felt the broken glass slide against my skin. There might be other things I had to do before that.

Jasper sent the light to the edge of the pond, where the chain link ran. "I know what you're thinking. But even if you make it out of the water, I'll take you down at the fence. Hundred foot shot. With this here fine rifle, I could make that blindfolded. You hear me?"

I didn't say anything, and the green dot from the rifle centered on my chest. I felt the raw skin on the inside of my wrist burn in the dirty water, and I remembered Trey, and I imagined him standing right there beside me, like we were running a scenario, like we were training. I even heard his voice in my head.

Timing and opportunity. Watch for the convergence.

I took a deep breath, straightened my spine. "What am I looking for?"

"Chain. Goodly length of it."

"And how am I supposed to find it?"

"Head out to the piling. I'll tell you what to do."

I waded in. The water was warmer than I expected, thick with coontail moss and lily pads. I slogged my way forward until the kayak got clearance, then I swung myself inside. It was muscle memory, a move I'd made a thousand times, only this was the first time I'd done it at gunpoint.

"Okay. Now what am I—?"

The bump came out of nowhere, like a torpedo. The kayak tilted crazily, and I screamed and grabbed my knees, pulling myself into a ball.

Jasper's voice was irritable. "What happened?"

"Fucking gator! What do think goddamn happened?"

Jasper sent the light down the bank, and a dozen pair of glittery red eyes stared unblinking back. "Probably a mama warning you off her nest. You gotta be more careful."

I muttered curses, wrapped myself tighter. Waited. The gator didn't return. Definitely a female then. The bulls would not be so generous. I moved like a reptile myself—sluggish, slow, dull. Trey had explained why during our drills at the gun range. Adrenalin shuts down the blood flow to the extremities, routing it to the core. Hands go numb, fingers get clumsy and thick. I could feel it happening to me.

I moved the paddle into the water, and it almost fell from my grasp. "I can't do this! I'm gonna get eaten alive out here!"

"I've seen you swim with sharks. You can do this itty bitty thing."

I heard another bellow, and felt my stomach go liquid. Jasper fired, and I heard a wallowing thrash. Then silence.

Jasper raised his voice. "You better hurry up. I ain't got a million bullets."

I tightened my grip on the paddle and stroked shakily for the middle of the pond.

Chapter Fifty-one

The kayak bumped up against the piling. "Now what?"

"Now you take that paddle and you stir around at the bottom until you hook the chain. Then you pull that up and grab hold."

I stirred in the soupy water, catching nothing. Every sensation sent a ripple of dread through me, every sound jerked my head in its direction. I could hear splashes at the banks, the hiss and glide of leathery bodies moving through the vegetation.

I tried to sound calm. "You could throw me a boat hook, that'd help."

He laughed. "Right. So you could throw it right back at my head. Make do with what you got."

I shoved the paddle back around the base of the piling, careful to avoid dislodging the hunk of glass up my sleeve. The water was even shallower than I'd guessed, only five or six feet, and I knew if I didn't find his freaking chain, he'd make me get in the water and dig around bare-handed. I heard another bellow from the weeds, and I jammed the paddle back down until it hit bottom, then raked the T-shaped handle through the mud another time.

This time I caught something. Something heavy and loose.

Jasper played the light over the water. "You got it?"

"I think so."

"All right now, be careful." He was all earnest and excited, like we were kids on a treasure hunt. "Pull that chain up nice and easy. Don't mess around with the box yet. It's loaded with fishing weights, and you pull that chain off, you'll be diving for it, you hear me?"

I shoved my hair out of my face. "Shut up and let me do this!"

He kept the light on me. I gritted my teeth and plunged my hands into the water, slowly pulling my cargo to the surface. I lost count of the minutes as I focused on my task. Hand over hand, I drew the paddle up, until I finally saw the end of it, thick with rust and slime. A length of heavy chain.

Jasper's boots clomped on the wooden boards. "You got it?"

"Yeah."

"Haul it up then, just the chain, until you feel the box tugging."

I did as he said. Soon I felt the resistance at the other end. I pulled a little, testing it, and felt the box give. It was heavy, but not buried completely. If it was still properly secured to the chain, it would come up without a problem.

Jasper's voice echoed over the water. "I'm gonna throw a buoy out. You attach it to the chain. It's solid line, so use a good knot, now. You don't want to be diving tonight."

I froze. The second I did as he said, I was done for. All he had to do then was haul on his end of the line until the box came free. But he couldn't shoot me until I did because the box would sink again into the muck and he'd have to dive for it himself in the sloppy sucking mud, with gators slavering all around him. He had to make sure my knot worked, which meant I stayed alive until he had the box in hand. I held the chain as the buoy splashed next to the kayak. I didn't reach for it.

I raised my voice. "You decided what you gonna do with me when I get done?"

Jasper laughed. "Lord have mercy, you don't ever quit, do you? How about this? You get that line attached to that chain, throw me the other end of it, and I'll let you get back on the pier and give you a running start. It'll be all sportsmanlike. That fair enough?"

"Ain't exactly sportsmanlike, you up there with your rifle and Kevlar and fucking Bowie knife in your boot, shining a light in my eyes."

"I didn't say it was fair, just sporting." Another laugh. "Come on, cuz. Don't you wanna die trying?"

The tattoo throbbed where the glass scraped it. Jasper had the rifle trained on me, the flashlight in one hand. I couldn't see him for the blinding light. I didn't want to swim for it, not with the gators riled up like they were, but I'd rather face them than Jasper. Of course, even if I reached the bank, I'd have to climb over the chain link fence, Jasper hot on my heels. Maybe staying in the water was best after all. At least Jasper couldn't—

Two splashes off the keel nixed that idea. I felt the almost irresistible urge to beat at the water with my paddle. My head was a slosh of panic and anger and desperation and confusion. I could only think one move ahead at a time. Only I didn't have any more moves.

Except one.

I tied the buoy to the chain with a sturdy bowline. Tugged it once to make sure it would hold. The box wasn't completely buried, but it would take two hands to haul it in. Jasper would have to put down the rifle to do it. That would be my time to make a break for it. I hoped he cared more about getting his money than hurting me. I was betting my life on it.

I coiled the line and threw it toward the pier. "There!"

The line hit with a clunk. The light moved with Jasper's footsteps. He picked it up, and the light wobbled, but I could tell he still had it trained on me. I was right, though—the box wasn't budging.

Jasper stopped tugging. I could see enough in the glare to know that he'd stooped to tie the line around one of the pilings. "How about you paddle on back here, and I'll give you that sporting chance we talked about?"

The green dot centered on my chest once more.

I almost dropped the paddle. "You don't have to kill me to get your money. Drag it in and go!"

"Get up here. Now." He paused. "Or not. You could just close your eyes."

So much for Plan A. We were back to Plan B. I picked up

the paddle, feeling the slide and shift of the glass. I'd get one chance, one, and the only reason it was a chance at all was that he wouldn't see it coming.

I paddled closer. The green dot shimmered over my heart. I started to breathe harder, getting light-headed. A fresh adrenalin rush. Overwhelming, stupefying. At least this way I wouldn't have to go through the gators. At least this way it would be quick, however it was going to be.

I stopped at the edge and climbed out, water up to my ankles, the trees twenty yards to my left on the other side of the chain link, the path to the house ahead, dozens of gators behind. And Jasper, on the pier, hidden behind the light. And the glass, sharp against my skin.

Jasper's voice was cajoling. "Oh, come on. Don't make me shoot you like a fish in a barrel."

I shook my head. Didn't move.

"You don't trust me." He laughed. "I promised you a chance, and I aim to deliver. See?"

He laid the rifle at his feet. I knew then that he was telling the truth, that he did want me to make a run for it. He was a hunter, after all, and he'd have the rifle shouldered and aimed in two seconds. It was no chance, running, and we both knew it. But he wanted me to try.

I started shaking worse, praying maybe, whispering *please-please-please* in my head if not from my lips. Die running or die fighting? Make for the woods or charge at Jasper? I walked toward him, stepping out of the hip waders. I dropped my hands and spread my fingers, and the broken glass slithered out of my sleeve and into my grasp.

I couldn't see Jasper for the light, but I could hear him. "Come on up, cuz."

I rolled myself onto the pier, stood. Shaky but on my own two feet. I started counting down. Three…two…one…

The noise came from my left, from the trees—a swift swish followed by a meaty thunk. Another swish, and I heard the heavy thud of a body. I was still blind from the light, but I listened hard, heard nothing except my ragged breathing.

Then footsteps from the woods, a soft tread. I heard splashing at the bank of the pond, just beyond the beam from Jasper's rifle. A lone figure stood half in the light, half in darkness, dressed head to toe in black, eyes blackened too in the manner of night hunters. The figure held a compound bow, a fresh arrow nocked and ready to let fly.

"You stay real still, you hear me?"

A woman's voice. One I knew.

Cheyanne.

I didn't move a muscle. "I hear you."

I stayed still as she slogged through the underbrush to the pier. She worked in darkness, her boots on the wooden boards. I heard the slosh of the box as she hauled it in. She'd put down her bow, I was sure. But I didn't move. She could have taken me out. She hadn't. I was damn sure not about to give her a reason to do otherwise.

Soon I heard footsteps up the oyster shell path. I guessed she was headed for the river, where she probably had something small and quiet waiting, a canoe or jon boat. She'd collect whatever sparse gear she had and slip into the night. Jefferson was in a Kentucky jail. And she couldn't let his land, their lives, all they'd worked for, all they wanted to pass down to their daughters, go to ruin. She had come back to protect it, to find the money she knew had to be there somewhere, so that she could give it back to the Klan. So they'd leave her family alone and not burn everything she loved to the ground.

I crawled forward until my fingers wrapped around the rifle. I could hear Jasper breathing, rapid and shallow. A whistling sound, not even a moan. I picked up the rifle and pointed the light his way, the broken glass still in my hand.

He lay on his back, a thick pool of blood spreading beneath him. The first arrow protruded from his throat, the second from his chest, right through the ballistic vest. It was made to stop bullets, not blades, something a hunter like Cheyanne had known since she was a child. She had good aim—either arrow would have been a kill shot on its own.

I sat cross-legged, the rifle resting in my lap, the green dot centered on Jasper. I kept it on him as my own breathing returned to normal. As his breathing grew fainter, shallower. I didn't move until there was an emptying sound, a last exhale released from lungs that had no more work to do. Until only the sounds of the night surrounded me.

Chapter Fifty-two

Trey beat the cops to the scene. He'd called them, of course, as soon as he'd heard about the explosion at the detention center. And then he'd violated every protocol and procedure that existed and taken the situation into his own hands, parking at the road and hurtling through the woods, fully armed once more. I'd heard him coming, for even though he was as silent as a ghost on concrete and pavement, in nature he was as unstealthy as a bull moose.

I remembered him taking me by the shoulders, saying my name. I remembered him trying to get me to stand, and my refusing, him peeling my fingers from around the gun, from around the broken glass. Eventually he sat on the pier behind me, my back against his chest as the sirens rose.

The EMTs managed to get past him, but he hovered just outside their circle. I cried out as they hauled me into the ambulance on a backboard, Trey at their heels. He stayed right behind them the entire time. I know because every time I called his name, he said, "I'm here." He said it over and over and over.

The EMTs, bless their hearts, insisted I be stabilized before I was questioned. They had no such qualms about Trey, and that was the second thing that separated us—his interrogation. It wasn't an interview. He endured it all stoically. He was told there would be more to come, once I got out of the hospital, which is where I was headed once the State Patrol opened the road back into town.

They let him sit with me in the ambulance while they made sense of the scene. I took his hand. Cameras flashed. The cops had asked a dozen times who had shot Jasper, and I'd said I didn't know, a dozen times. They'd found no trace of Cheyanne, and I knew they wouldn't—as far as anyone knew, she was in Kentucky, and I was willing to bet a dozen people there would swear she still was.

I didn't know why I refused to give Cheyanne up, except that she could have killed me and hadn't. But I did know that the authorities would shake down every militia nut and KKK big job and conspiracy-minded ranty secessionist in the whole of Southeast Georgia —and that would take some time—and they would end up with too many suspects to count. One of them might even get taken down for it. I didn't really care. They'd told me they'd found Train—alive. They'd told me everybody else in my world was accounted for and under protection. And Trey was sitting right beside me. I had everything I needed.

I squeezed Trey's fingers. "How'd you find me?"

He hesitated. "I tagged you with a small ergonomic processor. A prototype, impervious to water. It tracks without batteries using a GPS signal. And as long as it stays in motion, even movement as slight as respiration—"

"Where'd you put it?"

Another hesitation. "On your bra. In your bra, actually. I inserted it between the padding and the wiring, then used the hotel sewing kit to stitch it shut."

"Show me."

He slipped his hand under my shirt, his fingers following the line of elastic to the swell of foam lining at the side. He tapped a tiny hard disc. I'd never even noticed. If I had, I'd have thought it was part of the Italian engineering. I remembered the patdown he'd given me before I left his hotel room, checking to make sure it was still in place.

"When did you do this?"

"Wednesday morning while you were in the shower. It's the field sample from the meeting I walked out of at Phoenix, so I had it in my briefcase. I forgot to give it back."

"Forgot? You never forget."

"That day, I was a little…you know." He met my eyes. "I didn't activate it until a few hours ago, when I got the cell phone alert about the explosion."

His phone was always going off with warnings and BOLOs and APBs, Amber alerts and fugitive last-scene-in reports, any bit of danger a quasi-authorized law enforcement officer might need to know about.

"You didn't check, that whole time we were separated? Not even once?"

He shook his head. "I was questioned, repeatedly, as to your whereabouts, and what I didn't know, I couldn't tell. It was difficult, I will admit. But it was enough to know that I could check at any time. If I needed to."

So that was how he'd survived our separation discombobulation-free. And there I was thinking he'd gotten some new Zen technique, or some new tea, or some mega herbal relaxant thingies.

He sat very close but not touching, his spine straight, shoulders square. His eyes were on my face, however, a hesitant searching look from under his lashes. "They told me you couldn't identify the shooter."

"That's what I told them."

"Yes, but…is that true?"

I couldn't speak for a few seconds, like my heart was stuck in my throat. "Please don't ask me that."

"Tai—"

"Please."

Trey tilted his head so that he could track my eyes, my mouth, the whole truth or the lack thereof. Then he nodded once, final and decisive, turning his face toward the crime scene.

Jasper's body still sprawled on the pier. No sheet for him until the forensics team finished up. I tried to feel something, and couldn't. Shock will numb, I knew that, but it wasn't only shock I felt. There was a profound sense of relief, of pieces moving back into place. Of order, maybe even justice, slowly taking form. And something else, something undeniable.

"I wanted to kill him," I said.

Trey kept his eyes on the crime scene. "I know."

"I wanted to really bad. But then suddenly he was gone, and I'd lost my chance, and I got so mad when I realized I'd just sat there and listened to him die instead of slicing his throat with that piece of glass and—"

"Tai. Listen to me." Trey turned back to me, his voice soft. "If you'd had to kill him, it would have been the right thing to do. It might even have been easy, at the time. But it's better that you didn't. For many reasons."

I knew he was right. He understood the psychological repercussions better than most. But I knew that in a crowded world of seven billion, someone's existence could be justified in two ways—either of personal value, or value to humanity. And no matter which way the needle trembled on that dial, Jasper didn't deserve to live. And I regretted that I wasn't the one who'd put him down.

I leaned my head on Trey's shoulder. "I know. Still."

Trey reached for my hand just as his phone rang. Marisa most likely, ready to breathe fire. Or Garrity, ready to take my head off. Or Gabriella, ready to smudge away the negativity. Or Eric, insisting that he rush right down and psychoanalyze Trey and me back to full mental health.

Trey put his phone to his ear. "Yes?"

He looked puzzled. I mouthed *who is it?* at him. *Boone*, he mouthed back, standing up.

"She's fine," he continued. "Yes, right here, do you… No, I can't. Because it's an open crime scene with three victims."

Victims. That was cop speak, but it wasn't the right word. Did Ivy count as a victim, she who'd shot John in cold blood? Or Shane, who'd helped her dump his body into the river? Jasper certainly didn't make the cut. And now here was Boone on the phone, Boone who wouldn't need evidence to figure out who'd done it, but who'd keep that secret as surely as I was.

Trey kept talking. "I understand, but…" And then he went pale. "I'm sorry, what did you say?" He listened, blinking in confusion. "I can't…I don't…Don't you think you should…"

I heard coughing at the other end of the line. Trey stood up and started pacing, his fingers drumming a nervous rhythm on his thigh. My stomach dropped. Whatever this was, it was serious, and I wasn't sure I had it in me for another shoe to drop.

"Trey?"

He waved me quiet, his eyes tight, forehead wrinkled. "Yes. I see your point. I'll do my best. Goodbye." He stopped pacing and lowered the phone, staring at it like it was going to rear up and bite him.

I tried to keep my voice calm. "Trey Seaver, you tell me what's going on, and you do it right now."

He looked up. "The authorities have blocked access to the house until they close the crime scene. They've already taken Boone's papers and admitted them into evidence, including his most recent will. Which means the information there is no longer confidential. It's a part of the investigation now."

"And?"

"And you will be questioned about it."

"Why?"

"Because you're in it. Boone divided his estate down the middle, half to you and half to Jefferson."

I couldn't breathe for a second. "He did?"

"Yes."

I was still confused. "Okay, that's completely out of the blue, but why should the cops care? Jasper wasn't getting one red cent, so nobody can claim I did him in so I could get his share of the money. And Boone's not on death's door or anything, so..." I grabbed Trey's arm. "He's not, is he? You said he was okay, so—"

"Tai—"

"Tell me!"

Trey sat beside me, his expression tender and bewildered. "Boone's okay. What I'm trying to tell you is...he says you're in the will because he's your father."

Chapter Fifty-Three

One week later, we laid John to rest in the Atlantic Ocean, past the seventh wave as the Celts were fond of saying. Captain Lou took us out on a Sunday morning, with fair skies and a following wind. Train said words, plain simple ones that promised grace for the present and peace ever after. Hope stayed silent for the entire journey, her eyes dry and distant. When she shook out the box, the grit and ash flailed in the wind, graying and coarsening it, then swirled onto the water, becoming a part of the sea and sky. And of us, I supposed.

Hope left the boat before Trey and I did, but she waited for me to disembark. I sent Trey on ahead to the car, then joined her underneath the shade of a palm tree. She sucked in a long drag on her cigarette, blew it out slowly.

"Did they suffer? The two who killed him?"

I nodded. "Yes."

"And Jasper?"

"Yes. But not enough."

She took another lungful of smoke, dropped the cigarette to the sand. She ground it out with the heel of her sandal and left me standing under the palm tree. The personal protection detail that had brought her took her away again, and I knew that I'd seen her for the last time.

Trey waited for me at the Ferrari. He'd insisted on wearing a suit, but once again refused to strap on his gun, despite the fact that his suspension was over and he'd be returning to Phoenix the next morning. He was talking on his phone when I arrived, and from the way he looked at me, I knew who was on the other end of the line.

I got into the car without saying a word, shoved my sunglasses on my face. Trey got in, fastened his seatbelt.

"I'm still not ready to talk to him," I said.

"I know."

"Then why are you giving me that look?"

He took the Ferrari gingerly down the dirt driveway. "There was no look. You have explained you don't want to talk to him. I am fully supportive of that decision, as is Boone."

"Then why does he keep calling you?"

"To check on you."

I made some noise. I'd tried to come to terms with this new complication, this life-wrecking, world-cracking revelation. It made no sense, and it made perfect sense. It connected the fragments, the unexplained pieces that didn't fit anywhere. I'd tried to find my father in me, and had always failed. I had a sharp chin like he had, but it wasn't the dimpled Randolph chin, and my eyes were gray-boned hazel instead of clear green. Eric used to joke that I'd somehow managed to screw up gene transmission. I winced at the thought of telling him the news, which I'd have to do as soon as the DNA confirmed what I already knew in my heart. Assuming the story didn't leak before then. THE KKK KILLER DIDN'T KNOW HIS CAPTIVE WAS HIS SISTER. Film at eleven.

My mother had been the epitome of the house-proud, tight-mannered Southern society matron. I'd never seen her with a single hair out of place until she started dying, and the idea that this woman had had an affair with a bootlegging redneck like Boone boggled my mind. I remembered Gabriella's crumbling tower, and her admission that she'd misread that card, that she'd seen it through Trey-colored glasses when it had been for me all along. Score one for the French chick.

I watched the marsh roll by, fully ripe with spring now. "I'm going to sign my half of the estate over to Jefferson. When it's time."

"Okay."

"I don't want any part of it."

Trey didn't reply. He knew this wasn't true, that the marshland pulled at me, filled me with bittersweet longing, a peculiar nostalgia not for what had been, but for what could never be. It was more home to me than anyplace else in Savannah, but it was poisoned ground. It would shelter Boone through his final days, though, Jefferson and Cheyanne and the girls too. And then I could sever myself from it once and for all. I hoped so anyway.

"It's like who I was is gone, but I'm not even sure if I was that person anyway, and now I'm this other person, but I'm not sure if I'm that person either, and I realize none of this is making any sense to you, but—"

"Of course it does."

"What?"

"It makes sense. All of it."

Sometimes I got so caught up that I forgot this was his life too, only his before and after was much more violently rendered, a savage discrete line. Mine was fluid, a tide that washed in and carried out. Flotsam and jetsam, trash and treasure.

I turned to face him. "So how do you do it? Be yourself when you're not sure who that is?"

He slipped me an enigmatic look. "I'll answer that when we get back to Atlanta."

"Why then?"

"Because you told me I needed to figure out a way to tell you this part of the story. And I have."

He was being perplexing and evasive, but I didn't feel like cross-examining him. I was tired, and we still had four hours of travel ahead of us, through fields and small towns, past rebel flags and farm stands. And then would come the first glimpse of Atlanta, like a steel oasis, rising and falling behind green trees exuberant with spring. As if the winter would never come.

I rested my head against the window, closed my eyes, and let the rhythm of the road lull me to sleep.

◇◇◇

I woke when Trey pulled off the interstate. My neck ached from being slumped over, but when I blinked into the light, I got confused. This wasn't Buckhead. No smoked glass and gleam here. Instead we were on a tree-lined street in a residential area.

"Trey? Where are we?"

"Westview."

I sat up straighter. "This is where you grew up."

"Yes."

We passed the gates of Westview Cemetery, rolled to a slow crawl by St. Anthony's, the church where his mom had worked, where he'd been an altar boy. I knew his childhood home had to be close. His mother had never learned to drive, preferring to take the bus or walk, only consenting to a car ride when it was her son behind the wheel. Trey remembered nothing of the accident. In his memory, he was picking his mother up from a visit with a sick friend one minute, then squinting into fluorescent overheads from his hospital bed the next. They didn't tell him she'd died until weeks later, when they finally pronounced him capable of comprehending it.

He turned onto a smaller street, narrower, the sidewalks running like tributaries alongside. The houses sat sturdy and no-nonsense, with squared porch posts and tidy lawns, azaleas blooming in riots of purple and magenta. He stopped abruptly in front of a brick cottage. Instead of getting out, he remained behind the wheel, index finger tapping, tapping, tapping.

"You said you felt as if who you were was gone, and that you were suddenly this other person. You said you didn't understand. You asked how I did it. This is how."

"I still don't understand."

He opened his door. "You will. Come on."

"Where are we going?"

"The basement of my mother's house."

◇◇◇

The dark inside looked tangible, like I could grab a fistful of it, the air cool and damp and mineral-scented. Trey disappeared inside. I waited at the door until he switched on the lights.

The room was rectangular, with a small kitchenette at one end, barstools piled on top of a plain round table. Dozens of plastic bins were stacked like a weird cityscape in the corner, next to stereo speakers and a crate of dusty CDs. Photo albums lined the bookshelves, fake leather with gilt scroll trim on the spines. A framed and faded poster of the Atlanta skyline propped against the wall, the jutting spires of a Midtown that didn't exist anymore.

I stepped into the center of the room. "This is your mother's stuff?"

"No. It's mine. This is where Garrity stored my things while I was in the Shepherd Center."

And then I understood. After getting out of rehab, he'd bought a high empty apartment, a couture wardrobe, and a black-on-black bespoke Ferrari. Then he'd jammed every shred of his former self into this basement, like a message in a bottle. Upstairs I heard footsteps, the patter of soft-soled sneakers, the equine clippety clop of heels.

"She willed everything to the church," he said, "with one provision—that I got to keep the basement. The upstairs serves as the St. Anthony's parish house now. But the basement is still mine. Technically."

"Do you come here much?"

He shook his head. "I started to go through everything once. But none of it seemed to belong to me."

He ran a finger along the back of a hunter-green velour sofa straight out of the eighties, shiny at the armrests. I sat down, patted the spot next to me. He sat too, gingerly, as if he expected the sofa to give way.

"These things used to be mine. I don't understand why they aren't anymore. The doctors said that reconnecting with my possessions would help me recover. But it didn't."

I couldn't understand either. According to every theory I knew about cognitive recovery, he should have been using these belongings and the memories associated with them as a tool. They should have been paving bricks on his road back to himself.

He sent his eyes to the floor. "The apartment. The wardrobe. The Ferrari. The job at Phoenix. Those things are useful, but they're not me either. They're…I can't think of the word."

"Containers."

"Containers. That's a good word. And this room is a container too. It will hold all of this until I'm ready." He let his thumb brush the bone at my wrist. After a few more seconds, he interlaced his fingers with mine. "It seems as if you have a similar problem. You aren't you anymore, at least not as you'd defined yourself before."

I felt the tears spring into my eyes. "Yep."

"Perhaps you should find a container too, something that will hold things until you can deal with them." His eyes got very serious. "But you don't have to deal with things until you're ready. You're the one who makes that decision. Nobody else."

I squeezed his fingers. "So you're ready to dig into all this?"

A look of horror flitted across his features. "What? Of course not. This is too…No, absolutely not. But I wanted you to know that even though I can't tell this part of the story yet, you can still come here whenever you want. There is nothing off-limits here."

"No secrets?"

"No secrets."

"Not even why you kept this couch?"

He shot me a sideways look. "Okay. One secret."

I laughed, and he relaxed a little.

"My current life is a container," he said, "and I worry what might happen if it breaks. I think that's another reason I wanted you to come."

"To test the container."

"Right."

"And is it holding?"

He considered. "Yes. You're here, I'm here, and I'm okay."

"Much better than okay, I'd say."

He lowered his head, but I saw the flash of pleasure in his eyes. He took another breath, this one shakier than before. He'd gone pale, like he was on the verge of passing out, and he wouldn't meet my eyes. I was starting to get worried when he reached into his jacket pocket and pulled out his key ring. He laid it on the sofa exactly halfway between us.

"What I'm trying to say is…" He raised his eyes, squared his shoulders. "All in, Tai."

The keys to the Ferrari. His most precious container. The one where he really did come alive, even if he kept that thrill tamped down below the speed limit.

My mouth went dry. "Does this mean what I think it means?"

"What do you think it means?"

"That I finally get to drive your car."

"That's what it means, yes."

I wrapped my fingers around the keys. Then I leaned forward and kissed him. I kissed him like pressing down the accelerator, like revving the engine, with velocity and high-octane promise. I kissed him, and he responded in kind, a zoom-zoom kiss if there ever were one.

I pressed my forehead against his. His eyes burned blue, half from arousal, I imagined, and half from terror. And then I took his hand, and we went side by side back into the bright spinning world.

Author's Notes

Tai and Trey inhabit a parallel universe. Their world overlaps with mine, creating an interesting playground where the real-real and the book-real meet. You can explore my research for all five books on Pinterest, where I have boards about both Atlanta and Savannah (including interactive maps) plus other topics like the American Civil War and Trey and Tai's accessories (a collection of my protagonists' clothing, automobiles, and weaponry): www. pinterest.com/tinawh.

Tai's gun shop resides in my imagination; the city of Kennesaw is real, however. You'll find it slightly northwest of Atlanta, and it really does have a city ordinance requiring every head of household to maintain a firearm and ammunition. The city also has a store specializing in Confederate memorabilia—Wildman's Civil War Surplus (although any resemblance between Tai's shop and this one is purely coincidental).

As much as possible, I try to include current cognitive and neurological information about recovery from a traumatic brain injury and the neuroplasticity of the human brain. Enclothed cognition is a real thing, as is Trey's ability to detect lies, although science can't yet provide a clear how or why on the latter (it is linked to language processing difficulties, that much is clear). For an excellent first-person account of one scientist's recovery from a TBI, read *The Ghost in My Brain* by Clarke Elliot, a professor of artificial intelligence at DePaul University who shared his harrowing, humorous, and profoundly moving story of life after a debilitating concussion.

Trey's ergonomic tracking processor is, alas, still in the developmental phase, although it shows great promise as both search-and-rescue equipment and as an earthquake detection device. His Urban In-Ground Target Detector is also more theoretical than actual, although military-issue prototypes exist. (Like Tai, I have no idea where he gets these things.)

His ability to track sharks on his phone is totally real, however, as is Mary Lee the great white shark. Though not an app, the Global Shark Tracker lets you follow her and hundreds of other sharks on your computer or smartphone, and in the process, learn more about one of Earth's most magnificent and unfairly maligned creatures. Visit www.ocearch.org to see the Shark Tracker in action, and follow @MaryLeeShark on Twitter for a deepside perspective on our world.

Tai's Savannah and the real Savannah both include Bonaventure Cemetery, which is the final resting place for not only Gracie Watson but other notables, including Johnny Mercer. River Street exists (although Soul Ink does not), as does the DeSoto Hilton, which does indeed have a lovely independent bookstore across the street—the Book Lady Bookstore. Although I wouldn't recommend using it as a surveillance site, it is a marvelous place to spend some quality hours among books both spanking new and previously loved. And if you have Tai's taste in drinking establishments, visit the Bar Bar on Julian Street. If you have Trey's, don't. Just…no.

While Savannah's historic district's squares and parks are easily explored on foot, to see the Lowcounty marshes, rivers, and shores, you should get yourself on the water. And there's no better guide, both inshore and off, than Captain Judy Helmey of Miss Judy Charters. Like Captain Lou, she'll be glad to carry you on the fishing trip of a lifetime, and unlike Captain Lou, she's real.

Finally, though I have visited some nastiness upon the fictional versions of the Savannah Metro Police Department and the Chatham County Detention Center, in the real world, I have met only good people doing hard jobs with professionalism and respect. At both places, there are hundreds of dedicated people working hard to keep citizens safe, and they have my highest respect.

Thank you for sharing your time with Tai and Trey and the rest of their people, including me. If you'd like to read more between-novel short stories about my protagonists (including the epilogue to *Reckoning and Ruin* where Tai finally gets her fingers on the Ferrari), you can visit the Other Writings Section of my website—www.tinawhittle.com/pages/otherwriting—or Wattpad: www.wattpad.com/user/TinaWhittle.

To receive a free catalog of Poisoned Pen Press titles, please provide your name, address, and email address in one of the following ways:

Phone: 1-800-421-3976
Facsimile: 1-480-949-1707
Email: info@poisonedpenpress.com
Website: www.poisonedpenpress.com

Poisoned Pen Press
6962 E. First Ave. Ste 103
Scottsdale, AZ 85251